THE
ACHILLES HEEL

Karyn Rae

KARYN RAE PUBLISHING

Visit Karyn Rae's official website at www.karynrae.me for the latest news, book details, and other information

Copyright © Karyn Rae, 2014

Date of first printing: May 2014

Edited by: Samantha March of Marching Ink LLC
Cover Design by: James, GoOnWrite.com
Ebook Formatting by Guido Henkel, www.guidohenkel.com

This book is dedicated to my family:
Lance, Max, and Mia
Without you, I would have no life perspective

Life's tragedy is that we get old too soon and wise too late.
-Benjamin Franklin

ANNIE

*D*on't put your hat on. Please don't put your hat on.

Crossing my fingers like a grade school child wishing for a snowstorm in August, I watched him take his time as he gathered what looked to be papers, but I wasn't quite sure. He took in a deep breath and let it out slowly while grabbing his hat from the dashboard. For some reason, I had the notion if he didn't put on the hat to complete his uniform, this visit would be somewhat less official. He noticed me standing in the sliver of the window framing my front door. He paused, shut his car door, and straightened his trousers a tad—when one goes from sitting to standing and is between pant sizes. Finally, he put on that goddamn hat.

As he walked towards the door, gravel from the driveway crunched under his heavy black boots. Streaks of sweat ran down his sunlit glistened face. His heavily starched shirt sported a soaking wet "V" on the chest connecting to the wetness under both arms. With record high temperatures in Kansas City reaching 106 during the first week of June, I was secretly glad he was hot, and it almost made me happy to think he might be suffering a bit. Our eyes made contact when he reached the red-brick porch steps, and I knew. He could have turned around, got back in his police car and never said a word to me; his eyes told me the whole story. Maybe his eyes didn't tell me the entire story, but they certainly implied the most important part—the ending. As he stood on the opposing side of the window, the glare from his name badge which read GRADY shone in my right eye, causing me to wince.

"Ma'am," he asked through the double paned glass. "Are you all right?"

I just stood there, staring blankly. *Why is he here to ask me if I'm okay? Is this guy a fucking idiot? What cop comes to someone's front door, scares the hell out of them, and opens with a question like, "Ma'am, are you all right?" I was doing just fine before he pulled into my driveway.*

"Ma'am," he started again, as he tapped on the window trying to get my attention and break the paralyzing trance holding me motionless. "Are you okay? You're bleeding!"

At that moment, I tasted the blood. As I mentally calculated his every move from the car to the door, knowing he wasn't here to give me stellar news (cops don't randomly show up at your house for no reason) I hadn't noticed I was biting down on my lip. It must have been hard, because the blood was now running down the side of my chin.

I tried to answer, but only felt air pass between my lips; my voice lost in translation. I nodded my head up and down in a "Yes" motion.

Officer Grady asked, "Are you Annie Whitman, the wife of a Mr. Jack Whitman?"

Again with the up and down, "Yes," motion.

"Could you please open the door?" he asked. "I'd like to come in and speak with you for a moment."

I reluctantly but automatically obeyed, and the creak of the screen door was synonymous with a horror movie. Apparently, I was the main character.

"Ma'am, your husband was in an accident on the highway this morning. There were no survivors. We believe he was killed upon impact and have launched an investigation into the crash, but unfortunately, we don't know many details yet. I'm so very sorry to bring you this devastating news. Is there someone you can call to come be with you right now?"

"No, no, you're wrong," I croaked, with a broken and raspy voice like someone infested with the forty-eight hour flu. "My husband is at work, and this is a mistake." I tried again, but only fragments of sound spit into the air. I wasn't forming recognizable words. "I'll just call him, and we can clear this up. You'll see it's just terrible mistake," I stammered, as I pulled my cell phone off the deep-chested entry table and tried to will my hands to stop shaking enough to dial the number.

"Oh, no, Jack, no," I whispered through gritted teeth when the call went straight to his voicemail.

I dialed again. "Shit. No. Please, no," my voiced squeaked as I paced back and forth. With my right hand barely sturdy enough to hold the phone to my ear and my left hand tucked tightly under the opposing armpit, I filled my fingers full of skin, pinching down as hard as possible in an attempt to divert the pain of feeling my heart rip apart.

Officer Grady extended his arms and shifted his feet each time I shuffled near him, initiating words of comfort, but quickly realizing his efforts were powerless when dealing with someone who's rapidly sinking in the quicksand of denial.

Finally, he stepped into my path, and with a tight grip on both slumping shoulders, softly turned me around to face him.

The fact that I had bitten entirely through a small portion of my bottom lip seemed to startle him, and while the stream of blood continued to remain constant, he gently took control of my breakdown. "Mrs. Whitman," he whispered. "Who should I call? You need someone with you right now. Please, is there someone I can call for you?"

This time a small and childlike "Yes," escaped through my bloody lips. I felt like it shouldn't take so much effort to say one little word, a word we use a hundred times a day, but it *was* hard and completely exhausting. It was as if the sound from this three letter word had held my lips apart just long enough for my soul to escape.

He pulled out a bandana, applying pressure to my mouth, and in exchange, I handed him my cell phone with the contact name Jamie lit up in blue letters on the screen. Someone would need to tell my brother-in-law that his older brother Jack was dead.

As Officer Grady took the phone from my hand, a tiny, purple orb slowly drifted past my line of vision and across his chest. Confused, my eyes followed the speck, only to see it suddenly multiply a thousand times, and then each orb began to swell. The purple color faded to the outside of the circle and a bead of light replaced the center like the dimmer switch on an LED bulb. Trying to blink the beacons away only seemed to make them brighter, and within moments the fluorescent illumination blinded me. The weight of my body became too burdensome for my legs, even my hair felt heavy. As if I were riding on a roller coaster and cresting the highest peak, I closed my eyes to the brightness just as I felt myself plummeting to the ground.

My name is Andrea Whitman and those were the last moments of *this* life as I knew them.

KESSLER

We stood underneath the stage feeling the ground shake—the floors pulsing and vibrating in a rhythmic, stomping pattern. The noise was deafening, like a freight train rolling at full steam right over our heads. This was the final concert of a six month long, twenty-two city tour. The band huddled together backstage for what, unbeknownst to them, was going to be my final show—*ever*. Drew, my drummer, gave the pep talk tonight about living in the moment and doing our best, like our lives depended on it.

"Those people out there worked all week and spent their hard earned money to come see us play here tonight, so don't any of you fuck it up for 'em!" he yelled over the crowd screaming in the stadium. "It's the last show of the tour, so let's blow their fuckin' minds! All right? Now, everybody get your hands in and let me hear it on three."

Six hairy, snarled, middle-aged, yet talented hands stacked one upon the other as we all screamed "boo-yah," while throwing them up in the air.

I had to laugh. Drew was never much of a poet, but he could give one hell of a pep talk. Our usual routine for this tour was to have the band already set up and out on the stage before I made my grand entrance, but for the finale we're making a change. Tonight we're all taking the stage together; one family, one band of brothers, one last time. We crowded onto the pitch-black elevator, collectively took in a deep breath, and then I flipped the switch. As soon as the crowd saw us rising up from the floor, it was *on*, for all of us.

We always start out with a few favorites to get the crowd pumped up. They responded exactly how we had hoped; everyone went ape shit. Arrowhead Stadium in Kansas City is one of the best places to do a show; Midwestern folk who love country music and know how to throw one hell of a party. Fans started arriving in the stadium parking lot at nine o'clock in the morning, and the opener wasn't set to go on until six in the evening. People who love to spend an entire summer day baking on the black asphalt in the scorching sun, fishing out beer cans from the truck bed cooler, and smoking BBQ, just waiting to hear some live music, are my kind of people. I'm glad this is the spot for the final show—*my final show*.

During the first set as I looked out into the audience, I could see about ten rows in front of me from anywhere on the stage. I used to *always* look for the most beautiful girls, and inevitably, I would spot a couple in every city. I'd send my roadie out to the seats to ask them if they wanted to come backstage to meet me and the boys, have some drinks, and party for a while. This was an extremely useful tactic in no-strings attached one-nighters, and there were many, many one-nighters. When I was younger I was so proud of myself, thought I was the shit, a real big deal that all these girls wanted to sleep with me. A few years ago, I finally realized our night together was just a story to tell their friends or an article to sell to the tabloids. I don't regret the girls or mistakes I've made because they're part of my journey that's led me to this point, but I'm ready to move on now.

Tonight there's a group of six women having a ball together. I'd say they were mid-twenties, sitting in the third row, all of them singing along and cheers'sing each other after every song. I sent Randy out to schmoose on them during the set break and ask them if they'd like to come backstage after the show. That invite certainly revved up their engines, because I got all kinds of "fuck me" eyes during the second set.

A sixty foot screen flanks each side of the stage allowing a front row view from any seat in the stadium. This only amplifies my seduction of the crowd when Lacy, my camera girl, fills it full with images of just my ass—sixty feet (one-hundred and twenty if you count both screens) of my ass over and over again. I get it though, whatever sells tickets. My schedule over the last five years had become less about the music and more about the money my image brings in. Singer/songwriters, authors, actors, and anyone in "the business" have been bitching about this for decades. I went to Nashville to be a songwriter, and fifteen years later I've become sixty feet of ass in tight white jeans.

I always told myself, that when this dream of mine became too mechanical and I couldn't give every part of myself to the fans, I'd hang it up. It's been a great ride and only a handful of people have been with me from the very beginning. Those are the people who deserve all of me; they've earned it, but I can't give one hundred and twenty percent anymore. Don't I deserve a normal life again? I've earned that, too.

As the last song of the encore performance wrapped up, the spotlights put on a magnitude of a show and the fireworks shot up into the sky like rockets in flight. The crowd howled with gratitude for a job well done. Anyone who has ever had major success in business, particularly in finance, says, "Buy low and sell high," and that's exactly what I'm doing here tonight. I worked my ass off playing dive bars and LSU frat parties for years, eating at Taco Bell and Popeye's Chicken whenever I could afford it, and excited I had made the money to do so. Now, I'm playing in a sold out arena with fans screaming my name, singing my songs, and girls still wanting to come back stage to meet me.

Yeah, I'd definitely say I'm high.

ANNIE

I felt like I was floating in one of those kidney shaped swimming pools strategically placed in a well-manicured lawn. With my eyes closed and both arms stretched out like an airplane, my toes barely peeked out of the pleasantly cool water bobbing ever so gently up and down and side to side. My ears rested just below the surface of the water, and the only noise was the funneled sound of my own breathing in and out. For the moment, I was happy and safe, and could have floated in this spot forever. A muffled voice slowly invaded my peaceful breath, but I couldn't decipher the words. I wanted the voice to fade away or stop completely. Trying to block the noise out of my brain, my *happy* was fading, and I became more and more nauseated.

When my eyes finally opened, Officer Grady's round, sweaty face hovered over me whispering, "Mrs. Whitman. Mrs. Whitman, can you hear me?"

It took me a few seconds to even remember him or why he was at my house, but within moments the words: *accident, no survivors, and devastating news* came flooding back.

"Jesus, why am I wet?" I stuttered, wiping the water away from my eyes and feeling the soaking wet washcloth on top of my head. I slowly rose up until I was sitting cross-legged on the hardwood floors, took the rag off my head, and then violently threw up in my lap. Apparently, grief also comes in liquid form. Grady took the washcloth from my hands and tried to clean the puke off my blue maxi dress, but quickly realized wiping my tits and crotch with a dripping wet towel only made the mess worse.

"Oh, God, Mrs. Whitman. I'm so sorry."

"Is this real? Am I dreaming?" I asked, staring straight ahead and facing the door as I spoke. I didn't want to look at him, hoping that it might somehow force him to give me a different answer.

"Yes, ma'am," he whispered. "I'm real and this is happening."

I started crying which quickly turned into sobbing, as I held my face in my puke covered hands. There is a huge difference between crying and sobbing. Crying is when your face looks all screwed up, and you wipe the tears from your cheeks over and over again. Depending on where you're crying, you might even blot at your eyes to keep your make-up intact. Sobbing is when your *insides* are all screwed up, and you fight with your own body to breathe. It's a painful sickness that comes over you like a seizure, stopping every lobe of your brain from functioning properly. You do not recover from sobbing to finish what you were previously do-ing, or gather yourself to start a new project. Your only goal throughout sobbing is to get through each moment and remember to breathe; you are helpless, weak, and pathetic. This is a feeling I remember all too well, only this time, the subject matter was different.

It was obvious to me that Grady had never before been given this type of assignment which, I might add, he did confess to me later on that eve-ning. He spoke in fragments and constantly fumbled with the belt on his uniform. Although uncomfortable and shy, he ended up staying late into the night at my house, even though he had a wife and child who were most likely missing him at his own home. I have continued to tell him how grateful I am for the gracious way he handled my family throughout what I thought at the time was the worst day of our lives.

"Mrs. Whitman, your brother-in-law should be here any minute. You just go ahead and cry or get sick or do whatever you need to, and I'll be right here to help you as best as I can." He was bent down on one knee and lightly rubbed my back in a circular motion as he spoke.

He had a nurturing, fatherly tone to his touch and his voice. I could picture him lying in bed with his child, stroking his or her hair as he sang them off to sleep at night. The image made me feel guilty that I had been happy earlier, when he was miserably hot. I also confessed this to him later on when we became better acquainted, and my family was more manageable.

Jamie's wheels kicked up the gravel as he hauled ass down my long, circular driveway, both car doors slammed and then, the beeping of the door.

Thank God, Elizabeth is with him.

Only acquaintances come in our house through the front door. Family and friends always walk through the garage and come in through the laundry room, which is usually littered with dirty clothing that didn't seem to make it in the laundry bin, or half-finished craft projects clutter-ing the counters. Anytime a door in the house opens, a quick *beep-beep* goes off. Jack had the security system installed for safety precautions since he traveled often for work, and he also thought it would come in handy when we had kids. I admit, I thought it was a stupid idea, because the constant beeping drove me fucking nuts for the first few months. But like most of his ideas, I inevitability relented to his foresight in home security. After a while, the beeping didn't bother me as much. Actually, I liked the security of knowing when someone came in and out of my house.

"Annie!" Jamie yelled. "Ann, where are you?"

"We're in the foyer, Mr. Whitman," Grady called back.

Jamie ran to us, like a bull running straight for a red cape. "Oh, God, Annie," he exclaimed when he saw me in a crumpled mess on the floor, sobbing in a puddle of puke. "Liz, we need you in here!"

Officer Grady stood back against the wall and let our dwindling family have a moment. His superior was on the way over to give him a chance to escape the unpleasant experience of becoming the grim reaper's personal assistant and also, to provide us with any dreadful details of my husband's death.

KESSLER

After the second encore, every performer of the night came back out on stage to sign autographs on whatever people hand up to us, while the band plays in the background. I always try to sign something for the kids first. My family didn't have the extra money to send me to a concert when I was growing up, so I always try and make it the most memorable experience for any kid that comes to see one of my shows. Of course, we've had some mighty interesting items put on stage for us to sign: bras, panties, cowboy hats, T-shirts, a clock, a tube of KY jelly, a bottle of hot sauce, and once someone handed me a framed picture of their mama. Of the hundreds of shows we've done, the autograph that stands out the most was a pair of brown, knee high, Jimmy Choo boots.

I kept asking her, "Are you sure? Are you really sure?"

From what my best friend's wife, Hope, tells me, those boots are like a thousand dollars a pair, and this lady looked higher than a Georgia pine when she handed one of them up to me. After I got backstage that night and told Hope about the boots, she went on and on about how I shouldn't have ruined those beautiful Jimmy Choo's with my ugly signature. I felt so bad about what I'd done, and woke up the next morning still thinking about it. I'm pretty sure the owner of those boots woke up thinking about it, too.

After the show, when everyone had a chance to take off their sweaty clothes and get a quick shower in their dressing room, the party was on; especially tonight, with this being the final show of the tour. The music was loud, and the food looked amazing spread out on a twenty foot table. In each city where we do a show, the dinner served is the specialty of that city. In San Antonio it's Mexican food, in Seattle it's salmon, in Chicago we have Italian, and in New York we have monster-sized pizza pies. Tonight, since we're in Kansas City, the main course is meat and we had any and every kind of BBQed meat you could think of. My stomach was empty, the line was impossibly long, and I didn't know if the small amount of energy I had left would hold out long enough for me to pile a disgusting amount of food onto two over-sized plates. I'm always the last one to eat dinner after a show. Without all the support of everyone in my crew, this concert wouldn't be possible, and they need to know that I appreciate each one of them and the work they do to make me look good. Plus, my mama raised me right. She'd slap my face if she ever saw me go to the front of a line with women and elders standing behind me, so better safe than sorry.

After everyone was fed, the cocktails were flowing and the talking and laughter got increasingly louder. Finally, I ran into one of my oldest and best friends, Wade Rutledge and his wife Hope. I love it when my friends come out to my shows, especially since Wade just so happens to be a four time Grammy winner. I like to give him shit about that—only because I just have three.

"Hey, buddy," I smiled and said as we gave each other a man hug.

The "man hug" is when two very good male friends feel it's socially accepted to hug each other with one arm. Each man embraces the other with *only* one arm and slaps the shit out of each other on the back with their free hand.

"What's a Grammy winning, country music star like you doing at my little ole show?" I asked, laughing.

"The boys were driving me shit house crazy at home, and I've been promising my wife I'd bring her to see a sixty foot ass. Well, honey, here he is!" Wade clamored, while grabbing and shaking me. "Plus, the whiskey is free and she's driving," he added, pointing to Hope.

"Oh, baby, you're just jealous your tush has gone a little soft on your tour break. Look at his ass, Wade! Women all over this stadium would love to grab a couple of handfuls and give it a rub, like the Buddha belly at that horrible Chinese restaurant where you're always making me eat." I jumped back as she pinched my rear.

"Kess honey, don't you listen to him," she said as she put her arm around me. "It was a fantastic show, and I, for one, am having a great time! Now," she said, as she turned me around and started walking me towards a group of women. "These ladies have been staring you down since we started talking, and I think you should be polite and say hello." She pushed me towards the group of drunken women and walked back to kiss on Wade some more.

There was a time when Hope tried to fix me up with her friends, but it never seemed to pan out. Half of them were pissed off at me for sleeping with them and never calling again, and with the other half there just wasn't any chemistry. It seemed as though I kept having the same conversation over and over again, only with different women on different nights; same shit, different day, beautiful women, but boring just the same.

Tonight, forcing me over to this group of women, Hope was just being mean. I'm always happy to talk with fans and thank them for coming out, but this group was a mess. There was a point where a few of them stopped speaking English and the brunette was so worn out from standing, she sat on the floor in the middle of our conversation.

"OMG, Kessler Carlisle!" one of the blonde's screamed as I walked up to the disastrous straggle of women.

OMG, I hate that. Jesus, I'm getting old.

"You're my all-time favorite singer and so damn good looking! Can I give you a kiss?" the other one slurred, swaying from side to side, unable to master gravity. As she spoke, her right eye slowly began drooping until finally closing completely, making her a full-fledged cyclops.

"Oh, thanks, you're sweet, and I appreciate y'all so much for coming tonight. How 'bout we make it a hug instead?" I asked, praying this was over soon.

I gave her a hug and pretended not to notice when she started rubbing my ass, but once her hand moved around to my crotch and her tongue found my ear, I jumped back.

"Hey, all right then, y'all have a great night and thanks again. Drive safe!" I said, and as I turned around, Hope was grinning at me. I shot her a "you're dead" look.

Walking back to my friends, I heard the molester yell, "You don't say no to me, Kessler Carlisle, you fucking prude!" Hope and Wade were cracking up; holding on to each other so one of them didn't fall down from laughing so hard. I hung my head a bit and smiled, because it would only be a matter of seconds before that girl saw the outside of the stadium.

"Hey," started Hope in her slow, southern drawl. "She seemed real nice. You gonna bring her round for supper on Sunday?"

"Yeah, thanks a lot! I don't think she'll be sober by dinnertime on Sunday. She smelled like gin, and had puke on her shirt," I said in disgust.

"You should've been a little sweeter to some of my friends, Kess. Looks like you're wiping the bottom of the barrel at this point," she teased, patting my face.

"Come on y'all, this is a party, and I'm gonna dance with the most beautiful woman in the room," Wade said, as he took Hope's hand and led her over to the makeshift dance floor.

I stopped and watched them dance together for a while. He whispered something in her ear, and she threw her head back laughing like it was the funniest thing she'd ever heard. After twenty years of marriage, they're still giggling and teasing each other like they were a couple of high school kids. Whenever they're out together, Wade always has his arm hanging around her shoulder, and Hope's got her hand in his back pocket; they're a real-life John Mellencamp song. How they act together at home is no different than what they're showing people tonight. They never take their hands off each other. Hope and Wade were together before he got rich and became a celebrity. With one divorce under my belt, I just don't ever want to go through that again. My ex-wife ruined my trust in women and the desire to be married. Maybe if I didn't have fame or money, or maybe if she didn't know who I was, I could find a good woman and love her wildly for the rest of my days.

I found myself staring off into space, once again wanting to feel that fire for someone, but having no idea when or where I was going to find her.

The dance floor was heating up with people acting a fool when Wade left his wife in the hands of a drunken drummer, headed back my way.

"Goddamn you're boring, Kess," he said, poking me in the chest. "You need me to tuck you into bed and read you a story, or are you gonna go out there and dance with my hot ass wife?"

"Better be careful what you wish for, 'cause I just might be going home with her tonight," I said.

Wade bantered back, "Only reason you'd be riding in her car on the way home is because you live next door to us, and don't *think* we're taking you all the way to your front door either. You can walk from the end of our driveway." About that time Hope waved us over.

Wade offered up his glass of whiskey and said, "To an amazing tour and an even more amazing break from it."

Even though he had no idea how permanent of a break this was actually going to be, I raised my glass and added, "To life-long happiness."

ANNIE

T he night seemed to drag on endlessly. Officers took turns talking, and Liz and I took turns crying. Jamie showed no emotion whatsoever. Officer Grady, bless his heart, had turned into a concierge making coffee and serving drinks; it's the obvious sign of a good man. Anyone who takes on the role of host without asking a bunch of, "Where is this, where is that, what would you like," type questions, and especially without being asked to do so, is a person with a good heart. I could see the kindness in Officer Grady and realized how lucky I was that he was the one on my doorstep.

Liz had already packed a suitcase with all my necessities, big enough to last me a week.

"You're staying at our house tonight, and I don't want to hear another word about it," she said. Almost fighting her on it, my body and mind were too exhausted; I wanted sleep and to send this day straight to hell.

I just nodded in agreement. "Where are the kids?" I asked.

"My mom came and picked them up. They're going to stay with her for a few days so we can sort some things out."

Jamie and Elizabeth have two kids; Max is seven and Mia is almost five. My niece and nephew are the closest thing to having my own children I will probably ever experience. I love them madly and would walk through fire to protect them. Max is the spitting image of Jamie when he was seven, but with the personality of his mama—sweet and sensitive. Mia looks just like Elizabeth, but has her daddy's quick temper and is stubborn as a mule. These are terrible character traits for a five year old, but when she gets older, she's going to be the CEO of something. Ever since these kids were born, Jack and I have been a constant in their lives. We were the first ones at the hospital when each one of them was born, and the first ones at every birthday party they've ever had. We have date night with them once a week taking them to get ice cream or a movie, and they spend the night at our house at least once a month, not because we feel obligated, but because we truly love spending time with them. Since I don't work anymore, when Liz needs a break or is in a bind, I'm always happy to pick them up from school or head over to their house and make myself at home. This is the only family I have known for some time now, and I don't know how it's supposed to work without Jack in it.

The investigators had very little information at this point and spent most of their time asking me the same questions over and over again. Jack's Range Rover was found on a secluded stretch of HWY 29, wrapped around a massive pine tree. They can only speculate that the impact of the crash was what set the car on fire; the windows were blown out and it was burned to the ground. The only way they identified him was because the force of impact from his car hitting the tree shot his front bumper with the license plate still intact through the woods; again speculation. The officers who arrived first on the scene recovered only the license plate. Everything else was turned into ash. My only prayer at this point was that Jack had been killed in the wreck, not in the fire. I couldn't let my mind take me to the latter scenario; it was just too graphic, and strangely enough, physically painful to imagine.

One by one the officers left the house until it was just the three of us staring at each other in silence.

"It's two in the morning, let's go," Liz said.

"I'll just put Janet and Tito in their kennel for the rest of the night. Can you drop me off in the morning?" I asked Jamie.

"Yeah, okay. I'll get your bag, Annie," Jamie said, and he held my hand as we walked out the door.

As we slowly drove down the driveway, Jamie looked as though he had a slight smirk on his face. *Is he smiling?* I squinched my eyes to get a better look at him through the rearview mirror, but when our eyes made contact he instantly looked away. I couldn't even register what I thought I saw, but I haven't ever lost a sibling. Never even having a sibling, I can't imagine what it feels like to lose one. *I shouldn't judge.* The house grew smaller, fading into the darkness through the back windshield, and my gut told me nothing about this house would ever feel the same. I dreaded walking back into it.

KESSLER

As daylight broke free from the murk of night, our jet made a smooth landing at the Nashville International Airport at dawn the next morning. The three of us looked like hammered shit. We drank everything that wasn't nailed down, and I think Wade won the wrestling match we started on the dance floor, but couldn't be sure because that's when I blacked out. Thank God Hope's mother, Mama D, was waiting for us with the car when we arrived. As we rolled our bags towards our ride home, her face changed from happiness to disbelief, with her hands planted firmly on her wide-set hips.

"Good God almighty," she said, slapping her leg. "You three look useless as tits on a boar!"

"Pipe down, woman!" said Wade, rather annoyed. "Just drive the damn car until I tell you to pull over so I can puke."

"Well, well. Looks like Mr. High Cotton can't hold his liquor in his old age," cackled Mama D. "And you, young lady, I taught you better than this. You look like you got mowed down by the John Deere."

"Well, maybe I did. I don't remember a damn thing from last night, and might still be drunk. Please stop yellin', mama," Hope whispered.

"Oh, my baby, Kessler!" Mama D cried, as she grabbed me and squeezed my waist so hard I almost shit my pants. "Are you feeling okay?" she asked, while feeling my forehead for a temperature. "Now, you come on over, and I'll fix you a big breakfast and a little hair of the dog to get you feelin' right side up again."

"Thanks, Mama D. I sure do appreciate that, and you know how much I love your cooking, especially those cheesy grits, but the only thing I can think about right now is sleep," I apologized.

"I'll take breakfast," whined Wade.

"Only thing you're gonna take is a shower, Wade Rutledge, 'cause you smell bad enough to knock a dog off a gut wagon," preached Mama D.

There was a moment of silence and then we all busted up laughing.

Alice Deanna Kroy, (aka Mama D) spent all her life growing up in Lynchburg, TN—a southern Tennessee town with a ton of southern

Tennessee sayings, about five thousand people and one traffic light. Over the years, some notable celebrities have called Lynchburg home: Davy Crockett, Little Richard and the great Johnny Majors (head coach of the Tennessee Volunteers 1977-1992) but no one more famous than Mr. Jack Daniel. The Jack Daniel's Distillery has called Lynchburg home since 1956. Even though it resides in a dry county and the residents can't purchase this Tennessee whiskey in restaurants or stores, the distillery does sell commemorative bottles to enjoy at home, and I had more than my share last night.

Although I don't always understand Mama D's Tennessee sayings, I do know that anything she does for someone comes from love. She's a short, round woman; looks like an apple on a stick, with curly gray hair styled like a football helmet. She has her own rules of how she thinks life should run, and isn't afraid to put her two cents worth of advice in your piggy bank. Her heart is pure as gold, and she has mothered me from our first meeting over twenty years ago. I don't always take her advice, which I should, but she never holds it against me or steers me in the wrong direction. After Hope's daddy passed and right before their youngest son Kroy was born, Mama D moved in with Wade and Hope to help with the kids and the house since Wade is on tour six months out of the year. She's always cooking up something delicious, which is why I'm always eating at their house, and she usually makes enough food for twice the amount of people that are eating. She's the quintessential Southern Mama.

We headed down I-65 South to Franklin, a suburb of Nashville, with the windows rolled down in a vain attempt to dry ourselves out and to also keep Wade from puking in Mama D's new Cadillac. The blustering air charging through the windows restricted any amount of talking between the four of us and gave me some thinking time to reflect on the last few months. I needed to concoct possible ideas regarding my retirement and eventual vanishing act. Usually there's a progression of rules one follows when retiring, but having never been one for following rules, I'm just not ready to drop this bomb yet. I've been planning the escape to my house in St. Croix in the U.S Virgin Islands for some time now, and apparently, that's as far as I've gotten. For the first time in a decade, I have no plan. I'm hung-over, about to really piss some people off, leaving the states indefinitely, and haven't packed a single thing, but damn, it felt good!

When the woodsy landscape became familiar, I knew we were close. The final stretch of a tour can significantly age all the parts of your body.

The last tour for me was no exception, but once I inhaled the sweet smell of cherry trees, I relaxed. Finally, I was home.

Positioned at the head of the cul-de-sac in a classically charming neighborhood, with massive maple trees lining the street, is where my early 1900's Tutor sits. From the very first walk through, I knew I'd grow old in this house. Last winter I started renovations in the garage, and those turned out so well, I just kept going across the backyard with a new outdoor patio. Throwing a good party is my business, and the amount of work and people that seven acres of yard takes to keep up is daunting. The contractors laid a huge concrete patio which was stained and stamped to look like a hardwood floor. A new infinity pool was put in the middle of the entertaining space, with a stone retaining wall towering above, and the mist of a constant waterfall sprinkles the deck reminding me of my second home—the ocean. When finalizing plans for the back- yard, I was blown away to see how many options I had just on the con- crete. I realized I was in way over my head, and spent a week on the internet looking at different yards, trying to find a style I liked best. I printed myself out a picture and then hired someone to landscape it for me. Growing up on farmland in the bayou taught me hard work, not de- sign aesthetics, but I did help in every bit of the construction, and my daddy would have been proud.

My home in Nashville, like the rest of my life, has become a three-ring spectacle; all by my own doing, but done just the same. Maids, gardeners, chefs, and assistants are in a constant rotation through my kitchen, down my hallways, in my yard, and consistently around every next corner. I realize this is a first world problem, and one I certainly never thought would infuriate me as much as it does, but it's the reason I'm leaving. I want to open my curtains to the silence and spectacular of an ocean sun- rise, sit by a pool, strum my guitar, or just disappear into the tides with- out explaining why I'm going, and when I'll be back. This breakneck pace has finally worn me out. I'm ready to take my foot off the accelerator. It's time to just cruise.

Mama D pulled into the driveway, up to the garage and said, "Okay baby, home sweet home."

Wade was snoring in the backseat next to me, and I couldn't resist. I licked my finger, softly stuck it inside his ear, and swirled it around a bit. When his eyelids flickered with consciousness, I leaned in and whispered, "Mornin' sunshine."

"Get away from me," he grumbled.

"Looks like I went home with your wife, *and* made it all the way to my front door!" I teased him.

Wade opened one eye and looked around, then he punched me in the arm and smiled, pleased he inflicted some kind of pain on me.

I grabbed my bags from the trunk, kissed Mama D and thanked her again for picking us up and bringing me home.

"Come on by for supper tonight after you get some sleep. I'll make you some grits," she offered.

As they turned the car around, I heard Wade through the open windows ask Mama D, "How come you're never that nice to me?"

"Oh honey, Kessler doesn't have anybody, and you get to live with me," she boasted.

I stood in my garage and watched the doors close all the way to the ground, thinking how right she was. After I managed to shed the weight of my ex-wife, I successfully filled that void with things unreal, and in the process sealed myself shut. I'm surrounded by expensive things paid for in cash, but what I really long for the most can't be bought. Maybe it was time to get in the business of someday having a family.

ANNIE

The next afternoon, I awoke gagging to the smell of stale puke. The pitch-black room disoriented my location and time of day. I turned on the bedside lamp and caught a glimpse of myself in the mirror.

Well, that explains the smell.

Apparently, vomit acts as a bonding agent when mixed with human hair. Blond strands were clumped together in hard, jumbled and mashed sections, sticking straight out in every direction. The overall appearance resembled a poor attempt at homemade dreadlocks with little knowledge of the hairstyle to begin with. The rancid smell of undigested groceries decomposing on my scalp overwhelmed the picture perfect, Pottery barn guestroom and probably contaminated the entire second story of my brother-in-law's house. I obviously had not taken a shower after getting back to Jamie's and was disgusting and pathetic, inside and out. Liz must have put pajamas on me, but I was sleeping on top of the bed, not under the covers—probably too heavy for her petite frame to lift up and work underneath the sheets. After desecrating every probable square foot of this lovely area with my fragrant stench, I envisioned Liz burning the whole damn room down.

"Please don't let today happen," I whispered and then turned my face into the pillow, screaming as loud and as long as my breath would allow. This infantile display only made my throat hurt and tears well up in my eyes, not helping me to feel any better. I quickly came to the realization that nothing was going to make me feel better about having a dead husband. For a moment, fury rose from my heart like fire imploding the core of a hot air balloon, but the sensation passed as quickly as it came, and once again, I only had enough energy for exhaustion and numbness. I turned back over and closed my eyes, fully aware of my foulness but rejecting the thought of putting forth any kind of effort to rectify it. This was a preview of what I had in store for myself over the next few months: carelessness for myself, carelessness for others and quite frankly, for life in general.

***

Shooting up in bed, I heard myself make a loud gasping sound like some-one had just punched me the throat, knocking the wind out of me. The moment you wake from an intense dream and can't seem to distinguish fact from fiction easily muddles the next few minutes, leaving you in an almost alcohol induced haze.

Did I dream it? Is he gone? I thought, as it took some effort to begin breathing normally again. Without fail, truth came washing over me, along with a real-life movie trailer of the last twenty-four hours. After composing myself, I pressed the button on the clock to light up the time: 7:35 p.m.

Jesus, I slept all day.

I attempted to roll out of bed, but couldn't move my legs. The physical discomfort of becoming a widow rushed over me; the pain of a broken heart is sharp as a surgeon's scalpel.

Why does my body hurt?

I had to physically pick up each leg to swing them over the side of the bed and onto the floor. Holding on to the wall and slowly sliding my body down until lowered on hands and knees, my only choice was crawl-ing if I was going to make it to the bathroom. I turned on the shower and took inventory of myself in a hand mirror stashed in the vanity bottom drawer as the ice cold water filled around my lower half. My reflection was grotesque—the loser end of a bar fight. Where my eyes should have been were black, puffy circles that hindered my vision and reminded me of over-ripe plums. The sides of my face were stiff, like small curtain rods had been stuffed inside my cheeks. My bottom lip was swollen and cov-ered in crusty, dried blood, which was also smeared throughout the inside of my mouth causing my teeth to resemble the type of baked beans commonly served at a backyard barbeque. I didn't care, I wasn't even shocked; I felt nothing.

Liz must have heard the water running, and she came upstairs to check on me.

"Annie, I'm so glad you're up," she said with careful fraction. "Can I help you with anything, honey? Ann?"

When she pulled back the shower curtain, even though I didn't look her in the eye, her pity screamed at me. I heard it in her silence and felt it in her stillness. Like only a mom can, she fought back her tears and got to work. I sat in the fetal position against the side of the tub with cold water from the shower running on me. She adjusted the water temperature, filled up the tub, and gently washed me from head to toe; insert humiliation. Then, she walked me into the bedroom where a fresh set of pajamas were laid out. I submitted to her nurturing like a child, allowing her to comb my wet hair, dabbing at the ends with a towel until the beads of water finally stopped dripping.

I turned my face towards her. "Thank you," I whispered. She replied with a wink.

"Can I go back to sleep now?" I asked.

"Of course, and don't worry about Janet and Tito. I picked them up yesterday morning. They're having a great time here," she assured me.

"Okay," was all I said, and laid my head down on the pillow.

What I was thinking was a lot more than just okay.

I'm a deadbeat mother. How could I not even think about needing to take care of our dogs? Liz said, "Yesterday morning," so that means I could have left the dachshunds in a kennel for basically two days and not even noticed. I'm a horrifying person who can't seem to keep things I'm responsible for alive; a baby inside of me for more than ten weeks—twice, a husband from dying, and next up apparently are my dogs.

"What the fuck am I here for?" I asked aloud to no one in particular.

"Yeah," I started again, and this time I was speaking directly to someone. "What the fuck? What the fuck is this? Do you hate me or something? Have I wronged you in some way? Tell me! Give me a goddamn answer!" I growled. I waited through heart-pounding, heavy breathing for a reply but heard only silence. "Well, fuck you, too," I whispered, and then rolled over and went back to sleep.

ANNIE

I opened my eyes to the broken and scattered beams of sunlight shining in through the windows, and it took a while to adjust to the brightness, since I'd been asleep for two and a half days. Even though my mouth was beyond dry, a thick coating of saliva reminiscent of rotting fish had taken up residence, so I dragged my repugnant self into the bathroom, splashed cold water on my face and brushed my teeth seven times. It was time to face this new life.

"Here I go," I said aloud and walked downstairs.

Jamie and Liz sat on barstools at the granite island drinking coffee. The roman shades were open, everything was put away in its place, and the immaculate kitchen smelled of a recent cleaning. This is one of the differences between Elizabeth and me. When life gets tough, I curl up into a ball and cover my eyes; Liz gets busy making things right in the world, and has probably been like this her entire life. I used to be a strong woman, something Jack loved about me, but after the first miscarriage that part of me died along with the baby.

I walked up to my brother-in-law and hugged him tightly. "I'm sorry," I said.

"Me too," he replied.

The Jackson's, as Jack and I referred to them, came running up to me barking, jumping and peeing all over theirselves in delight. Jack always loved Michael Jackson's music and thought it would be hilarious if we named our dogs after his siblings. I chalked it up to another stupid idea, but truth be told, people always laugh when you call a wiener dog, Tito. The eighties weren't my favorite genera of music, I'm a classic rock girl, but the names seem to fit their personalities, so I didn't make a stink about it.

"Hey, guys, I missed you!" I told them as they started running in circles around the island, which turned into chasing, which then turned into Janet attacking Tito. This is their usual progression with any excitement that might occur in their wiener dog world.

"The kids are coming home today!" Liz said, with excitement in her voice.

"They'll be a breath of fresh air for me," I replied.

"Me too," Jamie chimed in.

Putting my hand on his shoulder, I said, "I'm sorry I've been asleep for so long. I didn't mean for you to be alone in this, and I'm ready to help in any way possible."

"It's okay, Annie. Jack would have wanted me to take care of you, and that's the least I can do for him. Actually, Jack had every detail taken care of for *us*," he said.

"What do you mean?" I asked feeling stupid, because I should've known what our plan was if something like this were to happen. Isn't this common knowledge to every wife?

"All you have to do is call Gail Adams, your insurance agent, and she will set the plan of action into motion," Jamie said.

"Is it normal for an insurance agent to be a part of planning a funeral?" I asked.

"I'm sure Jack just didn't want to burden you in any way. Don't think too much about the details and just stick to his plan laid out for us. Everything will turn out all right," Jamie assured me.

"I would have liked to be involved in that big of a decision," I admitted. "I'll call her today," I said, feeling annoyed but also ashamed that the last two days had slipped by me. "Does that mean he planned his own funeral? I guess I'm just a little confused," I confessed.

"Jack already picked out and paid for everything. We just need to set the funeral date and notify anyone we think might want to attend," he said. "I sent out a mass email letter yesterday and already have several responses; a lot of people want to be there for us," he added.

Did Jack think I couldn't handle any of this? Why didn't he talk to me and let us figure it out together? I thought, but at this point it didn't matter; it was done and quite frankly, it's obvious I could *not* handle it; I've missed the last two days of my life.

"Wait, what about his body? Is there a body?" I asked as I felt the vomit in my throat and the weight in my legs; picturing his mangled and burnt out black Range Rover hugging a tree on the side of the highway. I only allowed a flash of the image before forcing my eyes to immediately focus on the first thing I saw. I slumped onto one of the barstools.

"I spoke with Officer Grady this morning, and he said it's not good. There's nothing left, Annie," Jamie said in a slow and monotone voice as he stared down at the floor in a zombie like trance.

I already knew Jack's body was turned to ash, but hearing it verbally confirmed was a crushing blow and still something I couldn't actually get my head around.

Now we were both staring at the same spot on the floor.

"After you talk to your agent, I assume we will have the information we need to finalize funeral plans," he whispered as I softly cried.

"I'll call her now and get it over with," I said, while letting out a long sigh to stop the flow of tears.

I found my purse on the counter and began digging through it when Liz said, "It's over here. Your phone was out of juice, so I charged it up for you."

I forced a grateful smile, gently patted her cheek and asked, "What would I do without you?"

She took my hand, looked right into my eyes and very sternly said, "Anything you need, anytime you need it, Andrea, I'll be here to help you."

I froze, crippled with emotion. My whole life I've gone by Annie, even my parents used that nickname for me before I came home from the hospital. No one has ever called me Andrea except Jack. It was something special between us no one else shared, only us. I know she meant well, but to hear my formal name come from her lips was like hearing a crack in the galaxy, and I couldn't help feeling like she had just ruined a special memory for me; realizing now that Jack wasn't the last person to call me *Andrea*.

I turned on my phone and *Jesus Christ*, thirty-seven messages and twenty-two texts. I didn't even want to check my email; that was for another day. I scrolled through my contact list and found Gail Adams' phone number.

"This sucks!" I whispered in anger, opening the back door and walking out into the yard to smoke.

"Adams Agency, this is Cindy speaking, how may I help you?" chirped an overly blissful voice.

"Andrea Whitman calling for Gail Adams," I mumbled.

"Thank you, transferring, please hold," she replied, exuding friendliness.

How can my life be this fucked up and yet everyone else's just keeps on going without a scratch? Doesn't she know that the future I expected to have with my husband ceases to ever exist? Why is she so pleasant?

I'm not sure why I expected the first person I spoke with to be just as miserable as me, but I did. Instead, I got Cindy, the next Miss America, who loves sunshine and kittens.

"Mrs. Whitman, Gail Adams. How are you holding up, honey?" she asked.

"I've been better. My husband Jack Whitman has passed away, and I'd like to meet with you to discuss the details of his estate," I said, trying not to sound like a wife with no fucking clue.

Jack's dead. Jack's dead. Jack's dead. How many times am I going to have to say Jack's dead? Is there a point where it just becomes two words with less meaning, or is it always going to hurt this bad?

"Yes, I was expecting your call, and I'm so very sorry for your loss. I spoke with your brother-in-law, Jamie, and have all the paperwork ready for you to sign," she said. "Can you meet me at my office around three o'clock today?"

"Yes, that's fine," I replied.

"Do you know where my office is located?" she asked.

No, I don't know where your fucking office is located! Actually, there's a lot I don't know! For starters, I don't know where my husband has chosen to spend eternity or if he has a spot for me next to him. Maybe it was two for one day down at the funeral home, and he couldn't pass up a good deal. I also know nothing about the funeral he has planned for himself and can't wait to see how that unfolds. It's like one of those huge boxes you get as a kid on your birthday. You think it's going to be this amazing present, but really its several wrapped boxes, one inside the other. It takes you a half hour to unwrap all these packages, only to realize at the end, some asshole has a fucked up sense of humor, and all you got was some fake, gold studs. Well happy birthday, Annie! Here's your box!

Was what I really wanted to say.

"I can find it," was what I actually said.

34

KESSLER

That evening I woke up all stretched out with a smile on my face. I hadn't slept in my own bed for almost five months, and my God, there's nothing like a king size, pillow-top mattress. After trading sleep between hotels and a tour bus bunk bed (which just seems wrong at forty-three years-old) today was the best sleep I'd had since the tour started. I let out a ferocious yawn, cracked my toes and slowly made my way to the bathroom. While in the shower, my appreciation for how freeing unlimited space and time felt grew enormously. Sometimes on the bus, stress over-powered my mind and I couldn't pinpoint exactly why. Now, standing in my colossal shower which could accommodate five people, I'd figured it out. My smile crept all the way to my ears when I thought about the infinite space of driving my boat to the middle of the ocean and throwing out the anchor for a few days; freedom was so close.

My happy was short-lived when I visualized my "To Do" list which was getting longer by the minute. Call Lloyd, the manager at the concierge service in St. Croix, to get the house and the boat ready, unpack then repack my suitcase, close down my house here and ask Wade to keep a watch on it for me—and oh yeah, tell everyone that worked for me to get a new job. I guess a plan was needed after all. My thoughts were interrupted when the phone rang. It was Mama D calling me over for dinner.

Damn, I'm going to miss that family.

I threw on a shirt and went out the back door. It was a five minute walk across the field which separated my house from the Rutledge home. I'd made this walk so many times, I'd worn a path in the grass and could walk it on the blackest night with a face full of whiskey; I'd had plenty of practice. At one time, there was a six-foot privacy fence I'd have to climb over if I took the path instead of the driveway, but a few years ago when Wade was on tour, I chain sawed myself an opening. I got tired of climbing that damn fence, so I cut a hole in it and waited for Wade to notice. It took a while, but when he did, we all had a good laugh over his temper tantrum. I didn't want to upset Hope, so I built an arbor in the opening and filled it with colorful flowers and plants to keep me in her good graces.

As soon as I walked in, the smell of the best Southern food in the state smacked me in the face and turned me knock kneed.

"Hello?" I called out.

"Hey, sugar! Come on in!" Mama D yelled back.

A smorgasbord of food was spread out across the kitchen; it looked like they were filming a cooking show. Fried chicken, mashed potatoes—with brown gravy of course—coleslaw, deviled eggs, and cheesy grits—my favorite—caught my eye. It was apparent I was going to eat too much, and might need another ride home.

After saying hello to Hope and Mama D, I heard Wade start hollering from downstairs.

"What in the hell is this?" he demanded as he walked up the stairs into the kitchen, holding up a picture frame. "Well? Why is this hanging on a nail in my man cave?" he asked again, only this time he was walking towards Mama D and pointing his finger at her.

"I wasn't aware the basement only belonged to you. I thought that wall was for the *family* to showcase our awards," she answered condescendingly.

"Did you notice all those platinum records or any of the Grammy's on the shelf?" he shot back at her. "Even the boy's trophies aren't down there because that is *my* space!"

"I thought it was a nice addition and made the room feel a little homier," Mama D said, with a slight smirk as she looked over and gave me a wink.

"It's a pie recipe! Why in the hell would you think a framed pie recipe should be hung up in my cave? Don't you think it fits in a little better with the kitchen décor?" he asked her, slapping the counter.

"Hey!" she snapped back. "That is an award winning pie that dates back all the way to my Grandmama. Didn't you see the blue ribbon hanging next to it? And furthermore, since we're talkin' about awards, you're getting a little too big for your britches with your Grammy this and Grammy that. You sing, we get it, so you can just cool it!" she snarked.

"Y'all both need to cool it; you're givin' me a headache," Hope muttered under her breath, rolling her eyes.

Mama D and Wade had an interesting dynamic when it came to their relationship. They loved each other and would put their lives on the line

36

where the other was concerned, but they were both full of so much fire; Hope always needed to throw water on one of them. The battle of control over the homestead wages on year after year between the two of them, but the permanent bantering back and forth was a constant source of entertainment for me, and I was always happy to be a member of the audience.

Just then, the sound of a wild buffalo herd came stampeding down the stairs, making all kinds of racket, and a gang of Rutledge boys filled the kitchen—the volume increased twenty decibels. The boys have their mama's good looks and their daddy's fire. Samson, almost reaching six feet, is the oldest and tamest at fifteen years old and my personal favorite; I'm hoping to see him play college ball in a few years. Carson is twelve and a daddy's boy. He wants to do everything his dad does. Wade acts like it annoys him, but I know he wouldn't have it any other way. Kroy is the youngest and Hope's namesake. That boy has been spoiled something awful by Mama D. No ten year old boy should be more mischievous than coons around midnight and get away with murder day in and day out, but Mama D thinks he does no wrong, and he's got her suckered good.

"All right y'all, let's say a prayer before we eat. I'm going tonight, it's my turn," Hope said. "Dear God, thank you for this wonderful food and the hands who prepared it. Thank you for my loud and passionate family; please help me to survive them. Amen."

After around seven seconds of quiet, everybody started talking at once. It didn't seem to matter that no one was listening to anyone else; they all just kept on talking.

Hope was smiling at me from across the table, and yelled, "Don't you want to get a couple of these someday?" pointing at the row of boys overstuffing their faces with chicken like food had been withheld over several days as a means of torture.

I just sat back in my chair and smiled. *Maybe I do.*

After we cleared our plates from the table, and the boys scattered to who knows where, Mama D put me to work plating the leftovers in Tupperware. *No time like the present.*

"I want y'all to listen to what I'm going to tell you-all the way through before you start asking questions or interrupting. Okay?" I asked, catching them by surprise as I looked at all three of their nodding heads. "Here's the thing; I haven't been happy with where my career's been going for the last few years. Now, it's not what you think. I know I've made plenty of money, received lots of awards and bought more toys than one man should have, but that's not what I'm really looking for anymore. I'm not real sure what I'm looking for to tell you the truth, but I do know I need a break. Not a tour break, a permanent break. I'm going to retire."

Hope let out a sharp gasp, and Wade hung his head down at the table, shaking it back and forth while he let out a long sigh. I instantly thought I might be letting them down, but kept going.

"You three are the first to have this information, and I'd appreciate it if we could keep it in this kitchen until I have a meeting at River Rock Records to tell them myself. I've got six months off until I'm supposed to start going over songs for the next album and sign a new contract. That gets me a December deadline before I have to let anyone over there know I'm not going to renew. I'm spending that time in St. Croix, and I would love it if y'all came out to visit. Now it's your turn," I said, turning over the floor for questions.

They just stared at me in silence. The quiet was complicated by the ticking from the Granddaddy clock in the hallway, and every stroke seemed louder than usual; each second was clear as day.

Hope spoke first. "Honey, you've worked so hard to get to the top, why would you throw it all away?" she pleaded with me.

"Well, I really don't see it that way. I've gotten almost everything I could have ever hoped for and carved out a life for myself that far exceeds anything I ever thought was possible. I'm proud of my accomplishments in this amazing, sometimes dirty rotten, and insatiable, industry. It's been quite a ride, but I just don't want to spend half of the year traveling to city after city and the rest of the year glued to my phone. I hope y'all aren't too disappointed. It's not like I'm dying; just taking a break," I explained.

"I never thought I'd live to hear you say you're gonna retire. I don't agree with this decision and I think you're gonna get bored, but if it's what you want, then I suppose nothing we say is gonna change your mind; and you bet your ass I'm coming to the islands! St. Croix doesn't know what it's up against!" Wade yelled as he stood up and high-fived me so hard, my head jerked back and my hand stung.

"Oh, lord," I said, rolling my eyes. "All right then, I'm glad y'all know. I feel a hundred pounds lighter, but I've got to get home and get some things taken care of before leaving and only got a week to do them," I said.

Hope hugged me and told me she always had my back, even though her eyes said, "Big mistake!" As Wade followed me out, Mama D called over and said, "Let me walk you home honey, I could use the exercise."

"I would love that!" I beamed as we linked arms and headed back towards the path.

The night air was dark and thick, but the fireflies and the sky full of stars were working together to light the way for us. When we reached the arbor, Mama D turned me around so we were face to face. She looked directly into my eyes, put her hands on my shoulders and said, "I'm not out here 'cause I need the exercise. Hell, walking all the way to your door might kill me. I'm out here to tell you I'm proud as punch, Kessler Carlisle, and I want you to know that. I've been wondering for a while when you were gonna figure it out, and it looks like you finally came around. The first half of your life was a great success story. I don't deny that, but the second half, the second half will be your masterpiece. You go out there into the world and find what you're lookin' for and when you do, you bring her back here to meet me," she said as she gave me a big hug and smacked my face.

She just always knows.

My heart felt almost as full as my stomach as I watched her make her way back to the house, whistling a little tune as she skipped along the path.

ANNIE

J amie dropped me off at the edge of my driveway. I wanted to make the walk to my door alone. As I suspected, my two acres of land didn't have the same curb appeal, and my house seemed less like a home since the last time I was here.

Jack found this house in Kansas City over ten years ago, and I was floored walking through it for the first time. The red brick, walkout ranch sits on 2.5 acres, and was built in 1942. It has two creeks running the length of the property, one in front and one in back, and it sits across the street from the seventh green of a golf course. The craftsmanship and the location of this home are unparalleled, and for me, it was love at first sight. We'd put so much effort and money into renovating it year after year; customizing it to become our dream home and today, I can't even stand the sight of it. My hope was to grow old with my husband here, watch our kids play in the yard, take hikes in the woods behind our house, and now, it was an absolute certainty none of those things would ever happen. Fighting hard against the tears made my nose burn, but I still forced myself to go inside.

Everything and nothing were the same when I walked into the house. All the tangible items sat in their proper place, but suddenly, they each had a memory attached to them, telling me a story as I walked by. I kept my head down walking through the house, not ready to reminisce yet, and then got into the shower to clean the overwhelming stench of failure off me.

The water warmed my chilled skin, helping me to feel less like a corpse and cleared some of the pain of my thoughts.

I need to get dressed for the meeting with Gail, and I don't have a go-to widow outfit. I have: girls night, wedding, running and church outfit's, but seem to be fresh out of clothes for a new widow to wear. This is such bullshit.

I finally decided on a white button down, three-quarter sleeve shirt, a black pencil skirt and turquoise Brian Atwood heels. For a moment, the clothes helped me to feel like a real person that wasn't consumed with tragedy, and I prayed to God that feeling would last, at least until my meeting was over.

After plugging the address into my GPS, I was surprised to find that Gail's office was located on the bottom floor of the Allen Enterprise building, in a popular and quaint shopping district known to Kansas City locals as "The Plaza." Her insurance agency was only three doors down from where Jack and Jamie ran a capital funds management company.

I guess that explains why he chose her.

I also knew why her office was on the back side of the Plaza instead of the main street-money. Lord knows the rent throughout the fifteen blocks of couture merchandise, espresso bars, luxurious linens, and trendy restaurants is astronomical, and it's baffling how some of the boutiques have stayed in business over the years.

As I turned onto Ward Parkway heading towards the Plaza and Gail's office, a wave of urgency came over me causing me to lose all interest in dealing with the responsibilities of Jack's afterlife-which also happened to be my present misery. I busted a U-turn and caught HWY 29 north. The thought to turn around never fully registered in my brain; it just happened, as if I was the passenger in the car, not the driver. I had to see where he took his last breath, had his last thought and touch the scars on the tree that captured the last moment of his life. The thought of feeling his last earthly location was dreadfully agonizing and sickly comforting; the spot consumed my focus.

Daydreaming is a yin and yang personality trait passed down to me from some distant ancestor; I have been known to "lose time" in varying amounts depending on the situation. For some reason, driving a car almost always puts me in a functioning trance. Sometimes, I wake up in the parking lot of my destination; other times I have missed a turn and had to backtrack. This appears to be a dangerous habit, but even though I'm not always aware of my surroundings, the fact that I'm still driving a car never escapes me. Often, it's the music from the radio that takes me away before I even realize I'm gone.

Heading to Jack's actual grave, not the one we are manufacturing at the cemetery, I lost time; remembering the little things, private things, which only a wife of ten years would notice about her husband. Even though my eyes were on the road and my foot was on the gas, my mind was gone. Memories fluttered by as fast as the centerline markings on the highway, flashing in and out so rapidly-the swollen knuckles on his hands, his infectious smile, his smell; I had a hard time keeping up. I pictured the way his fingers rubbed together when he was in the middle of a story and momentarily at a loss for the right word, or the heavy sound of

41

his boots on the hardwood floors as he carried wood in for a winter fire. The big one though is the smell of Cartier cologne; it's unmistakably Jack Whitman.

All these images and sound-bites are stored inside of me, triggered by something greater than just my memory. My grandmother took me in when I was twelve years old after my parents were killed by a drunk driver. Every time I eat red grapes, I'm suddenly a teenager again, sitting on her kitchen counter. With every bite I can remember her voice; the taste connects me to her and it's a comforting feeling that usually warms my insides.

The images projected of Jack were much the same; so real, so lifelike that if I could just reach my hand through the windshield, I could touch his shirt or stroke his beard, but I'm not so far gone to know driving seventy-five miles per hour down the highway, trying to stick my hand through a windshield at the hopes of physically grasping a hallucination is the definition of insanity, although insanity might feel a little comforting right now.

What am I doing? I'm going to ruin him, ruin the memory of us! I thought as I woke up less than a mile from where Jack died. *Jack's dead. Jack's dead. Jack's dead.*

Everyone is on this fast-paced track of confirming Jack's death. Officer Grady has confirmed that Jack doesn't have an earthly body anymore. Gail Adam's is waiting to confirm my new financial situation as a result of Jack's death. Jamie is ready to put what's left of my husband in a metal box and stick a headstone on it, confirming his life and his death.

As far as I'm concerned, I have the right to live in denial for a few more days. I don't need any more confirmations, unless it's the paperwork confirming my psychosis and inescapable maddening spiral into lunacy.

Suddenly, I'm panicked at the thought of seeing the tree and knowing exactly where his death took place. I took the next exit and then got back on the highway, headed south, headed for home. I feared that going to the scene of his death would inevitably make it impossible to celebrate his life; the unwanted images would consume the welcome ones, like a slow moving cancer, eating away the happiness from my past. A constant about-face of my thoughts was something to which I would need to become accustomed. The light switch flickering from good idea to bad idea was on the fritz, and I was not an electrician. Right now, I didn't know who I was or who I was supposed to be.

My button down shirt was soaking in sweat, and I actually heard it peel away from my skin as I again stood in my closet searching for another outfit to wear. I was already late for my meeting with Gail, but she could suck it; I was playing my widow card today.

I finally decided to compromise with my favorite James Perse, white T-shirt, the matching tuxedo jacket to the skirt I was already wearing and the very first necklace Jack had given me-which also happened to be the very first diamond I had ever owned. The two carat, round stone hung brilliantly from a silver chain, and when precisely reflected in the light, sent tiny fragments of color spraying in every direction. Once again, I was ready for my meeting with Gail.

I pulled into an empty space at the front doors, which never happens on the Plaza. A usual routine when searching for parking is to drive around a five block radius for twenty minutes until finally giving up and pulling into a garage; I'll do anything not to park in a garage. The dark enclosure always feels like nighttime, and whether day or night, never feels safe. Jack put a bottle of pepper spray on my keychain around three months ago to help me feel more at ease. In reality, I'd probably never be able to get the cap off and the safety unlocked, much less spray it in someone's face; but was kept on my keychain to make him happy.

After feeding my meter, I stood back to admire the mature brick build-ing. Seven separate suites total, and Jack's office sat at the pinnacle of the structure with a few retail stores and agencies adorning the lower level; Gail's office was one of them. Older buildings in Kansas City which have been painted with logos or murals on the outside, probably from the 1900's or earlier, are in no short supply, and those have always been my favorite pieces of architecture in the urban area. Many tourists and locals alike flock to some of the two hundred manmade fountains around the city, helping to immortalize Kansas City's nickname, "The city of foun-tains." However, I'd take admiring the craftsmanship and imagination of masonries from long ago over bubbling puddles of water any day. Actu-ally, there's a National Trust fighting to save these buildings, so perhaps, they are favorites of others as well.

Touching the gold plaque drilled into the mortar of the building that read, "Allen Enterprises" was somewhat of a habit when visiting Jack at work, like an athlete slapping a sacred sign before running out onto the field. This visit would break tradition. My eyes never looked in the gold plated direction.

I entered through the glass doors and heavily shuffled my heartbroken body to the reception desk. The woman in the office was bent down searching through a file cabinet and had her back to the door, not realizing she had a client waiting. The moment she turned around, I knew this had to be Cindy.

Good God, it's worse than I imagined.

Cindy was a very blond, petite woman in the waistline and super-sized everywhere else. Her hair was sprayed heavily in an up-do that looked like dinner rolls stacked in a bread basket, and that's probably the nicest part of her description. The clothes she had on might actually fit a toddler, and not to mention, completely inappropriate for an insurance agency. Stacy and Clinton from "What Not to Wear" would have a field day with Miss Cindy.

"Good afternoon, Mrs. Whitman! Mrs. Adams is expecting you. Can I offer you some soda or water?" she asked me, with that giddy and familiar voice.

I only heard the beginning of her greeting because her make-up, especially the mascara, was applied so thick her eyelashes kept sticking together. As she leaned over the desk greeting me, she used her long, white, fake nails to separate them; pulling her eyelid out further than a doctor might advise. It became difficult to focus on her words, only on her jabbing that stark white nail into her eye and her twenty year old tits staring me in the face.

"What?" I asked as I came out of my Barbie coma. "Oh, a drink; no thank you, I'm fine," I stuttered, recovering poorly.

Just then, a tall and slender red head with outstretched arms came into the lobby and began hugging me tightly. I just stood there, my arms hanging down like egg noodles, as she swayed me from side to side.

"Gail Adams I presume?" I stated, still in her embrace.

"Oh my, yes! Where are my manners? Annie, I'm so sorry to hear about Jack. Come in, come in and take a seat," she said, as she directed me into a chair. "I know we've never met, but I knew Jack from the building, and am sincerely going to miss our morning chats," she acknowledged lovingly.

"Thank you, I appreciate that," I replied.

"Now, let's get down to business," she began as she opened the manila folder which was sitting on her desk. "I have a twenty thousand dollar check made out to the Parker Family Funeral Home, and you just need to endorse the back before you take it over there. I have already spoken with Joe-that's who you will be contacting—and they have started the preparations for the funeral," she informed me.

"Do you have a pen and paper? I guess I didn't come prepared," I asked, embarrassed and already exhausted.

"Oh, honey, don't you worry about it; every detail is listed in order of the steps you need to take when you leave here," she said as she patted my hand and smiled. "Here's my card, and if you get tripped up on any of these directions, you call me anytime, day or night, and I'd be happy to help you. I have also informed Life INC of your policy claim, so you can expect a check to come to your home by registered mail in a month or so," she informed me.

"Can I ask how much the check is for?" I asked, almost in a whisper.

"Of course you can. Annie, it's for two million dollars!" she exclaimed. "Now you're going to have to pay tax on this amount, because you know the government will have a conniption fit if you don't, but that should leave you with well over a million. This amount is just the life insurance policy; it doesn't include any stocks or bonds and company policies from Jack's business."

"Oh, my God, I had no idea," I said in complete disbelief, trying to fathom where that substantial amount of money was coming from.

"Next is the Will. Who is the executer of the estate?" she asked.

The overload of information and the barrage of questions felt like a jail house interrogation, and it all became just too much. I started to cry. "I don't know, I don't know! Mrs. Adams, I don't know anything!" I sounded like a whiney child and a complete idiot. "Why don't I know *anything* that's going on?" I asked myself aloud, but hoping for an answer from Gail.

She handed me some tissues, ripped them right out of the box and yelled, "Cindy, get in here with water and Excedrin, now!"

Cindy came in with that stupid smile on her face, carrying a first aid box and a glass of water. In her defense, I can't imagine she is a workaholic around the office, so I'm pretty sure she thought she had this task nailed, but she just stood there smiling at us until Gail looked up at her and yelled, "Why are you just standing there? Get the hell out of here and close the damn door!"

I looked at her in surprise, not accustomed to seeing a button-upped employer go off on an assistant.

"I'm so sorry you had to see me get upset, Mrs. Whitman," she apologized. "She's my brother's kid, and I'm trying to help her out, but Jesus, with the outfits and the make-up and God, she's just not smart! I think she gets dumber every day she works here," Gail complained, but now was talking more to herself than to me.

She paused, realizing I was still sitting in her office. I stopped crying, and we just sat and stared at each other, letting the ridiculousness of Cindy sink in. Spontaneously, we both busted up laughing; not just ha-ha funny, but no noise, table slapping, face hurting laughing. Five whole minutes must have passed before one of us could speak.

"I'm so sorry, Annie, that was an incredibly unprofessional moment and it's okay if you fire me after today. I'll understand," she said, dabbing the tears away from her eyes and letting the last of her giggles escape.

"Gail, you have no idea how much I needed that laugh; I was on the verge of a nervous breakdown. I've either been crying or sleeping for three days now and quite frankly, I'm just sick of being around myself. Fire you? No, you might have just saved my life. Now, Cindy is a different story!" I said, and we both started laughing again.

"Would you like to get a drink with me? Brio has a great happy hour, and it's right around the corner. I'll understand if you say no, really I will, but we can discuss more details, and I'll walk you through the list one by one," she offered.

"You know, I would really like that, and anything sounds better than going home right now," I sincerely told her.

ANNIE

We found a seat inside Brio, each ordered a glass of La Crema Pinot Noir, and sat quietly while watching people pass by the wall of windows. Some strolled nonchalantly down the double-wide sidewalk and some hustled to bang out the stores in a hurry; most of the pedestrians carried their signature lattes and shopping bags.

"I love coming down here, especially when they turn the Christmas lights on," Gail said breaking the silence.

"Me too. It's fascinating how the relatively short distance from my house to the Plaza can transport me to a completely different continent, especially during the months of November and December. Every Thanksgiving when they turned the lights on Jack and I came down here, hopped into a carriage right before dark, and clinked our flasks together the moment the lights made their debut into the night sky," I said, painfully remembering. "Thank goodness it's only June. I might need to be out of the country when the holidays roll around."

"Yeah, it's nice to remember some good times with a husband," Gail said, as she stared across the street.

"Oh, I'm sorry. Has your husband passed?" I asked.

"No, and that's really my biggest problem with him. The only thing he could pass is a kidney stone," she said, smiling. "He's a junkie, a two-time loser. He blew through most of our savings before I knew it was gone, and I couldn't get a divorce fast enough to save the rest. I'm not really even mad anymore; he was sick, fighting a nasty addiction and once I accepted that, it was easier to leave," she confessed.

"I'm sorry. That sounds terrible," I said.

"Oh please, don't be sorry, it's the best thing that ever happened to me. Sure, I was scared at first, but the nice thing, and I mean the *only* nice thing about being at the bottom, is swimming to the top. I built this business by myself, and it only has one name on the sign: Adams, and that feels pretty good," she boasted.

"I bet it does," I agreed.

"You know," she started carefully. "I saw Jack almost every day around the building and would have never guessed he was sick. Although, living with my ex and his bullshit drugs might have skewed my perception of what authentically sick people look like."

"Wait, what? Jack wasn't sick. Why would you think that he was sick? Did he tell you he was?" I asked; more like demanded as my voice got louder, my heart beat faster, and I immediately started to sweat.

"Well, no," she paused, "but I just assumed. With over twenty years of insurance under my belt, the only people who prepay for a funeral and hand pick the details are usually the ones that have a terminal diagnosis and know the insurance company is going to put the family through hell before they pay them a dime. I guess when I saw on the death certificate that the cause of death was an automobile accident, I just assumed Jack was sparing you the horror of watching someone you love waste away," she said. Her voice trailed off like she immediately regretted opening up this line of conversation.

"Are you telling me you think Jack committed suicide?" I yelled out of shock, while the noise of the happy hour crowd silenced, and people began to pretend they weren't watching us. "Just because you chatted with him some mornings doesn't make you a fucking expert on his mental state or his health! Got it?" I was leaned so far over the table yelling at her, I smelled the Pinot on her breath. Grabbing my purse, I stuck my finger in her face, bellowing, "Oh, and yeah, you are fired!" I turned to storm out the door, but not before purposefully knocking over her wine glass into her lap.

Running back to my car, trying to escape the scene of my life, I got behind the wheel and pulled out of my parking space, clipping the car parallel parked ahead of me. I reached into my purse, rolled down the passenger side window, and threw an Adams Agency business card on the windshield. Clearly a danger to society—having never driven that fast and reckless in my entire life—I just needed to get home. She was wrong about Jack, she had to be. He wouldn't do this on purpose; but the seed had been planted, and now it was all I could think about.

ANNIE

The funeral was an intimate and unavoidably sad affair, with only immediate family present; Jack's explicit request. He obviously didn't want a congregation of people standing around crying over him, so he didn't invite anyone. The five of us stood stoic as we gathered in the rain staring at a freshly implanted headstone. Tiny, shimmery flecks in the black granite glowed around the silver lettering and lit up Jack's name like a marquee in Times Square. Jamie chose the style of headstone and within that process, had to also pick the color of granite. I was grateful for his attention to detail, but unfortunately, it was an exact match to my kitchen counters; another crushing blow.

Over the last two weeks, plenty of people touted a plethora of advice concerning: my grief, my mental state, and most importantly, my future as a widow. Most tried hard to sympathize with my anguish, reaching into their bag of thoughtful and poignant Hallmark expressions; knowing as they walked away, I was left feeling exceedingly hopeful about my future. After the first two days of fielding phone calls, I realized that any words of comfort relayed were much like a boomerang revolving around me, but ultimately landing back into the hands of the do-gooding adviser. I became a master at blanketing my reactions and began to play a sick game with myself. I found that when someone began to speak to me about Jack's life or his death, I would focus on cramming my heartache deep inside and choking the oxygen from my emotions. This kept my tears from falling, having to hear the words coming out of their mouth, and also successful in escaping a public breakdown.

The Parker Family Funeral Home held a respectable ceremony, and I was grateful to them for honoring Jack's wishes with the highest of standards. His ashes were laid to rest on a Tuesday afternoon in a corner plot, under a colossal oak tree and honestly, it didn't look like there was room for me next to him.

After the ceremony, I spoke with Joe Parker, the General Manager and resident accountant. "Thank you so much, it was really very beautiful," I told him.

"Of course, Mrs. Whitman, I'm glad. I know Mr. Whitman had specific requests, and we are happy you're pleased with the outcome," he stated, trying to make me feel better, but only twisting the knife to help me feel worse.

I wouldn't say I'm happy about the outcome, because the outcome is that I'm standing in a funeral home and my husband is dead. Jack's dead. Jack's dead. Jack's dead. I've got to be up in the hundreds by now.

"However," he continued. "I do need to speak with you about the payment, if you have a moment." He nodded his head and extended his hand towards an open office door.

"Is there a problem with the check, because twenty thousand should have more than covered the expense," I stated, as I felt my face flush with anger.

"Oh no, no, ma'am. The check is just fine, except," he paused, "well it's almost four thousand dollars too much. I'm extremely embarrassed to tell you this, but I can't reimburse you your change until the check clears at the bank. I can offer you a credit though, if you'd like to take advantage of pre-planning for yourself. I'm so sorry to give you this news today of all days, but we just don't have the immediate funds with the tanking of the economy. The bank will hold the check for ten business days and once it's cashed, we can get you the rest of your money. This is not how we like to do business, but it seems we are at the mercy of a third party in this instance and I just wanted to be honest with you," he said apologetically.

"Tell me how much the amount is again."

"Three thousand, six hundred, eighty-two dollars, and nineteen cents."

I took my time before I responded. "Joe, do you have a wife?" I finally asked him.

"Yes, ma'am, married twenty years in October," he answered.

"I'll make you a deal. I'm going to skip the credit to the funeral home; I think that's just asking for trouble, but I want you to keep the money and spend it on your wife. People say Jamaica is nice in October, and you know we ladies always enjoy something sparkly. It was a pleasure to meet you," I said as I shook his hand, walked down the hall and out the door, leaving him to pick his jaw up off the floor.

ANNIE

The day after the funeral, I was obligated, almost forced, to go to the reading of Jack's Will. Scheduling this meeting only one day after burying my husband was insensitive. Jamie and I argued about the overwhelmingly asinine timing, but he wouldn't budge; he insisted we get it over with so we could start moving on. I didn't even know what this reading fully entailed, who was going to be there, or what they were going to say; I only wanted to be alone, not in an office with strangers.

As we pulled up to the bungalow converted office space, the sign on the door read Graville Law Office. It was humble and unassuming; nice, but not elaborate, and I felt my anxiety slowly start to fade as we walked through the front door. The receptionist's greeting was warm and polite, and her tits were appropriately covered; a one-eighty from bread basket hair-do over at Adam's Agency.

She escorted Jamie and me into a large office, more like a living room with a desk, and showed herself back out the door. Three gentlemen dressed in suits occupied the club chairs as they waited for our arrival. The youngest man came around from behind the desk to introduce himself. "Mr. Whitman, Mrs. Whitman, my name is Robert Graville, and I'm overseeing the reading of Jack Whitman's Will today."

"Hello, Annie Whitman," I said as I shook his hand. I allowed a customary pause for Jamie to say something or even acknowledge Robert's presence, but when I looked over at him, his face was turning a pasty white color and beads of sweat were forming at his temples and upper lip. Turning back to look at Mr. Graville, I swear I saw some kind of silent exchange happen between them.

"This is David Perry, a partner in my firm, and he will be sitting in on the meeting," Mr. Graville explained.

I glanced at Jamie again, who at this point still hadn't said a word, but his sweat was running in trails now, and he began to look physically sick, like the first effects of food poisoning were setting in.

"This is Guy Townsend," Robert began. "As of May 1st, he is the new Executor of the Will. I think you both might find some recent changes and should probably be sitting down from here on out," he said, as he offered us a seat on the couch.

Guy was an uncomfortably gray and slim man. His hair was silver with a horseshoe swoop around the low back of his head; shiny and bald on top. He wore a gray, pinstripe suite with a gray tie and gray suede bucks on his feet; he looked more like a restaurateur from Tavern on the Green than a Kansas City lawyer.

I smoothed down my black skirt, took a seat and wondered what in the hell is going on. Jamie needed the arm of the sofa to help him keep his balance as he slowly lowered himself down onto the couch, as if he had just celebrated his hundredth birthday. By the white of his skin and sudden bloating of his face, he knew exactly what was about to happen.

"Like I said, some recent changes have been made to the Will, so let's just get started. Guy, if you would?" Robert encouraged him.

"Ahem," Guy cleared his throat. "Here we go."

"I, Jack Allen Whitman, being of sound mind and body, request my wishes be carried out to the exact detail. The house, cars and all personal belongings are left to my wife, Andrea Whitman. All stocks, bonds and personal investments are also transferred to her name and belong solely to her. I have two personal trusts set up; one in the name of Max Whitman and one in Mia Whitman's name, both minors. Each trust contains one hundred thousand dollars and can be accessed when each child turns twenty-one."

I felt the tears well up in my eyes. True to form, Jack had thought of our niece and nephew and the continuation of bettering their lives.

"Whitman Capital Funds has gone through some crucial changes and as CEO of the company, I am responsible for protecting our business as well as our clients at all costs. The "Key Man" Life Insurance contract owned by Whitman Capital on Jack Allen Whitman has been changed. Andrea Whitman, as beneficiary, will receive 100% of the proceeds, of which she will use immediately to pay 50% of Whitman Capital Funds booked liabilities as of the date of my death." He paused from reading and said, "That means after the debt is paid, Annie will receive the remaining amount of money from the company."

Guy glanced up from his bifocals to see how my side of the room digested the news. Jamie sat motionless with his face cupped in his hands; his usual brown hair was now black and soaked in sweat. It was obvious this information did not sit well with him, but I didn't fully understand the gravity of his affliction yet. Without warning, Jamie sprang out of his seat and lunged toward Guy Townsend, like an ambush predator moving in slow motion until it strikes its prey and then attacks with full force. I rolled off the side of the couch, crawled across the floor and hunkered down in a corner covering my face with my hands, leaving slits around my eyes to watch the train wreck happen. David and Robert sprung to Guy's aid and surrounded him before Jamie could land an actual punch; this was a side of Jamie I had never seen before. His eyes were as gray as Mr. Townsend's suit, and the physical characteristics in his face changed; I would have never recognized him as my brother-in-law.

He kept advancing on Guy who sat curled in the fetal position, still in the leather club chair. David had a grip on Jamie's tie and repeatedly tried over-taking him, pulling his face close to the carpet, while Robert held his arms from behind. Jamie kicked his legs and swung his torso, trying to free himself and rip the papers from Guy's hands; literally foaming and spitting as he screamed into the air, "You pinstriped cock-sucker! You can't do this to me! They'll kill me goddamn it, they'll fuck-ing kill me!"

Jamie's screaming shifted to sobbing as he dropped to his knees, then completely onto the floor while David jammed his knees into Jamie's back, pinning his chest down into the carpet. Now everyone in the room was sweating and breathing hard, not just Jamie. As the officers kicked open the French doors, Jamie had exhausted his fight and looked as though he had just finished a marathon. He was hand cuffed, led into the lobby and out the door as one of the policemen read him his rights. I stood up and steadied myself on a bookcase watching through the window as an officer ducked Jamie's head and put him in the back of the police car. The blue flashing lights circled as they pulled out of the parking lot and eventually became non-existent as the car got smaller and smaller the further away they drove.

Mr. Perry tended to Guy; although shaken up he only wore a few scratches and seemed to be fine. One of the officers stayed behind to get our statements of what occurred during Jamie's lapse of sanity.

"Grady?" I asked as the officer walked towards me.

"Mrs. Whitman?" he replied in shock. "If you don't mind me saying so, you've had a hell of a month." He put his hand on my shoulder and brought me in close for a hug. "Was that Jamie we took out of here? What got into him?" he asked.

"That's a great question. Something is happening in this family, and it's obviously been going on for a while; everyone seems to know about it but me, and it's pissing me off," I said, punching my fist into my hand.

"However inappropriate this may be, I'm having a drink. Does anyone else want one?" Robert asked as he opened the dark stained, wooden doors to the hutch, and poured himself a glass of Johnny Walker Blue.

Three other hands shot up, including myself. "Drinking sounds like the *only* way to spend the rest of the day," I stated as I took my glass, tossed the liquid fire down my throat, concentrating on keeping the whiskey inside my body; I didn't want to puke on Grady twice.

"Are we done here, because I'd really like to go home?" I asked Robert.

"Not quite, Mrs. Whitman, one more thing," he said, as he took a small manila envelope out of his top desk drawer. "This is also for you," he added, dropping a peculiar key into my hand. "I wish I had some information about this key, but I don't, and I'm hoping you know what to do with it. My only written instruction from the Will was to give it to you in private, but I guess it's okay if Officer Grady is here. It's clearly a key to a small lock; my guess would be a pad lock or a lock box," he said.

"I have no idea what this goes to, but what else is new," I stated, putting the key back into the envelope and put it in my pocket. "I'm done here; no more surprise Will readings or surprise street brawls, I'm going home to continue drinking," I said rather matter-of-factly. "Do I need to call Jamie's wife, Elizabeth, or has that already been handled?"

"Don't worry about that detail; I think you're done for the day. Although, with the way it's going for you…" he trailed off. "I'm sorry, that was rude. I didn't mean to be insensitive, Mrs. Whitman," he said, looking ashamed.

"Hell no, Grady, you couldn't be more right!" I yelled, grabbing my purse off the sofa.

I slid into Jamie's car since he got a ride from the cops and drove home; it was the first time in weeks my house was a welcoming sight. I shut the garage and locked all the doors, went into my closet, put on some sweats, and then went back out into the kitchen to make another drink.

I've always been partial to vodka and when my good friend Claire Kingsley told me I should drink it with Crystal Light (no calories and all) I was smitten with the first sip. It's not fancy and can be somewhat redneck to drink in certain upscale situations, but it's refreshing, it reminds me of good times with my girlfriends, and I never claimed to be fancy.

KESSLER

By the time my jet landed in St. Croix, I had a firm buzz and couldn't stop smiling. The driver was waiting for me, courtesy of Lloyd, my concierge, and the thirty minute trip across the island to Cotton Valley Estates gave me time to knock off for a quick nap.

The more exclusive homes in St. Croix have proper names according to their location. Since I live in Cotton Valley, all the homes around me have the word Cotton in them; mine is called Cotton Falls, because there is a water-fall on the back balcony that runs into the ocean. However, the realtor neglected to tell me what a pain in the ass it is to keep it functioning properly; a small over-site on her part, I'm sure. When I first viewed the property, I was bowled over by the immediate connection between the land and the ocean. There is no backyard, the exact opposite from my house in Nashville, but the patio is an extension of the home and almost runs right into the water. Even though the salt from the ocean clogs up the waterfall on a monthly basis, it's what sold me on the property and today it was working, so nothing was going to spoil my mood.

The combination of jerked chicken and Pine Sol greeted me as I walked in through the front door. This was another courtesy of Lloyd who obviously got in touch with Rosie, my housekeeper, and let her know I was coming. Rosie is a class act. She's lived on the island her entire life and makes a respectable living cleaning homes and cooking for families. She took me under her wing right away and gave me the low down on where to shop for groceries and how to blend in with the locals without looking like a douche bag. She cleans my house once a week when I'm in town, and twice a week she'll cook me some of her fine, local cuisine. You could say she's my island Mama D, but I'd never tell either one of them about the other. They might have a fit if one of them thought someone else was feeding me better.

I laid my carry-on bag by the back door, grabbed the bag of Community coffee and shoved a beer from the fridge into my favorite purple K & B Pharmacy koozy. I like to surround myself with trinkets from my past; they help to remind me where I came from and where I'll eventually end up. I made a promise to myself that if I ever got rich or famous, I'd never forget my dirty south Louisiana roots and the people from my parish that helped shape me into a man.

Heading down the rock path, bag slung over my shoulder, beer in hand, towards the dock, my newest toy awaited me. Last year after my third Grammy win, I bought myself a fifty foot Sea Ray and named her Sue. My parents played Johnny Cash records throughout my childhood, even when technology surpassed the record player. Anytime his voice comes over the radio, I'm suddenly seven years old again; dancing in the living room with my parents, green shag carpet between my toes. Mr. Cash was the beginning of country music for me, and the reason I chose this career. I figured I owed him something and naming my boat after one of his biggest hits was the best I came up with.

Sue idled in her dock slip as I stood back to admire her beauty. The shine off the hull stung my eyes and immediately called for aviators; the glare from the sun was a long-awaited and welcomed pain. After a long day on tour, I would lay in bed (if you can actually call it a bed) and stare up at the darkness, thinking of my girl Sue. Since I had no real connection to an actual woman, my thoughts usually lead me back to her. Lloyd already had the boat gassed up, scuba ready and the fridge stocked enough to last me at least a week. As I pulled out of the dock my engines revved, due east.

My dive gear was already assembled and just back from the scuba shop. I once had a drowning scare in the Cayman Islands while diving with my ex-wife. I lost all my oxygen about thirty feet under the water. Panicked and suffocating, I grabbed the first person I saw, ripping the respirator right out of her mouth. Luckily, it happened to be an instructor, and she very calmly took me to the surface while I breathed out of her second respirator installed on all dive vests. If narrowly escaping drowning doesn't help you appreciate the next sunrise, nothing will. After that day, I never dive without having my equipment first checked at a certified scuba shop.

My plan was to dive the reef off Buck Island and then head out into open water. It's been months since I actually had an entire day free from circus life, and I couldn't wait to get back into the water to watch the other half live. Today was about enjoying the moment and I planned on doing just that.

I was finally relaxed-in a wild and reckless sort of way.

ANNIE

One at a time, my eyes slowly opened, and I was terrified to move. I ran through my "morning after" mental check list: shitty taste in my mouth—check, pounding headache—check, puke bucket beside my bed—check; yep, a severe hang-over. Half walking, half crawling, hunched over like a caveman to the medicine cabinet, I chugged some aspirin, cavemaned it back to bed and pulled the covers over my head.

Later on, must have been mid-afternoon, and finally feeling like I could move without instantly hurling, I grabbed my phone and tablet and moved myself onto the couch in the living room. Returning calls or emails was not a priority to me; they were untouched since the day Jack died—*Jack's dead, Jack's dead*, and the voice mails were really piling up. Instead of listening to all those messages, I pulled up my recent calls list and started to scroll through. Of course, the first thirty were from one of my very best friends, Leslie Abbot. I could just see her sending out a mass text to rally the troops. She had probably been sitting in her car just waiting to get the green light on "Project Save Annie."

I met my closest group of girlfriends in college. They were already friends, and I was the last to join the group having transferred in the winter semester. The five of us worked at The Fieldhouse; one of the busiest college bars in Columbia. Those three years were the most fun I've ever had. We worked every Friday night; Leslie and I behind the bar and Jenna, Claire and Tori waiting tables. In college, Friday night was girls night, Saturday night was date night and Sunday's were designated as fun days, but I pretty much drank myself through the weekend. I always spent the better half of Sunday morning making phone calls (this was before I had a cell phone) trying to find out first, where my car was parked and second, who had my keys. Sunday evenings were spent at the softball fields, watching the guys play ball and drinking buckets of beer. Yes, they sold beer at the ballpark! It came in a plastic bucket, much like the ones you get when you buy Super Bubble in bulk. It was usually warm after one cup, but we didn't care; it was cheap and there was a cooler iced down with more in someone's car. When the games were over, we'd sit on the tailgates or in lawn chairs with The Stones playing in the background. After recapping the best plays on the field, the only decision left to make was who's hosting the after-party.

It was comforting now to think about my college years. Carefree and brimming with time, I never gave much thought to what my life would be like fifteen years into the future. I'm glad, because if my twenty-year old self could see me now, I'd punch myself in my thirty-five year old face.

Because Leslie lives in Kansas City, I get to see her more than any of the other girls. Once a year we all take a girl's trip somewhere to catch up on each other's lives, but mostly to talk. Jack used to make fun of us when we got together because we could talk for five days straight and never once come up for air. I have found (I think it's the same for a lot of women) that as the years go on, your group of friends might fluctuate, but the core stays the same. The difference between your twenties and thirties is quality over quantity, and time weeds out the friends that don't share the same philosophy.

I knew I needed to call her. "Hi, love, it's me. Call me back when you get a chance, and don't worry, I'm all right," I said on her voice mail.

The house is so quiet.

The Jackson's had made a permanent move to Jamie and Liz's house, and the kids were thrilled; it was the right decision, but I missed those wieners. After mulling over the events of the last week and the way they had unnaturally unfolded made my stomach sick; tied in a thousand knots. I'm sure Liz had a fit about Jamie's arrest, and I felt bad about not calling to check on her, but still didn't make a move towards the phone.

Why would Jamie freak out like that? Is he in financial trouble? Does he think Jack committed suicide too? What does that key unlock? I asked myself these questions, but hundreds began to fill my head, and I was suddenly drowning in insecurity and doubt. I wasn't ready to put forth any kind of intellectual thinking yet, so I made myself a drink instead.

As the Crystal Light dissolved into my vodka, the chimes of my door-bell rang.

Now what? I thought as my spoon banged down on the counter.

I walked to the door and saw Leslie peering back at me through the side window. At five foot three in heels, she has always been the shortest one of the group, but certainly the toughest, and there she was on my front porch with her arms full of groceries. I couldn't help but smile.

"Hi, love!" I said, taking the bags from her hands.

"Oh, Annie, you look terrible!" she exclaimed.

"Yeah, I know, but thanks for mentioning it," I said, as we both giggled through our tears.

Leslie has the most infectious laugh of anyone I have ever met; it can transform your mood in an instant, and it's physically impossible not to laugh with her once she gets on a roll. She's also wildly inappropriate, and honestly, I couldn't think of a better quality in a best friend.

When we took the groceries into the kitchen, she saw the mini bar and my tall drink starting to sweat on the counter.

"Are you drunk?" she asked, wide eyed.

"Not yet. Why, you want a drink?" I asked, as I held up my glass and choked down the first sip.

"I'll pass, thanks, but I did want to bring you some food in case you didn't feel like getting out. I made you a pan of lasagna for dinner and monkey bread for a snack. Now, how are you holding up? You look like you haven't eaten this week," she said, sounding like a mother would.

"Well, I made it through the funeral, but started smoking again; I almost forgot how much I loved it!" I confessed.

"Really? Damn, you were doing so good. Okay," she said, drumming her fingernails on the table. "Give me one; no one should smoke alone."

Leslie and I were always smoking-or quitting smoking-on any given day.

"Come sit, and let's talk," I said, as we walked over and sat on the built-in bench surrounding my kitchen table. I filled her in on everything so far; the funeral, Gail's accusation, Jamie's arrest, and the inheritance I was going to receive.

"Well, that sounds like a lot for anyone to absorb. My professional advice is to not do anything irrational, but I realize we *are* talking about you, so that's probably out the window. I see you're having a hard time, which is completely normal; I just don't want to see you go off the deep end. Please keep the drinking in check, and don't lose yourself in what seems to be more and more of a mess. My advice as your friend is to take care of yourself because you have so much to offer this world, and selfishly, my life wouldn't be the same without you," she said, as she reached over the table and took hold of my hand.

"Well, you're the doctor, so I'll consider it all, thank you. Now, tell me about one of your patients—a real nut-job therapy session—and don't leave any crazy out!" I begged her.

"Only because you're in a bad way. It might make you feel better to know there are worse situations you could be in, even though it doesn't feel like that right now," she said.

Leslie stayed for a few hours and made me eat some lasagna in front of her; she knew she had done what she could to help me as far as today was concerned. Actually, I felt better after she left, but there were so many ends to tie up-so overwhelming to think about any of them.

ANNIE

June and July crept by like two long years were crammed into those sixty-one days. The kids and I started having date night again, but I found myself watching the clock and counting down the hours until my first drink. Even with my distractions, we did begin to have our own kind of fun, although the three of us together certainly didn't feel like the old days. I tried to keep up with Liz, and we randomly had lunch together, but the elephant in our room was two ton. Our visits were awkward, and the small talk began to dwindle, as did our time together. She made it very clear never to mention Jamie unless it was going to be in casual conversation; everything else was none of my business. I respected her boundaries, choosing not to spend time with him if possible. Besides, the further away from him I got, the clearer he became and something in him had shifted. In passing, he looked like he had his shit together-nice car, big house, custom suits and a beautiful family. Although, it seemed like every time I saw him, he was off another inch; his ship was sinking, but I didn't know why, and I was too busy ruining my own life to find out.

After I received the inheritance, my days became more and more a waste of time. I let the inside of my house overtake me, and Jack's belongings were still untouched. I was the perfect candidate for an episode of Country Club Hoarders. I drank every evening and into the night; blaming God for not caring enough about me. People were kept at a distance, but I pulled together a mental front to fool the circle of friends around me. Looking back, I was the fool; the cliché Monet-lovely from afar, a straight fucking mess up close.

Experts in mental health fields allege a person needs to hit rock bottom before they regain the stability to begin the tedious climb back to normalcy. A trip I took to the grocery store one afternoon qualified my bedrock status. The exuberant amount of effort it took to free a shopping cart from the plethora of chain-ganged buggies immensely pissed me off, and set the tone for my thirty minute downward spiral.

A blast of frigid air belted my face as the automatic double doors opened to the land of the living. To me, a scary place where fluorescent lights illuminate excessively loud conversations amongst nicely dressed and happily naive people. There was an immediate and obvious separation from myself and these "high on life" dopes. If donning tragic, gray sweats coupled with long, unwashed hair wrenched in a knot on top of my head while wearing sunglasses inside the store did not solidify this obvious separation, I'll add this fun fact; I was drunk. It took every ounce of brawn or stupidity, (it's a toss-up) to walk inside.

I stood lost in thought among the pitiful cardboard-boxed dinners kept in the frozen foods section, my shopping cart wedged in between the door holding it open. An attractive woman, probably in her sixties, dressed in a lovely silk pantsuit with her face and hair completely made up, turned the corner into my aisle. She slowly pushed her cart towards me with a *tisk, tisk*—such a shame expression on her face, and the judgmental little nod of her head expressed exactly what she was thinking.

I ignored her as best as I could and jammed my arm as far back into the freezer as possible, dumping all of the Lean Cuisine boxes into my cart with one fell swoop. Cooking for one at my house consisted of a hundred dollars in microwaveable food. The brand wasn't much of a concern either, because at this point, food had no taste, and life had no joy. After I carefully replaced the vodka bottles on top, I moved on to the toothpaste aisle, because God forbid I should neglect my gums. *Christ*, there she was again!

For a moment, I felt embarrassed and small. The realities of letting yourself go don't happen overnight. You have to work at the negations between your head and heart, but blaming others for your own misfortune is a sure fire way to seal the deal.

Who the hell is she to make me feel bad? She doesn't know me or my troubles. Fuck her for judging me.

I worked myself into a rage over the pretend conversation I was having with this woman, all-the-while, actually staring at the excess of toothpaste brands. She would say that I was disgracing my family, I would tell her to mind her own business, and then really rip her a new one. In reality, I just wanted someone to feel as bad as I felt. I wanted revenge on someone whether they deserved it or not and this time, I just couldn't help myself. I mocked her snotty attitude, and as I rolled up on her, noticed a box of Massengill sitting on top of her groceries as she compared hemorrhoid creams.

I slowly walked by, pulled my shades down to my nose, and casually said, "I guess my cart isn't looking so bad after all. Good luck with the rotten crotch, Grandma; I hear it's a real bitch to cure."

Her hand covered her mouth, but I still heard the gasp of disbelief she let out, and unfortunately, it made me smile. This woman would probably have never given me another thought after she left the grocery store that day. I'm pretty sure she's going to remember me now.

Sadly, this was the most fun I'd had in weeks.

ANNIE

A lot of my time was spent avoiding phone calls or lunch dates. Summer had faded, fall had arrived, and I'd successfully built up enough walls to keep people out and my phone from ringing. I used to love having watch parties on football Sunday and would decorate the house for any occasion, but this year was different; I just wasn't ready to associate myself with anything fun.

Liz called me in mid-September and asked to borrow some decorations for the upcoming holidays. I was more than happy to loan them out, and knew Max and Mia would have a great time decorating their house this year. I needed some time to root around the crawl space in the basement, find all the boxes and get them organized for her, so I went downstairs to rummage through the holiday decorations. Thank God I'd been so anal about putting them away the year before; I knew that would pay off at some point. Dragging the boxes out one by one and stacking them together by label and color in a line on the basement floor was more work than I expected. As I stepped back to survey the most physical labor I'd done in months, I noticed all the boxes weren't there.

I'm missing one. Where's the Halloween box?

I squeezed myself back into the rectangular opening, and let me just say, this is not a place you'd like to spend time. The pea gravel floor is covered with a tarp, in an attempt to minimize the mouse droppings every foot or so. The thick and dingy air is a scene straight out of an Alfred Hitchcock movie, but I was doing it for the kids and since I hadn't been very charitable lately, it was worth it. The box was lodged in a far corner, not with the other decorations or even where I remembered storing it. I heaved and pulled on this damn box, but it wouldn't budge. The corner clung to a mass barely sticking out of the gravel. I tried to move the bouldering stump, but it was lodged too deep into the ground. The terrible lighting offered no assistance, so I ran upstairs and came back down armed with a light in each hand, a headlamp, and my gardening spade. Honestly, this project released the first stirrings of my former self since Jack died—*Jack's dead, Jack's dead.* Tracing the shape of this rock with my spade—trying to free this Halloween decoration box—was the first attempt at completing a task from the beginning, through the middle, and all the way to the end. It wasn't the cure for cancer, but it was something positive, and to me, it was a tiny victory—but the more I chipped away at this rock, the more I realized it wasn't a rock.

What the hell is this thing? It's metal. I banged the gardening tool on the unidentified object. *Wait, it's got a latch.*

I bore at this metal doohickey trying to free it from the ground; oblivious as to what time it was or how long this chore was taking, but managing to continuously fling bedrock into my face. After jimmying what looked to be an old tackle box back and forth long enough, with one last hard pull, the box launched out of the hole and sent me rolling in mouse shit. Being that my house was built in 1942, I was excited about the prospects of what could be hiding in this little box. Forgetting the decorations altogether, I took the case out of the crawlspace and into the light of the basement, when I caught a glimpse of myself in the floor-to-ceiling hallway mirror. A dirty and shit covered grayish transient stood in my reflection and instead of being shocked, I found it hilarious. In fact, I laughed my ass off. It was appropriate to be rescuing a Halloween box, because at that moment, I was decorated in my best horror costume ready to scare the pants off some little kids.

I wiped the dirt off the top of the lockbox, but unfortunately, a key was needed to open the latch. I took it upstairs and tried to pry it open with every household item remotely useful, but no luck. Exhaustion began to settle in from my homespun archeological dig. I was filthy, and a shower was mandatory, so I left the mystery box on the counter to look at with fresh eyes the next day.

***

At 6:30 the next morning, suddenly and unannounced, my upper body shot up and out from underneath the covers as if a running hairdryer had fallen into a bathtub with me. Clapping my hands together, I shouted, "The key!"

I whipped the covers off my legs and started pacing the bedroom floor, poking my head with my index finger trying to clear the mental fog. *Think, think! Where did I put it?*

My nightgown was soaking in sweat, and my hands shook as I wrung them together. This coping mechanism was something I had done since high school. The constant interaction between my hands created a diversion for my thoughts and a portal to channel my hyperactive energy. I was so amped up trying to think straight, I couldn't think straight.

I must have been dreaming of Jack again. When he first died—*Jack's dead, Jack's dead*—I couldn't wait to fall asleep; a place free from reality where life made sense and we were together again. When falling asleep at night, I forced myself to picture his face while laying in the dark, but lately his presence had become an unwelcome feeling, especially when I woke up alone in-between the sheets of an empty bed. Anxiety consumed the mornings following a dream about him, and it usually took a few hours—and some denial—to shake it off.

I sat down on the foot of my bed, took in a long deep breath, and folded my hands in my lap. I embarked on a serious conversation with myself to tap into the intellectual part of my brain which had shut down four months earlier.

Okay, Annie, what did you do with the key Robert Graville gave you? The investigator side of me asked.

I don't know, maybe I put it in my purse? The victim in me quickly replied.

No, no. You would have come across it if it was in your purse. Think back to when you came home from the reading of the Will. Investigator Annie pushed.

Yes, I drove Jamie's car home and came in through the garage. Annie the victim was now physically retracing the steps, starting at the garage.

I was furious with Jamie and wanted to have another drink, but my skirt was uncomfortable and my heels were pinching my feet. Yes, my skirt!

It was coming back to me as I sprinted across the house, barging into my closet, pushing pants and shirts aside, looking for that black skirt. My hands were trembling so hard, I could barely get the skirt off the hanger when it was finally found. I jammed my hands into the pockets and screamed, "Yes!" as I pumped my fist across my chest, giving my best Tiger Woods impression after making a tough shot.

I ran back across the house to the kitchen and found the metal box exactly where I had left it the night before. Carefully removing the key from the manila envelope and softly slipping it into the lock, I whispered, "Come on, God, please, help me."

The vacuity of space and oxygen around me suddenly dwindled, and the notion of time collectively stopped as I gently turned the key and heard a brash metal "ping" sound as the lock came apart and the box cracked open.

"Holy shit, it worked!" I yelled in disbelief.

When that lock snapped open, the investigator and the victim merged together, and it was finally a break-through, instead of another break-down. After being stuck on the road of life, senility on the left and serenity to the right, I finally made the choice to hang a right and was rewarded with a sensation of the old me again. My twenty-year old self would have patted me on the back.

Holding my breath, I eased the lid back and looked inside. Two small, black checkbooks and one of those mini American flags with yellow fringe around the edges were the only items showing. However, when accidentally knocking the box off the counter, the false bottom popped out, revealing more.

The corner of a Ziploc bag peered out from underneath the broken box. When I opened the bag, there were six pictures inside; one of a long pier, and the rest were underwater pictures, five of them, taken from different angles of what looked like the same flag I found in the box. The tattered flag was on the ocean floor, plunged into the sand and sitting against the concrete support columns that keep the pier from caving in. The pictures showed two long rows of columns running the length of the pier; it looked as though the flag was sitting in front of the very first one, on the right side.

"I know this pier!" I bellowed.

Jack and I spent our honeymoon in St. Croix in the U.S Virgin Islands and successfully tested for our Advanced Diving Certification while on vacation. We did five dives over a two week period; the ship wreck was Jack's favorite, but the pier left the biggest impression on me. We talked about our experience for months afterwards.

My heart raced.

Next, I inspected the two generic looking black books. I flipped through the first one, and on the top line of the first page were a series of handwritten letters followed by numbers, but they meant nothing to me. The second book appeared to be a passport without any stamps in it, and when turning to the front page to see who it belonged to, my heart stopped. The person I saw was me. Well, it was almost me; my face, but someone else's name. Andrea Bozeman from Lincoln, Nebraska smiled back at me, and she looked like she wanted to talk, but that would be just too damn easy. In the bottom of the box there was one last item, and it was the cherry; another small manila envelope holding a key.

My head began spinning and surely, the centrifugal force would pop it right off my neck. I felt like I had just taken ten shots of Rumpleminz at the Fieldhouse bar. I quickly plopped down on the kitchen floor. Paranoia began to set in, and I needed to be in control of *something* or the compass of reality would be lost here in my kitchen.

I hadn't been running in four months-hadn't done much of anything-and suddenly felt an overwhelming need to feel the autumn air rush past my face and sting the tip of my nose while whistling an organic tune in my ears. What I needed the most was clarity.

Running became a part of my life in my late twenties, and I'd even done a few half marathons; a full was on my bucket list. It's a love/hate relationship though, always hating the first few miles, even when I'm in shape they seem to be endless, but after working through mile three, I could go to Virginia and back. Something in the rhythm of my feet and the sound of my breath allotted tunnel vision, and the sounds of the city no longer existed-only clear, concise thoughts. Psychological therapy can run upwards of two hundred dollars an hour; running will only cost you a pair of shoes.

I need to run.

I slipped on my favorite neon yellow Nike's, walked out the front door and took off. My high hopes of certainty were short-lived after only making it a mile and a half. As I turned around and started to walk home, my only thoughts were of the stabbing pains coursing through my midsection like fire ants on a march. Peace and clarity had eluded me once again, along with any answers to the question, *"What the hell do I do next?"*

ANNIE

Surprisingly, it only took a few weeks before I was running five miles at a time, four days a week. Control was a tool I consistently lacked on a daily basis. Deciding to quit or push on during a run was totally up to me; I was in control. It doesn't seem like much, I certainly wasn't conquering the world, but the old saying, "If you're going through hell, keep on going," seemed to embody my life, and linking the miles together one by one were small victories for me.

I finally organized my house, although Jack's personals were still untouched as I continued to clean around them; his ties hanging on a coat rack, his Rolex on the nightstand. However, I seemed to notice his things more and more, and the voice of serenity inside my head began to speak louder when it came to boxing his belongings and moving on with my life, but denial was still a warm blanket I liked to snuggle with at night. An attempt was made to clean myself up, but I wasn't ready to let go of the drinking yet, vodka was snuggly, too. The discovery of the lockbox was kept secret until I made some sense of the contents. The thought to call Officer Grady for his assistance crossed my mind, but from the first moment my life was turned up-side down almost five months ago, I was only certain about two things. Having an illegal passport in my possession was a felony, and a plan was laid out for me; I just had to put the pieces together.

After an overcast fall morning run, I came inside to an unfamiliar voice leaving a message on my answering machine.

"Hello? Annie, are you home?" the voice whispered.

I tried to pick up, but am the first to admit I suck at technology, even a simple answering machine usually has the upper hand on me.

"Hello? Hello? Damn it!" I yelled into the phone, while frantically pressing random buttons.

After a long and annoying beep she said, "Annie, is that you? Are you there?"

"Yes, this is Annie. Who's calling, please?" I replied.

"It's Gail Adams, Annie. Listen, I know our last conversation ended terribly," she started.

"Gail, I can barely understand you. Why are you whispering?" I asked.

"Just listen! Something is going on in the Whitman Capital Funds office. Jamie has been in there for the last hour completely trashing the place, and I don't know if I should call the cops or what, but I have some information that concerns you." she said, still whispering.

With Jamie's increasing shadiness and reluctance towards me, I knew confronting him in the office would turn out to be a poor decision on my part, but I was positive Gail should get the hell out of there.

"Don't call the police; I don't want any trouble from him. Can you meet me somewhere?" I asked.

"Yes, of course. I was hoping you'd ask!" she exclaimed.

"Okay, meet me at Willie's downtown, Fifteenth and Grand, in thirty minutes. Gail, get out of that building, and don't let Jamie know you were there!" I begged her.

"I'll be there," she whispered, and then hung up.

I ran to the bathroom for a quick shower, long enough to rinse the sweat off, then put on my most comfortable skinny jeans, an oversized cashmere sweater, my favorite Frye boots, circa 1999, and headed out the door.

Willie's is a classic Kansas City sports bar with exposed brick walls, neon lights emitting an emerald hue, amazing hot wings and plasma screen televisions hanging on every inch of available wall space. It's my favorite pub downtown and usually so crowded that no one would ever give us a second look. Ten years ago Kansas City made a contracted effort to rebuild downtown. A private company bought a slew of buildings, renovated them-restaurants and boutiques on the bottom floor, condos and loft's on top; they named it The Power and Light District. To make the area stand out from Westport and the Plaza, they added some great design features-like old school lanterns, cobblestone streets, string lights that crisscrossed the street from one side to the other, and beautifully arched windows. When walking through the district, you truly feel as if you are in another country with a nineteenth century twist. Jack and I often met our friends at Willie's to watch Mizzou football games on Saturday and Chiefs' games on Sunday but I hadn't been back there in a while, and it felt strange going without him.

Arriving first, I picked a tall table in the corner under a buzzing neon sign and ordered a beer. I didn't really want one, but knew the waitress wasn't working for fun, and didn't want to piss her off by taking up a table without spending any money. My days of waitressing were still crystalline. The only thing worse than someone who didn't buy anything, was someone who paid their tab with a wad of cash, and then didn't leave a tip. Once you work on the employee end of food service, it makes you a humble customer for life.

Gail walked through the heavy wooden doors a hot mess. I waved her over. Her mass of red hair looked like an angry wasp nest, she completely missed outlining her lips with the lipstick, and her hands were shaking so much she could hardly hang her purse over the back of her chair. She sat down with a thud, closed her eyes and stuck her hand straight up in the air.

"What are you doing with your hand?" I asked, somewhat confused.

"I need a drink, and if I hold my hand up long enough, the waitress will come over," she explained.

"Fair enough," I said, as the waitress immediately stopped at our table, her arms filled with beer bottles, as she took down Gail's dirty martini order.

Gail gulped her martini down in two swallows, quite impressive actually, and then stuck her hand right back up in the air as if she was back in high school with yet another question for the teacher. The waitress just nodded, and when Gail was satisfied another drink was on the way, she focused her attention on me.

"Annie, let me tell you about my morning. I've gone into work on Saturday mornings since my agency started; I'm always the only one in my office and usually the only one in the entire building. The quiet keeps me focused, and I usually bang out twice the work in half the time of a regular work day," she said as she took a sip of her second drink.

"I got there about 8:30 a.m. and started on my usual routine; nothing out of the ordinary. I worked my standard four hours and began to pack up when I heard loud banging; it sounded like a filing cabinet being opened then slammed shut over and over again. I was glad to be leaving because it was extremely annoying, but then the walls rattled when a powerful *boom* went off, made me jump up right out of my chair. Now it gets strange. Jamie was clearly having a heated discussion with someone on the phone. I knew it was him because our offices sit next to each other and are connected by the same air vent. I've heard him talking before, and Jack has given me a tour of their office space, so I'm familiar with the layout." She paused for another sip and took out a sheet of scratch paper. "This is exactly what he said; I wrote it down so there were no mistakes."

71

"No, it's not here! I've looked everywhere; tore the whole fucking office apart and made it look like a break-in. Don't worry, she doesn't know anything. I keep tabs on her through my wife, and she would have mentioned a large sum of money. Please, I need more time to finish the job! Yes, I know what I have to do. Once again, Jack really fucked things up, and Annie's going to have to pay his debt."

"After I finished writing," Gail continued, "I grabbed my bag and took off. I hid in front of the brick column, peeked in the glass double doors of his office and saw the disaster; a real shit storm. Papers all over the floor, every door and desk drawer open, a filing cabinet laying on its side, and Jamie standing in the middle of it all."

I'm all too familiar with the repulsive feeling that began to swirl inside of me; a fake passport with my picture on it buried in my basement, a doctor telling me I have a dead baby, a cop telling me I have a dead husband and a friend telling me I might be next. I just sat there and stared at Gail. I couldn't begin to form words, because I had none.

Gail broke the silence. "I can't begin to understand how you're feeling right now, but it sounds like you're in trouble. You need a plan, Annie. Do you think it's safe to go back to your house tonight?"

Butchering my words and trying to form a sentence, "I don't know," was all that came out.

"Why don't you come home with me tonight? I have a comfortable guest room; you'll be somewhere safe. We can stop by your house to get whatever you might need. Come on, I'll drive," she offered.

ANNIE

We pulled into the driveway of a modest home in a lovely neighborhood, and I was really very grateful to Gail for taking such an interest in my well-being, especially since the last time we met, I'd caused a public scene and fired her in a crowd of people. When we stopped at my house for some over-night personals, I decided to take a chance and grab the metal box. Gail's an astute woman, who passed along some very valuable information concerning me, and she's far removed from the gossiping ladies of the south-side; solid motives in trusting her.

"Let me give you some space to put your things away, and please, make yourself at home. I'll brew some coffee in case you're interested in a cup," she said.

"You're a busy woman; I don't want to be a bother or intrude into your life too much, and yes, I would love a cup," I said, thanking her and grabbing my bag to move into the guest room.

"Oh please, today's events were the most excitement I've experienced in a long time," she said as she led me down the narrow hallway. "It's been years since I had a sleepover. Besides, I work too hard and don't get enough girl time. Believe me, you're the one doing me a favor," she assured me.

I returned to find Gail's kitchen transformed into a tiny Starbucks as she busied herself with brewing espresso, steaming milk and making the prettiest cup of homemade coffee I'd ever seen.

"It's a gift; I was blessed with barista's hands," she said with a smile as she stretched out on the couch and covered her toes with a blanket.

"I'd like to explain this situation to you, and I'm open to any advice you might have for me," I said.

"I'm all ears; I love a good mystery," she answered.

Starting from the beginning, when Officer Grady knocked at my door on that god-awful day, I recited every detail—each moment still blisteringly raw.

"Hold on," she interrupted, as she ran into her home office and came back with two large dry erase boards, one in each hand. She propped

THE ACHILLES HEEL   KARYN RAE

them up against the living room wall and started a list on one board and boxes on the other; the box on top had Jack's name on it and underneath was my box.

"Okay, ready," she said.

I told my story to the best of my recollection; everything up until tonight, and as I talked, she scribbled short hand abbreviations on one board, names with boxes on the other. It all looked very official, and I can't believe I hadn't thought to do the same thing.

She must have sensed my disappointment and lack of self-confidence, and said, "Don't worry about it, honey, I'm a master of organization. It's necessary that we see everyone involved and can start to put the pieces together." She stood up and started circling the coffee table, making a path around the living room and tapping the dry erase maker in the palm of her hand as she spoke. "We need to make sure we ask ourselves the right questions. Who was Jack Whitman? Is Jamie's intention to harm you, and why does he want or need to? Why that box was buried in your basement, and was it put there for you to find or was that a coincidence? What are you supposed to do with the information in the box; obviously that passport is of crucial concern-and the keys—what's the story with the keys? We know the first one led you to the contents of the metal box, so my gut tells me there is another box to unlock. Where is that box?" she asked, still pacing the room like a track horse warming up for a race.

Now, it was my job to write while she spoke. As I scribbled furiously trying to keep up, connecting boxes together, the finished product looked like the Periodic Table of Elements.

We both stepped back to admire our work, and Gail turned to face me. With severe honesty, she asked, "Annie, are you sure you even want to know the answers to any of these questions? You have the option to hide that box, forget about it, and start a new life. If that sounds at all appealing to you, you should say so now. Of course, I'm one hundred percent committed to helping you get all the answers you need to move on and live happily ever after. Are you?"

I thought about the different possibilities of my situation. I could have let it go and moved on; stuffed my feelings down deep inside and pretended nothing had ever happened. I could have gone to the police and let them sort this whole mess out (I had gotten good at sitting on the bench and letting others play for me) or I could sack up, wipe the sand out of my vagina and be the person I used to be; the one who wraps the job up in a tidy little bow and serves it on a silver platter.

"I'm in," I said, with my best game face on. "Besides, if Jamie is ready to hurt me over something he feels I deserve, then he is capable of harming his family, and that means I'd be turning my back on Max and Mia, and I'm not going to do that, not anymore. If he ever hurt Liz or the kids, then I would essentially be just as responsible as him, and I don't want to live with that thought."

"I was hoping you'd give me an answer like that! Now we need a plan; any thoughts?" she asked.

"The only thing I am absolutely sure of is that I will be on a plane to St. Croix as soon as possible, because I have a gut feeling what I'm looking for will be under that pier. I want the trip to the Islands to appear as though I'm going away for some much needed R & R though, and I certainly don't want any red flags to go off in Jamie's head. He should know as little as possible about how I spend my time. I need an excuse." Now I was pacing. "A reason, think damn it!" I yelled. "I've got it! It could be hard to pull off because I'm going to need the help of my girlfriends, but if I can get each of them on board, it just might work," I said.

"What are you thinking?" Gail asked.

"My annual girls' trip. We normally take a trip during the summer; however, we didn't go earlier this year because of Jack's death." *Jack's dead. Jack's dead.* "I think the girls felt bad taking a trip without me, even though I begged them to go ahead and make plans, but I hear the Islands are lovely this time of year," I said with a smile. "I'll start making calls tomorrow to see who's coming with me. That passport will need some serious consideration; getting it through security is going to be a challenge, and I'll have to get creative," I added.

I felt hopeful yet nervous about the trip, and the thought of being back in St. Croix was somehow comforting. I knew exactly where I would stay, and was sure the owner of The Cotton House would give me a great deal, especially if I rented it for a few months. Being a repeat customer couldn't hurt either.

KESSLER

My least favorite chore when owning a boat is the packing and meticulous organization of the gear. I wanted to be a responsible boat owner, so after buying Sue, I made a check list, laminated it and hung it on the cabin door. It turned out be pretty handy, and being that I have the guy gene, I now time myself to see how fast I can get everything back in its proper spot; today was a personal best! I still had to dunk my diving equipment in the pool to wash off the salt water, but I wasn't counting that today; again, I'm a guy.

The fresh water pool was liberating after swimming in the ocean for the past two weeks. It doesn't seem to matter how many showers I take on the boat, I always have a thin layer of ocean stuck in my hair and a sea water aroma clinging to my skin.

I was glad to be back on dry land. These weeks were the best I had ever spent in St. Croix, and I had owned my house long enough that I really did feel like it was home. My fridge was stocked again, and Rosie had whipped up some incredible chicken salad, so I made myself a sandwich, which I doused with Tabasco sauce—and then ate while taking a quick rinse in my outside shower; washing the sandwich down with an ice cold beer. I had only left Nashville a month ago, but it felt like years, and I hadn't stopped smiling since getting here.

My guitars were parked in a corner of the bedroom, waiting patiently for some attention. I threw on an LSU T-shirt, grabbed another beer, my Martin D28 twelve string and ambled out to the patio to play for a while. The guitar hadn't made it on the boat with me because I wanted it to feel fresh and new when holding it in my hands again; like a lovelorn couple waiting for their first embrace. Attachment to tangibles such as a boat or guitar wasn't a problem for me; they never change or let me down, but the attachment to a woman—especially when I'm at her mercy—is where I'm lacking. I'd been mulling over a few songs on the boat, and couldn't wait to finally hear them out loud. Song writing had always been the favorite part of my career; touring was fun in my younger days, but at this stage of my life I always looked forward to the finale, so I had more time to write.

Digging my fingers into the fretboard and strumming the strings with my calloused thumb, my heart began beating a little faster and then swelled up a bit. I was really enjoying myself when the goddamn phone started ringing. I tried to ignore it, but was already fucking up the song, and the little moment I was having was gone.

"What?" I yelled into the phone.

"Hey, buddy! It's your old pal, Wade! Do you miss me yet?" he asked.

"No, not yet. I'm gonna need more time for that," I joked.

"What's wrong? I need to hear more excitement outta you. Oh shit, I didn't catch you jerking off did I? Damn man, I'm sorry! You wanna call me back?" He laughed into the phone.

"Jesus, have you even hit puberty yet?" I asked him.

"Well, I've got hair on my balls, but that's the extent of it!" he yelled. "Listen, we're coming your way."

"Who's coming and when?" I asked.

"Me and Hope are coming in two days, and if you don't want to put us up I totally understand; I'll think you're a douche, but I'll understand. We're only staying three nights; Hope doesn't want to murder the boys, so she figured she'd better get to relaxin' somewhere, and I think that sounds boring as hell, so we're compromising. You up for it?" he asked.

"Of course! I can't wait for y'all to get here! Let me know when your flight comes in and I'll pick you up from the airport," I told him.

"Sweet, thanks, buddy. And hey, I hear there's a casino on the island. You should know I'm feelin' lucky! See you soon!" He was laughing as he hung up—not a regular person ha-ha laugh but more of a psychotic, I don't mind jail Muwhahaha!

Shit, I'm going to need a nap.

***

Forgetting how traffic only exists on the island during Pirate week or the Iron Man Triathlon race, I arrived at the airport way too early but thoroughly enjoyed the Jeep ride, and the warm breeze blowing through my dirty brown hair.

In high school, I drove a Jeep; you could say it was the first time I fell in love. She was a used, silver '87 Wrangler soft top with black interior,

77

and I practically cried when she lost her mojo and died on the side of the highway. I had wanted another Jeep ever since, but driving one around Nashville isn't too practical. St. Croix was the perfect place to recreate my high school glory days; cherry red, soft top with tan interior, and she's a beaut.

I parked and went in through the double doors, found their gate and waited at security for them to arrive, when an unusually large cluster of people began gathering around the luggage carousel. Not too many people fly directly into St. Croix; St. Thomas has the larger airport. Confused and apprehensive, I moved closer to the crowd, and that's when I heard the commotion. In inappropriately loud voices, two passengers were having an argument about why country music does or does not suck, and I knew one of those voices.

"Oh, lord, no," I whispered, and that's about the time Wade saw me standing there waiting for him.

"Kess!" he shouted across the lobby at me, waving his arms around like some stupid, country Sasquatch. "You tell this sonabitch Yankee that this God-fearin', mother-lovin', greatest country in the world was founded on country music!"

I just stood there and smiled, waiting for Hope, because I knew she'd be bringing up the rear, pretending she didn't know Wade; after all, this wasn't her first rodeo.

She came over and hugged me tight. "Hey, honey, you look great! They've been at it a while now. You gonna step in or let it work itself out?" she asked.

By now, they were real close together, up in each other's faces, and the guy started poking Wade in the chest, calling him a redneck among other things.

"Uh-oh, better get in there," Hope said, with no urgency in the least.

I went over, grabbed Wade's arm and pulled him to the luggage carrousel; I had a feeling I'd be carrying all the bags since he smelled like he bathed in whiskey.

"Aw, my best friend, I missed you, buddy!" he slurred and then slapped me on my ass, completely forgetting about the guy he apparently challenged to a fight behind the airport dumpsters. "St. Croix, let's do this, baby! Woo-Hoo!" he hollered at the top of his lungs.

There's a few people who aren't fans of Wade Rutledge; shocking, I know. He's the biggest, loudest and toughest guy in most rooms, but he also has the biggest heart. To be friends with Wade, you need to hate him before you love him, that's just how it works. There's one in every group of guys, and mine happens to be Wade. Our first meeting almost ended in a fist fight, and when he saw I wasn't going to back down to him, even though I'm four inches shorter, he decided he liked me and came in for a hug instead. I still punched him in the face; I didn't want some drunk asshole I didn't know hugging me, but he just laughed, told me I was all right, and we've been friends ever since.

I made him sit in the back seat with the luggage, and played tour guide as I drove them around and pointed out interesting facts about St. Croix to Hope. In between sips of whiskey from his flask, Wade kept yelling at me to get on the right side of the road; after a while I stopped trying to explain to him that you drive on the left side of the road here. He either figured it out or just stopped caring if we wrecked.

I brought the luggage into the house—the heaviest item being Wade—and got Hope settled into one of the guest rooms.

"Don't trouble yourself, darling.' I'll put Wade to bed and come back out so we can catch up. A quickie will knock him right out and he'll be snorin' until the sun comes up." She laughed, giving me a wink.

"Yeah, that's more than I needed to know, but you take your time. I'll be outside on the patio pretending y'all aren't having sex in here," I stated.

"All right, baby, give me ten minutes." She gave me a wink as she closed the door.

Wade started hollering, "I can go all night!"

Needless to say, Hope was sitting on the patio with me, drink in hand, less than ten minutes later.

"Well, this was an exciting evening," I declared.

"Oh, Kess, he just got so excited to see you; he needed to channel that excitement and unfortunately for you, me, and the people on our plane, he channeled Jack Daniels. You know he's missed you not being next door the past few weeks, even though he'd never admit it. Now, let's get to the good stuff. How's the lady situation down here?" she pried, her eyes wild with excitement.

"Why are you and Mama D always trying to find me to find a woman? To tell you the truth, I haven't even looked. I've either been writing songs or out on my boat since I got here and haven't really done much else; you know I'm a homebody. Y'all worry too much about me, and believe me, if I see anyone remotely interesting, I'll talk to her. Okay?" I asked.

"All right, but I hope you see her while I'm here, so I can be your wing man and size her up!" she exclaimed.

"Simmer down, Maverick, let's talk about you. What's been going on in Nashville?" I asked her, way more interested than I should be.

We sat outside on the patio, drank beer and talked into the night. Once we were both sufficiently tipsy, we decided to hit the hay. Tomorrow, Wade would be rearing to get into some trouble, so tonight I outta get all the sleep I could, if I was gonna survive a whole day on the island with him.

ANNIE

I stayed the night at Gail's house, but sleep didn't come easy. The constant ticking of the clock on the nightstand was a cruel reminder of the dragging hours until sunrise, and after what felt like years lying awake with my thoughts, I was ready to go home, too exhausted to care if I was in any physical danger.

We stood in the doorway waiting on my cab, and I promised Gail I'd fill her in on a plan when I had my ducks in a row on the St. Croix trip. My next step was to get the girls to commit to a few days at the beach, and with this group, I knew I could get at least one to come with me. As soon as I got home, I carefully crafted a mass text to my best friends, not only apologizing for my lack of contact over the last few months, but also explaining to them that I was ready to start my life over, and needed them with me on this trip. Of course, I would pay for our accommodations; I missed them dearly, and I mentioned that this was the best way to find myself again, but said nothing about my suspicions of Jamie or the questioning circumstances surrounding Jack's death. A text message was certainly not the appropriate avenue to spill my guts and divulge my secrets; the beach seemed like a far better place for that.

While waiting for the replies, I accessed the Cotton House website to check availability for an extended stay. Crossing my fingers and saying a mantra, "Please, oh please, please, oh please," it worked! It was booked only for the week of Christmas and available for the next two months starting next week, so I called the owner and got a great deal. Usually, high season rates run three grand a week, but I haggled him down to total of fifteen grand for two months; a nine thousand dollar savings is a deal in my book any day. He didn't remember me—even though I've stayed there twice—which kind of hurt my feelings, and I'm not really sure why. The house was booked along with an airline reservation; I was set to leave next week with or without my friends.

I'd been thinking about the possible scenarios on how to get Andrea Bozeman's passport on the plane while also carrying my own and avoid being arrested, but none of my ideas sounded fool proof. I considered putting it in a hard back copy of a book and carry the book in my purse, but I don't know anything about the make-up of a passport; for all I know it might have some high-tech, built-in sensor. Another option was to cut a slit in a seam of the lining of my suitcase and then re-stitch it, but again, I know nothing about the journey a suitcase takes from the time it leaves my hands until it gets on the plane. This sounded too risky, and I'd be a mess of nerves on that flight. I wasn't thinking outside the box; there must be an easier way to get that passport past security.

Wait, I'm going about this all wrong. I don't need to get it past security; I'd just bypass that step all together. I had the blueprint of a perfect plan and started to make a list of all the things I'd need to take on the trip. As the list grew longer, I resigned myself to a Walmart trip.

The next morning I awoke to four out of four *yes's*. The girls were in— all for the same reason; using me mourning my husband as an excuse for a vacation, and I was using them for a reason to go to St. Croix. I was thankful they pulled out the big guns, and that I was important enough to be considered ammunition.

I knew their husbands would be the major roadblock in my plan, especially Leslie's husband Carl; when he heard the words 'plane ticket,' his ass probably puckered so tight he wouldn't be able to shit for a week. Carl Abbot is the kind of man you wish for your best friend to marry. He's responsible and kind, a loving father to their girls and always puts the best interest of his family first. With that in mind, he's also a card-carrying conservative in khaki pants who doesn't let two nickels leave his pocket without anal consideration first. I'm really surprised he agreed to this trip; she must have laid it on thick, maybe even cried.

Jenna was the other one who might of had a difficult time stealing away. Jenna and her husband Paul are both chefs in Denver, and recently opened a farm-to-table restaurant appropriately called The Farmhouse. It's only been up and running for three months now, plus its football season, and the Broncos just traded Tebow for Manning, which means fans are partying in downtown Denver. With a usually packed restaurant, Paul is probably pissed she even considered the trip in the first place.

I knew Tori could make the trip, because Tori always does whatever she wants, and even last minute plans usually work out to her advantage. Even though she walked in on her shit-for-brains husband banging the office coffee girl on his desk (only three months after Tori gave birth) she is already back in her size two jeans, her Botox looks amazing, and she was recently awarded several million of his dollars by a San Diego judge in the divorce. She was married to a successful architect and signed a prenuptial agreement which would be nullified by an affair from either party, so she got full custody of their son and half of his money.

Last but not least Claire, the soft spoken, very regal and put together southern belle who runs an interior design company and antique furniture store in Charleston. Her husband Scott is retired from the Army, and he helps with the businesses on a regular basis. I knew she'd have no problem taking a vacation. Claire is the epitome of sweetness with never a cross word to say about anyone; I'm surprised she can stand to be around the rest of us. She's been married the longest, and has an eight-year old daughter who is an identical duplication of Claire at that age. It seems as though she has made a damn near perfect life for herself and I don't know anyone more deserving.

Even though I did have ulterior motives for getting this girls' trip together, these women warm my heart, and when we are together, all seems right in the world; we laugh, eat and drink until someone pukes.

I'm always impatient the day my vacation actually starts since it's usually booked so far in advance, but this trip was only a week away and I was going to be gone for such an extended amount of time; I was in a bit of a panic with my long list of errands while trying to tie up all the loose ends here. Once finally getting to St. Croix, I'd be riding solo until meeting the girls at the airport.

The company of my best friends is something I *so* look forward to, especially since we would all be together at the Cotton House. I needed their support because this time I wouldn't be a new bride, and it wasn't my wedding anniversary; Jack wasn't going to carry me over the threshold. On this visit I'd be a widow. I could do this trip by myself, I knew I could, but just didn't want to and my girlfriends will be a great comfort as I ease my way into a new period of my life; ready to make new memories. Hopefully, I'll want to keep going back to the Islands. Plus, this is the first activity I'm actually looking forward to since he died—*Jack's dead, Jack's dead.* First things first, continue checking things off my list and figure out how much luggage I needed to take.

Dread is an understatement when the possibility of a Walmart trip rears its ugly head; I loathed it, and usually procrastinate shopping in that store for as long as possible. While in route, I suddenly remembered my new financial status. *Forget it, I'm going to splurge.* I turned the car around and headed to the other side of town.

Even though Jack and I lived a comfortable upper-middle class lifestyle, I still clipped coupons and shopped at Target only for home décor specialties like linens and table lamps; everyday grocery items are seriously overpriced there. Walmart was meant for basic groceries and Hy-Vee has the best meat and produce in town; even the butcher knows my name. Obviously, I lead a very exciting, upper-middle class lifestyle since I have time to categorize grocery stores. Before I knew it, I had a Target cart filled with all kinds of crap; most of which wouldn't even make the trip, but a little retail therapy never hurt anybody.

At home I set out the most important items purchased, lined them up on the kitchen table and thought about the best way to fit them into a large Halloween tin. After filling the bottom of the tin with black and orange shredded paper, I then added marshmallow peeps in the shapes of pumpkins and ghosts. Next, was a bag of seasonal coffee called Witches Brew and the last item to go in was a puffy black Halloween cat that made a hissing sound when you rubbed its back. First, this kitty was going under the knife. Using an X-acto knife, I meticulously cut the stitching around the tail, pulled out the noise making device along with the stuffing, and replaced it with Andrea Bozeman's passport; shoved it right up that cat's ass. Even though the noise maker was now sitting on the counter, I swear that cat hissed at me as I replaced some of the stuffing and carefully stitched the seams back together with a needle and thread.

Not half bad. I proudly thought. *Maybe I missed my calling as proctologist.*

Everything fit snugly into the tin, and with a serious amount of packing tape around the edges, there was no concern for spillage. My plan was to mail this box to myself at the Cotton House. Since Halloween was only a week away; my hope was that it would look like a care package for someone, and if it did get searched, I supposed the coffee bag would be the obvious smuggling receptacle, not the cat. Maybe I watch too many drug cartel movies, but it's the plan I was going with, and if I pulled this off, I'd be sharing cocktails with this little kitty, watching the sunset fade with my worries into the ocean. But it's a little early to get cocky.

KESSLER

We were all slow getting started the next day; Hope and Wade didn't creep out of their bedroom until close to noon. I have to admit though, it was a comforting feeling waking up and knowing I wasn't the only one in the house; a conversation with someone else was only a few feet away. I went into the kitchen, opened the fridge and moved things around until I found all the ingredients for a big southern breakfast. Starting with a sausage log, I shaped little patties and started frying them in an iron skillet, while simultaneously grinding the beans to put the coffee on. I had a little payback for yesterday waiting for Wade in his coffee cup this morning. Getting the better of Wade, especially when he's in the vulnerable state of a hang-over, is better than Christmas.

The smell of breakfast cooking always reminds me of my mama bustling around the kitchen; one woman doing the work of three. For the life of me, I'll never figure out how she managed to prepare all those different dishes and have them ready to eat at the same time; she always made it look so easy.

I poured myself a cup of Community coffee with chicory, and poured one for Wade, too. Community coffee is a Louisiana staple; you can't find it anywhere else, and chicory has been around the French quarters since the mid 1800's. Chicory is the root of a wild flower that when roasted has a similar taste to coffee, but it's incredibly strong, so a little goes a long way. Obviously, a wild flower root is a hell of a lot cheaper than a coffee bean, and Southerners are no stranger to a bargain; we pride ourselves on it. The outside of chicory is that if you aren't accustomed to its bitter taste it can feel a bit pungent in your mouth. I knew Wade was going to walk out of his bedroom hung-over and feeling like a big ole pile of shit; I couldn't wait to blindside him, and hopefully, get a temper-tantrum reaction.

"Hey, buddy, looking good this afternoon!" I boasted when Wade finally emerged from his bedroom wearing a ratty wife beater and Hawaiian print boxer shorts.

"Coffee," he grumbled.

"I've got a cup of Louisiana's finest, freshly ground and piping hot, just for you," I said with my thickest accent.

Wade took the cup and put it to his lips, never once taking his eyes off me. "Well, just what in the hell's wrong with you? Why you actin' so chipper? You have sex with my wife last night and feelin' guilty about it?" he accused me, as he set the coffee cup down on the counter without actually taking a drink.

"What? Jesus, no!" I protested, trying to mask my excitement of watching him choke on a swig of that coffee. "I'm just trying to be a good host and start your day off with a nice breakfast."

"Uh-huh." He hesitated suspiciously. "Now," he started to say, as he took a huge gulp of the steaming coffee and immediately spewed it out of his mouth and across the counter. "What the hell was that, Kessler?" he yelled, as he searched for a towel to wipe the stream of drool running down his face. "You put that chicory shit in my coffee again? Who the fuck drinks that stuff? It tastes like somebody pissed in my mouth," he yelled, still choking, but also rambling now.

I bent over, laughing so hard I couldn't speak.

"Oh, okay, you're a funny guy today. That was mean, but well played," he said as he came over and gave me a hug, along with the hardest nipple twist I've ever received.

"Ahhh!" I screamed, as my laughing stopped all together.

"See, I can be funny too, Kess," he noted with a smile as he stuffed two sausage patties in his mouth at the same time, clapping his hands together yelling, "Wahoo!" and sending half chewed sausage bits across the kitchen island. "It's gonna be a great day! What's on the agenda?" he asked with a childish grin.

"First, you're going to put some pants on so I don't have to see your tiny dick peeking out of those boxers. Second, I've got something real good in store for you; might be even better than Christmas, but first, pants," I ordered.

"Ooh, I'm intrigued; be right back!" he wailed, as he galloped into the bedroom.

He was back in less than ten minutes; apparently the same amount of time he takes in the bedroom with his wife, and dressed like a manager at the Tommy Bahama store. Wade had covered himself head to toe in palm tree prints that were a variety of different colors; all of which were awful. Atop his fat head was a wide brim, straw hat.

"Oh, Wade, nooo! As your friend, I can't let you leave the house dressed like that. If the tabloids get a picture of you, it's career suicide," I pleaded.

"I don't give a good goddamn if I'm on the cover of every magazine in the Piggly Wiggly with this outfit on; this is what I'm wearin'! Now tell me what Santa Claus has in store for me today," he cackled with serious excitement.

"Okay, I thought that first we'd drive the Jeep to a bar called The Domino Club; way out on the west side of the island and totally submersed in the jungle. We have to take a tiny dirt path off the main road to get there. This little gem is a St. Croix icon, and you're just the kind of guy who can fully appreciate all the amenities packed into one tiny restaurant. They have the best Johnny Cakes you've ever put in your mouth, and the house specialty is a drink called a Mamma-Wanna. It's some kind of rum concoction that will certainly bring out your stellar personality, and after a few of them, you'll fit right in with the pigs," I said.

"Pigs?" he asked with a raised eyebrow, stroking his handlebar mustache.

"The main attractions at the Domino Club are Patty and Gus; two, four hundred pound, beer drinking pigs," I said with a smile, pleased that I'd just made Wade's dreams come true.

"Ha-ha!" he squealed with a high pitched laugh, slapping his knee. "No fuckin' way that's true."

"Swear it, and I'll even buy you and the pigs a round," I offered.

Just then Hope came out of the bedroom in her swimsuit, with a towel wrapped around her waist, carrying a book.

"Why are you dorks so excited?" she asked, never once looking at us as she started to line up all the fixings for a Bloody Mary on the counter.

"Baby, me and Kess are fixin' to drink some beers with real pigs at a jungle bar today! Can you believe that shit?" Wade asked her, still speaking in an excited and squeaky voice.

"Pigs, huh? Well, maybe you'll see some of your family members there, and it'll be a big ole reunion. I have two rules for you today, Wade Rutledge," she said as she looked up at him and directly into his eyes, pointing a long skinny finger in his face. "One, do not get arrested, and I could not be more serious about that rule. Two, if you do get arrested, do not call me, because I ain't driving all over St. Croix to find some tiki hut hoosegow in the jungle. Today I'm taking the day off from boys. I don't care what dumb shit y'all do today or the pigs y'all do it with, just don't involve me in any kind of trouble you stir up, and I mean that with every fiber of my being," she cautioned in a very calm but stern tone. "Now, I can see you're excited, baby, and I'm excited for you, so take off that stupid Clark Griswald outfit and go have some fun with your friend," she urged as she finished stirring her drink, smacked Wade on the ass, picked up her book, and went out the sliding glass door to the patio.

Wade turned to me with a shit eating grin and gloated, "If I can make it through the entire weekend during Mardi Gras in a jail cell filled with vomit, piss and the craziest bunch of fuckers to ever leave their houses, then I guess that pretty much makes me invincible. I'll take my chances in the jungle. Woooo pig! Sooie! Let's go call those hogs!"

ANNIE

The UPS parking lot felt more like a penitentiary than a place to park a car, as I changed my mind about mailing this felony package about a thousand times. Last year on my birthday, Jack surprised me with a white Ford Explorer, and I have loved this car every day up until now. Today, I was a prisoner in my car, enslaved by my desire to commit a substantial crime. After some research, I found that the penalties consisted of a considerable amount of jail time (I guess any amount of jail time is probably defined as considerable) and a permanent record if I mailed this package containing a fake passport. If caught, I was facing a minimum of ten years in jail, and the thought of that made the sweat collecting along my hair line start to run down the sides of my face; it physically sickened me.

Please God; help me make the right decision.

I don't know if God necessarily puts the people who are praying about whether or not to commit a felony at the top of his "Prayers to Answer" list, and I'm pretty sure when beckoned, an automatic eye roll is in order, but it hasn't deterred me from asking for help on a daily basis. My little chats with God have gone through quite the roller coaster of emotions in the last four months; screaming at his lack of caring for me as a person, to begging him to show me the way. Now my prayers sound more like, "I'm really sorry to bother you, but it's me again…"

We all face a series of "fork in the road" choices throughout our lives, the seriousness of the choice and the magnitude of the punishment becoming greater as we age. This was certainly the biggest fork in my road, and it had been jammed into the ground right through my shoes, leaving me stuck in one spot and unable to choose which road to walk down. This wasn't a hand in the cookie jar type of punishment; this was ten years of freedom taken from me by the choice to get out of my car or to simply drive away.

I began to undergo an out-of-body experience becoming a spectator to an argument between the angel and the devil, the good and the bad, the right and the wrong sides of myself; both of which debated very valid points. Could I live the rest of my life thinking that my marriage might have been a sham, only knowing a shell of the man Jack Whitman, and was I prepared to live in a world exchanging pleasantries with a brother-in-law who quite possibly wanted me dead? No matter what excuses I could make for my actions, above all else, what I was planning to do was not only against the law, but morally wrong. Strangely enough, the morality of the issue bothered me more than a prison sentence. In the past thirty-five years, I'd had my moments of stupidity, and made some foolish decisions, but nothing this high-caliber. I was pissed at Jack for putting me in this situation, angry at Jamie for always being Jack's shadow and riding his coattails right into some kind of fire he couldn't put out, but I was mostly mad at myself for having sat in this torture car with still no decision made. One of my biggest concerns is Max and Mia; how would they would perceive me if they visited with me through a glass wall? Would I ruin their innocence with the sickly smell of a prison waiting room or shame myself enough so that they would completely write me out of their lives? I would never forgive myself if the loves of my life were lost over this decision; hindsight would certainly be helpful right now.

As I pondered these questions, something started to happen inside my body; a clearing of the mind if you will. A slow moving warmth entered into my stomach and spread to my head and toes at a rapid pace. I'll call it a shot of clarity, but it felt very similar to a shot of tequila. I grabbed my package, opened the car door, and went inside.

How could I not do this? I thought, although, it was more like self-imposed encouragement.

This is their life, too, and they should grow up knowing the truth about their family; I'll be damned if I let them down. Besides, if Martha Stewart can make it in a white collar jail cell, than so can I. Maybe I'll start a crafting club; make curtains for the bars, doily coaster sets, and all the inmates can scrapbook our yard-time memories together. If I'm going down, I'm swinging. I walked into UPS with an ear to ear grin and peace in my heart.

After I mailed the box, I returned to the car and immediately called Gail.

"Hello?" she answered.

"The package is on its way to a lovely vacation spot, and its ETA is the day after I arrive," I said, with some resident bad ass in my tone of voice.

"Annie, you did it! You really did it! I have to admit, I thought you might bail on the whole idea once it came time to mail the package, but damn girl, you've got balls!" she exclaimed.

"Thanks, Gail; this master plan couldn't have been concocted without your help. Let's meet for drinks before I get out of town and run through the rest of the details."

"Sounds great. I could use a rare steak and strong bourbon. How about The Majestic around eight o'clock? We can sit in the lower level; I absolutely love the darkness down there, it has the feel of a 1920's speakeasy. It's Friday, so we can listen to the jazz trio; they fire up about nineish," she said.

"You certainly are skilled at coming up with a good plan, and it's quite impressive. I'll see you there," I said, hanging up.

I went home and set my alarm for six o'clock; my body needed sleep in the worst way. All the build-up of that one crucial mailbox moment was draining out of me and taking my energy with it. After four hours of solid sleep, I would be able to enjoy one of my last nights in Kansas City with great food and a good friend.

***

The Majestic is located in downtown Kansas City in the historic Fitzpatrick Saloon Building; a handcrafted masterpiece built long before strip malls in a time when integrity was more important than a paycheck. Eye candy is everywhere, and each time I eat there, I'm still not sure what impresses me more: the copper façade on the exterior of the building, the molded tin ceilings throughout the interior or the show stopping forty-foot long mahogany bar which was shipped in from New Orleans in the early 1900's; that's just the décor. They're famous for their dry aged steaks, handcrafted cocktails and a selection of over a hundred different kinds of whiskey. If you took a poll of Kansas City locals, you would find they believe The Majestic is the overall experience and damn hard to beat.

It was sprinkling as I started the walk from the parking lot to the front doors, and Gail was standing under the awning frantically waving me over. I hurried along, crossed the street, and when I reached her, she put her arm around my waist and said, "Hurry, let's get inside!"

"What's the rush? Do you need a drink that bad?" I joked.

"I couldn't tell for sure because of the rain, but it appeared someone was following you through the parking lot and then turned that corner over there when he saw me waving to you," she said as she pointed across the street. "Come on, it shouldn't be much longer on our table, and when we're ready to leave, we'll have security walk us out; you parked right next to me."

Could that be Jamie? I wondered, realizing that only when peering through my rectangle airplane window, the wisps of white clouds replacing the brown, flat topography of Missouri, would I finally relax.

Over a rib-eye and some Kentucky Bourbon, Gail and I hashed out the details of what was to come in St. Croix, and we were both shit-canned when we stumbled out of there. Our waiter called us a cab, and we laughed and talked over each other at a deafening volume the whole ride home. After that, I don't remember much, except I'm positive I had a great time! The Majestic didn't disappoint, it never does.

KESSLER

As we cruised down the highway enjoying the scenery, I advised myself to take a mental picture of this moment; the jungle to our left, the ocean on our right and the wind blowing through the Jeep, beating my shirt against my skin. Wade hadn't stopped smiling since he found out there are such things as alcoholic pigs, and he's acting so pleasant, he didn't even try to tackle the keys away from me in the driveway. This morning was a wake-up call for me. It was extremely evident how much I liked having people in my house again. After living a bachelor's life for almost eight years now it had become somewhat lonely, and even though Hope has only been here a day, a woman's presence is unmistakable. Southern women can be stubborn, pushy, and mean as hell, but I've come to realize that Mama D and Hope are right; these same women can also be what makes life worth living.

I finally found the dirt path after only circling the area twice, which is pretty good for someone who doesn't live here year-round, and Wade was hopping all around in his seat barely able to contain his excitement. Wade grew up in Arkansas and has been a die-hard Razorback fan since he was still in diapers, so he has a kindred spirit towards hogs. I guess he felt like he would be among family today. The burgers here are deliciously famous and almost as big as my face; the smoky smell of the grill wafted into the grass parking lot and invited us inside.

There are no windows per se at the Domino Club, only square cutouts around the outside of the hut and screen doors every few feet. The thatched roof is a handmade sensation and jets out five or six feet from the walls to act as an awning, keeping the rain from blowing in during storms.

"We'll have two beers, two Mamma-Wanna's and a menu, please," I ordered from the voluptuous, friendly woman standing behind the bar.

We clunked our plastic cups together, and Wade toasted, "Thanks for having us out, buddy." After slamming our cocktail concoctions, we chased them down with the room temperature beers.

"You know, I've been sent out here as somewhat of an informant on behalf of the women," he opened. "Are you still gonna announce your retirement to River Rock Records in a few months? I'm only asking 'cause you know what a pain in the ass they're gonna be if you do, and you're probably gonna get railroaded if you ever want to sign with someone else. Even if your contract is up and you have no legal obligation to the company, they still own your early songs, and you'll be taking a gamble if you ever want to perform any of them. Let's be honest, if you do have a change of heart and want to tour again, you know the fans will be pissed if you don't sing the songs that made you famous; John Fogerty is a perfect example. Even Paul McCartney had to buy back some of the songs he wrote with the Beatles 'cause Michael Jackson owned them."

Wade may be a lot of things considered country, but when it comes to business, he's an urban tycoon. Just because he grew up around tractors doesn't mean he can't figure out how to drive a Bentley. Grossing around ten million dollars last year off royalties, promotions, appearances and endorsements, I'd say he's got the music business figured out. When you're dealing with a cowboy, there are three things you don't fuck with: his woman, his money and his hat; that's just a fact.

"Listen, I'm going to say this once and then we drop it. I'm happy right now, but I won't live out here forever. Music is my life and that will never change. I'm just ready to do things on my terms, and if that means going to court and gearing up for a fight, then so be it. You can report back to Hope and Mama D that I'm open to another relationship, but certainly not gonna call out a search party to find her. I ran after the last girl and really thought she was worth the chase, but she turned out to be a self-seeking bitch that became obsessed with everything I'm trying to get away from; the money poisoned her," I recalled. "No running this time, I'm gonna just let it happen. All right?"

"Good enough for me. I'll help you in any way I can," he offered.

"Okay then, let's get another round of drinks for us and a couple for the pigs out back," I said with a smile.

Patty and Gus are kept in a pen across from the restaurant during business hours, and after a long day's work of beer drinking, they're let out to roam free or pass out (depending on the work load at the office that day) in an enclosed pasture. We walked out to the pig pen and they were both on the fence; big, black heads stretched way out and ready for a brew. One must follow a specific set of instructions when giving one of the pigs a beer; they don't know they're novelties and will crush your hand along with the beer can if you don't follow directions. Wade placed the unopened beer can (it's actually O'Doul's, rehab must have been a necessity) vertically in Gus's mouth and the second it hit his lips—*pow*, that pig bit down hard, smashing the can and sending a spray of foam all over Wade. He tipped his head back, as we all do when chugging a beer, but left some of it to run down his thick, hairy neck. When the can was empty, the pig chucked it ten feet to the side, and we watched it roll a few times before landing on the ground. Gus was showing his experience or maybe just showing off, it was hard to tell. I thought Wade was gonna split his pants; he was doubled over laughing like a lunatic. Since there was a crowd of people waiting to feed the pigs, we bowed out and went back inside where our burgers were waiting.

"Well, I feel like I've just about seen it all and can now die a happy man. Hey, maybe I'll retire too, and bring this little act back to Nashville; we've got the space!" Wade cheered.

"Before you get too deep into a new business venture with farm animals, you might want to run it by your wife first," I replied.

We talked while we ate, mostly about football and Wade's delusions of getting Hank Williams Jr. on the ballet for presidency, but we've both been working on some songs and wanted each other's opinion on what—if anything—was missing.

"Damn, that was one hell of a burger! What's next on the list?" he asked.

"I know how much you like to let it ride, so let's go check out the casino. It's back on the East end of the island and a little closer to home in case you get yourself into any trouble," I said.

We ordered two more Mama-Wanna's for the road, paid our tab and found our way back to the highway. I knew Wade would have fun with the pigs at the Domino Club, but taking Wade to a casino was a whole new level on the trouble scale. Wade takes gambling (at least the winning part) very serious and could be an honest to God professional if he wanted, but he doesn't have the best track record when it comes to mixing alcohol, slow dealers, and amateur gamblers. We finished our drinks in the Jeep, but as soon as we heard the ping-ping of the slots and saw the twinkling mini-lights outside the casino, I lost Wade. He's like Pavlov's dog salivating at the sound of a bell, knowing when he hears the jangle of the machines, he's going to get fed. The ping of a slot and the twinkle of a light can put Wade in a trance of aggressive pleasure, where his only focus is winning.

The Divi Carina Bay Beach Resort and Casino is small as far as casino's go, but it fits perfectly on the East end of the island where competition for the tourist dollar is minimal and the casino can really shine—moths to a flame. It's nestled into a semi-circular crook in the bay, with million dollar views from every table. Blackjack was usually our game, but Wade put a hundred dollar bill into the first slot he walked past and bing-bing-bing went the alarm, accompanied by six or seven flashing red lights.

"No way did you win already," I said, astonished as the coins kept shooting out of the mouth of the machine.

Wade just stood there, quiet, with a big smile on his face, but I saw the twinkle in his eye and knew we might be here the rest of the night; which meant we were gonna get a talking to from Hope in the morning.

He collected his winnings in a plastic bucket, turned to me and said, "Now, it's on."

Cocktail waitresses came at us from every direction, like linemen advancing on a quarterback, and because their hands were full of drinks, our hands were full, too. We sat at the blackjack table with a hundred dollar minimum bet, and I watched my chips disappear faster than my drinks. Wade had an entirely different experience. Seemed as though the faster he drank, the more he won; his chips just kept piling up in front of him. The pit boss took notice, came over to introduce himself, and offered us a free room and buffet if we decided to spend the night.

He was a severely tan fellow with a gut that might of housed too many free buffets and his slicked back hair, packed with gel, looked like those Lego pieces that are interchangeable. He was very professional though; he recognized us but didn't draw any attention our way, and I was grateful to him for using discretion.

The gambling had stretched on for five hours. Wade was up about twenty grand and I was out of chips; I couldn't sit at the table any longer, my mind and my ass were starting to go numb, so I wandered onto the veranda for some fresh air. Outside, a young guy picked the guitar and took requests. Someone asked for one of my songs; I froze and felt like everyone on the patio was suddenly staring at me, but when no one paid any actual attention, my muscles relaxed. The kid butchered my song—it was hard to listen—but I didn't feel like giving a guitar lesson, and the fact that someone took the time to learn it makes any musician feel grateful. St. Croix is a place where I blend in and am just Kess, not Kessler Carlisle the country music singer; so far, the only one to recognize me was the pit boss inside.

I'd probably left Wade alone long enough; it doesn't take much time for him to get into some kind of trouble, and at this point, he'd been

96

drinking for around eight hours. As I walked back to the table, I saw him standing up pointing his finger at a new dealer, another young guy, and Wade was really letting him have it.

The pit boss arrived at the table about the same time I did, and as Wade turned to express his grievances about the new dealer, hair gel said, "Sir, your time here tonight is done. I can exchange your chips at the counter for you, but you're too drunk to stay in the casino."

"How do you know if I'm drunk?" Wade asked, with terribly slurred speech and little flecks of spit landing on the Lego man. Wade is a close talking drunk which is *so* unfortunate for the face that ends up in his line of fire.

The pit boss raised his eyebrows and discretely pointed to Wade's crotch. Wade and I both looked down, and it was apparent to both of us that Wade had pissed his pants.

"Jesus, dude. Let's go," I whispered into his ear, but he thought it was incredibly funny and couldn't stop laughing. He was on the verge of making a scene; the two of us in that casino—with piss all over Wade's pants—was the last image I wanted to see on E! News tomorrow.

The pit boss came back with a check for seven thousand dollars, which means that during my time on the patio, Wade had lost around thirteen thousand dollars. He was still laughing when we got into the cab, but as soon as we pulled into my driveway, he turned to me and asked in a very sober voice, "You're not gonna tell Hope, right?"

"No, you big baby, I'm not going to tell on you. Get your wet ass out of the car, you're starting to stink," I said, pushing him out of the door and paying the cabby.

Lying in bed that night, a gush of laughter came over me, thinking about Wade's wet pants. Over the years, I thought I'd seen his best work, but tonight he really upped his game. I wouldn't need to tell Hope about it tomorrow; he loves that woman so much, he always comes clean in the morning.

ANNIE

For the last few weeks, every morning was the same ritual; wake up, walk into my office, open the fireproof filing cabinet, and go through the contents from the lockbox downstairs. I've looked at the pictures of the pier a thousand times; burning them into my mind to make sure that when jumping into the balmy waters of the Caribbean, I knew exactly where to dig.

Today was my last chance to finalize the preparations for my trip, and normally, I'm way behind schedule when it comes to leaving town; running around like a mad woman trying to get the last of my errands done. The only thing left for me to do was to retrieve my car from The Majestic parking lot and pack my toiletries bag.

Not too shabby old girl. Annie gets a gold star today.

I took my findings outside on the screened-in-porch to go over them again, checking the dates on the Life Insurance policies—three months before Jack died; the same week he made me the beneficiary of the business and also the same week he insisted I start carrying pepper spray in my purse. The chance of Jack dying in freak car accident became less and less a possibility I was willing to consider. All signs pointed to suicide, and I needed to find out why.

Wrapping a cardigan around myself, a breeze blew through the screen and gave me a chill as I lit up a smoke. I heard the lock on the gate unlatch and saw the door start to open, but get caught on a large chunk of unmown grass. A hundred scenarios had played out in my head regarding how to handle myself if attacked, and today, when it quite possibly could be happening this very moment, I just sat there, cigarette in hand and petrified with fear. The gate creaked loudly as it slowly opened.

Move damn it! Get inside! What the hell are you doing?

A slender frame with long blond hair carefully stepped over the grass and into the backyard. Liz silently closed the gate and looked around the yard as she walked up to the patio.

I waited until she stood adjacent to the porch and my fear had trickled down into relief before I called out, "Elizabeth!"

"Oh!" she gasped, jumping back and clenching her chest. "Annie, I didn't see you sitting there!"

"Why are you coming through my back yard? Can I help you with something?" I asked with a snarky tone.

"I knocked on the front door, but no one answered. I'd like to talk with you. May I come in?" she asked softly, bowing her head and clasping her hands behind her back.

"Okay, have a seat," I responded, feeling a bit leery but extending my hand to an empty chair.

It was obvious she was extremely uncomfortable. She kept tucking her hair behind her ears over and over again saying, "Well, let's see..."

I waited. And waited.

"I have a confession to make to you," she finally started. "I've been following you for a few weeks now, and don't know how good of a job I've been doing at staying out of sight, but my conscience is weighing pretty heavy on me these days. I just really needed to explain, in case you've noticed me."

"Jesus Christ, Liz, that's you? You had me scared out of my mind and a nervous wreck. My friend Gail saw you in the parking lot at The Majestic last night. What the hell were you doing out there in the rain?" I demanded.

"I know, I know. I figured you had seen me a while ago and you'd already written me off, so you didn't care why I was following you," she protested.

"Excuse me, but I remember you distinctly telling me to stay out of your family business unless it had to do with Max or Mia, and that is exactly what I have done," I stated emphatically.

She started to cry. "I know I said those things to you, and I'm so sorry I did. I thought you and Jamie were having an affair, and wanted to find out for myself, so I started following both of you," she admitted, as she took a tissue out of her purse and dabbed at her eyes.

I almost fell out of my chair. "Why on God's green earth would you think we were fooling around? We don't even talk anymore," I said in disbelief.

"After Jamie got arrested at that lawyer's office, something changed in him. He stopped spending time with me and the kids, he talked about either you or Jack incessantly, and then he started getting these mysterious late night calls on his cell phone. The first couple came when we were going to bed. He told me they were work calls, but after a while I knew he was lying. I think he was afraid I might be on to him if they kept happening around me, so he started sleeping on the couch; although neither one of us was actually sleeping. His phone buzzed at all hours of the night. I sat in the hallway at the top of the stairs, straining to hear who he was taking to and what they were talking about. I'm sorry I treated you so badly. When you needed family the most, we all just deserted you. We were consumed with ourselves. I now know that you and Jamie never had an affair and I'm so ashamed to have ever considered the option. I guess I just needed a reason for his erratic behavior change and resorted to making one up in my mind," she said.

"Thank you, Liz. I know it was hard for you to open up to me, and you are completely forgiven. As far as Jamie goes, no, we absolutely are not having an affair, but I certainly understand your need for answers." *More than you could ever know.* "Are you done following me?" I asked with a smile.

"Yes, I'm done," she said in a whisper, like a child after a good scolding; promising not to misbehave again.

"Then do you want to go inside and get something to drink?" I asked her.

"No, thank you. Although, I do have something else to tell you, and it just might stop your heart because it did mine," she stressed. "Once I started following Jamie around trying to catch you two together, I learned a whole lot more about my husband and the man that he's become—or maybe the man he's been the whole time. I'm not sure which yet."

"What do you mean?" I asked, as my palms instantly filled with sweat.

"Annie, he's become a stranger to me. Twelve years ago, I married a good and moral person, but in the last year, eight months specifically, that man has left my life and some guy who resembles my husband eats at my house and showers in my bathroom. In my opinion, Jamie is in some kind of trouble that seems to me he can't escape. He's lost around twenty pounds, his face is usually the color of glue and he sweats profusely. He doesn't even wear a suit anymore, and the only reason he goes to the office—if that's where he really goes—is to get out of the house."

I felt a twinge of guilt poking me since Liz was here spilling her innermost secrets. Letting her in on any of mine was an absolute no; it could bring my whole tower crashing down, and I wasn't going to take that risk over a little guilt.

"The business," she started again. "Whitman Capitol is empty, but not just empty, more like non-existent."

"It's only been four months since I paid off the investors and turned the business over to Jamie; he started with a clean slate. I find it hard to believe he lost all of the clients and messed everything up that bad in four months," I said as I fired up another smoke.

She grabbed my arm, held on tight and enunciated, "Annie, there are *no* clients. I followed him one morning. When he went north on the interstate, I knew he wasn't going to work, so I drove down to the Plaza and let myself into the office and God almighty, it was a disaster. No secretary, no appointments on the calendar, no phone line. Electricity was the only utility working in the office. I started going through his filing cabinet looking for anything that might help me understand what's going on. It took me about two hours, but I think I found something important."

At this point, I was chain smoking and on the edge of my seat. Liz had no idea how valuable this information was to me.

"Well... what did you find?" I asked her, giving my best attempt at casual.

"A little black book that Jamie had locked in the wall safe; idiot left the keys to the safe in the desk drawer. That jackass thinks I'm just a pretty-faced housewife with the brain capacity for folding laundry or carpooling children, and that I live to think about baking pies and cleaning house. I'm a college graduate, goddamn it!" She was starting to ramble now; clearly trying to validate her self-worth.

"Wait, wait!" I said, as I took her by the hand to get her attention. "What was in the black book?" I asked, ditching the casual conversation route and going right for desperation. I held my breath as she answered.

"There was a phone number to some farm and feed supply store and a bunch of account numbers. Well, I'm assuming they're account numbers; two pages of accounts starting with three letters, followed by a bunch of numbers. Only problem is, I can't find any bank in Kansas City with the matching call letters to any of the ones in the book. They *must* be banks located in a different city or something like an offshore account," she said, proud of her detective work.

"Can you excuse me a second?" I asked her calmly. "I'm going to run to the restroom."

I felt the blood rushing down towards my toes and the color melting from my face. I got out of my seat and walked inside through the kitchen and around the corner. Once I hit that hallway, I took off running towards the office, grabbed the keys to the safe and unlocked it. My hands were shaking so hard, they might have had a stroke. I pulled out my little black book and already knew what I was going to find, but I had to make sure; three letters—STX, before some random numbers.

Account number! This is a bank account! I screamed inside my head. *Okay, Annie, keep it together. I need to compare the number in my book to see if it matches any in Liz's book. The account must have been set up by Whitman Capitol which means both Jack and Jamie had access to it. But why does my book only have one account? What's so special about that specific account? Liz has just proven there are numerous accounts with numerous banks. I have to take a look at those numbers, but have a flight to catch in seventeen hours—and unless I'm dead—I'll be on it.*

I shoved the book into the safe and walked back out onto the porch with two glasses of lemonade, offering one of them to Liz.

"Everything all right?" she asked me. "You look sick."

"Yes, I'm fine. I'm so sorry for what you're going through right now, Liz. If there is any way I can help, promise me you'll ask. Listen, I have to go out of town for a few days, but will call to check on you. Do you feel safe at home, especially with the kids there?" I asked.

"Yeah, I don't think he would ever hurt us. I just think he's gotten himself into some real trouble," she said.

"Let me give you some money, Liz."

"Oh, Annie, no. Jamie is the one in trouble, not me. When my dad passed away a few years ago, he set up a trust for me, and it *doesn't* have my husband's name on it. I have plenty of money to take care of my kids, but thank you so much for offering. I really hope things can go back to the way they used to be concerning us," she said as she gave me a hug.

"They already are," I replied. "Hey, would it be possible to get a copy of those account numbers you found? I know it sounds strange, but I just want to double check something," I said, crossing my fingers.

She reached into her purse and pulled back the lining on the inside. "Sure, I've got them right here. I figured if they were important enough to put in a safe, then I should make copies," she said with that same proud smile on her face as she pulled two small pages of Xeroxed numbers out of her purse and handed one of them over to me.

After walking her to the door, I went back to the safe to confirm my suspicions. The number was a match; second page, fifth line from the top. The pieces were starting to fit together.

ANNIE

My stomach dropped as the plane descended into Henry E. Rohlsen Airport in Christiansted, St. Croix. Heartache, unanswered questions and meticulous planning were coming to fruition. Finally, I was in St. Croix, and prayed to God that I didn't leave disappointed and empty handed.

While my bags took a ride on the luggage carousel, I checked in to get the rental car. A thick woman with an accent to match drove me out to a parking lot littered with convertibles. It seems everyone has the same mental picture of themselves in the island: a nice tan, wind-blown hair, and a carefree attitude. The carefree attitude was still up in the air, but I'd take the brown skin and effortlessly tousled hair, so I rented a Jeep. In high school, I had a boyfriend who drove one. Actually, all the guys within my group of friends did; must be a boy thing. I loved the amount of noise it created when rolling down the highway; too noisy to talk, so we'd just crank up Pink Floyd and ride.

I pulled out my GPS and plugged in the address to the Cotton House, nervous about seeing it again, but I wasn't here to pine over Jack. I had packed away the confusion and anger to my innermost crannies, at this attempt, to put my life back together. Clarity, truth, and evolution; these are what matter most on the trip. No matter how I felt about the way he died, the outcome would always be the same; Jack was dead, and that wasn't going to change.

Driving on the left-hand side of the road did not appear to be a problem for me, so I checked it off my "Things to Worry About" list. I pulled into the steep driveway of the Cotton House, turned off the engine and just sat for a few minutes. The outside hadn't changed since my last visit eight years ago, and the surroundings aired a sense of belonging.

Opening the front door was like stepping into a time warp, and I was suddenly ten years younger. The months of lugging around a heavy heart, which felt as though it was dipped in concrete and shackled to my chest, certainly did not make me feel ten years younger. However, I did have high hopes that the weight of the world would no longer rest on my shoulders. After dropping my purse on the counter, I went back to the Jeep for the rest of my luggage, and had forgotten how far back the front door was set from the street; all the beautiful landscaping around the front completely hid the fact that a house sat on this lot. I rolled my suitcase into the master bedroom, immediately pulled out the documents which had become a hinge pin to my future and locked them into the wall safe.

Jack had found the safe by accident, when knocking a picture off the wall the last time we were here. Now, a scene from carnival, with bright blue-faced people on stilts sat in replacement, but this time the picture was on a swivel, and it easily swung open.

Well that's just genius. My first lucky break, let's keep that going.

Within the first moments of arrival, unpacking is a necessity, or I absolutely can't relax. Since my Cotton House stay was extending into months, the persnickety placement of clothes and toiletries seemed essential. Once the suitcases were emptied, under the bed and out of site, I drew back the curtains to open the sliding glass door that lead onto the patio. As the warm breeze fluttered in and out of my room, so did the sound of a guitar. The rear balcony stretches across the entire back side of the house, and has the most beautiful concrete balustrade railing. A complex structure that looks to be plucked from a sixteenth century Greek mansion and placed here for my own personal enjoyment. Leaning over the railing, I saw two guys in cowboy hats next door, singing and playing their guitars. The song they played sounded familiar, so I sat down in a rocking chair and melted into the music while the sun warmed my face. After a time, a woman's voice called out that lunch was ready, and they both got up and turned around to head inside. The shorter one of the two noticed me and just stood there for a second, holding his guitar and staring. I wanted to run inside. I was horrified he had caught me listening and didn't know what to do, so on impulse, I gave him a quiet golf clap, applauding his performance. He smiled and tipped his hat my way, then disappeared into the hedges framing his back doors.

Speaking of lunch, I had forgotten to eat today. When renting the house, I paid an extra fee for a concierge service to stock the fridge with the food and booze of my choice. After six months of microwaved dinners, the inside of a refrigerator overstocked with real food was overwhelming, but truly glorious. Pulled pork and potato salad sat front and center, begging to be my first meal, and I was happy to oblige. Speaking of obligations, a quick courtesy text was sent to the girls to let them know I had made it to the beach house. I popped open a beer, turned on the radio—reggae of course—and went outside to enjoy lunch on the veranda.

The view from my balcony appeared to be endless, and the brilliance of the sunshine made the ocean water sparkle like thousands of tiny diamonds. I have a good idea of what flowers experience in the spring. They've survived the harsh elements of winter, flourishing through the dirt to feel the warmth of the sun; gathering strength, growing tall and finally blooming. I was so close to blooming; I just needed a little more sun.

My sandwich hit the spot, and I devoured it in a matter of seconds. The barbeque sauce was thick and sweet, and the chilled beer warmed my stomach. My neighbors were back outside again, this time splashing around in their pool. Our backyards were separated by more balustrade railings, but the hedges weren't tall enough to offer complete privacy. From what I could see, the neighboring landscape was phenomenal, and obviously, a full time job to keep the foliage trimmed and the flowers in bloom; this truly was paradise.

After cleaning up my mess, I went through the house opening curtains and windows to make sure every room would smell like the sea before closing them up that night. The beach and the mountains have two very distinct smells that linger in my clothes and my mind long after the vacation is over. I wanted to experience as much of that smell as possible for as long as I'm here.

Next, I dialed in the interior of the house, and headed for the downstairs patio to set up the lounge chairs around the pool when the woman next door yelled, "Hey!" with a hefty southern drawl. It wasn't her accent that gave away her heritage, it was the fact that she spoke to a total stranger for no reason other than to be friendly. This behavior is significant to the South, and the further north you travel, the rarer it becomes.

"Hello," I said shyly, pulling an umbrella into the corner of the patio.

She walked over to the railing and introduced herself. "Hey, neighbor, I'm Hope. You need some help with those chairs?"

"Hi, I'm Annie. It's a pleasure to meet you. Oh no, thanks for asking, but I can do it," I said.

The same guys I saw earlier were floating on rafts in the pool until Hope let out the loudest whistle I have ever heard come from a woman's mouth. One of them was so startled, he flipped his raft over into the water.

"Damn, baby!" he yelled as he shot out of the water coughing. "You scared the hell out of me!"

"Well, I'm sorry, honey, but Annie here needs some manly strength," she yelled back as she gave me a wink. "They've been acting a fool for two days now, and it's high time I get some work outta them."

The men jumped out of the pool, dried off and put their cowboy hats back on before they came over to the railing.

"Hey, I'm Wade," the tall one said as we shook hands. "And this is Kess." He pointed to his friend.

"I'm Annie. Nice to meet you both," I replied.

I waited for Kess to come over, but he stood quietly behind Hope and gave me another tip of his hat.

"Let us do this for you, Annie," Wade offered, as he and Kess hopped over the railing and started lining up the chairs along the pool.

I got caught up in watching the shirtless men lifting and moving heavy furniture and realized I was staring.

"Thank you so much." I grinned, forcing myself away from the long-ing of a shirtless man and back to the present reality of looking stupid on the pool deck. "You really didn't have to help me, but I certainly appreci-ate it. Can I offer you all a beer or something to drink?" I asked, failing miserably to recover from my hot-flash.

"Darling, you're speakin' my language," Wade jested with a hefty smile.

"One second, be right back," I gushed, smiling like a freshman girl on the first day of high school.

We made small talk over our beers, everyone but Kess. He didn't have much to say, and it worried me that I had upset him. Hope and Wade mentioned they were only here a few days before heading back to Nash-ville, and I know what it's like when you don't get to spend a lot of time with your closest friends, so I certainly didn't want to intrude any more than I already had.

"Well, thanks again. You guys enjoy the rest of your trip and safe trav-els on your way back home. It was nice to meet you," I said to Hope and Wade. "And I guess I'll see you around, Kess," I added as we shook hands.

"Yep," was the only word he said, but the look in his eyes said so much more. They were a gut-wrenching blue; soft and warm, yet serious and guarded. Our hand shake seemed to last an awkwardly long time, and at one point our hands weren't even moving. We just stood there and stared at each other until Wade broke the silence and giggled, "Okay then, you two!"

Jesus, Annie, you've already pissed off your neighbor and you've only been here four hours; that's got to be some kind of record. Why is it so hard for me to act like a normal person instead of a malfunctioning shut-in? It's like I have some form of social tourettes. Get your shit together and remember how to carry on with company. I scolded myself as I walked back up the stairs. *Ugh, I need a drink.*

After putting on comfy clothes and going over my agenda more, another list was born. I needed to hire a dive master to take me on a private dive, my UPS package was coming tomorrow (God willing) the girls will be here in a few days and tonight, I would start plugging in every bank address in St. Croix into my GPS. Once the girls left the island, I would get down to business and the real reason I'm spending two months in paradise.

"Hey, Annie!" I heard Hope yell from outside.

Walking out to the patio and stretching over the railing, I saw Hope standing underneath my balcony, double fisting beers and spilling them all over the concrete as she waved to me.

"Hey, hon, the boys are playing at this beach bar tonight, and I'd love it if you came along and kept me company. It gets old watching women drool over your husband when you don't have any back up with you!" she yelled.

"Oh no, I don't want to intrude. Sounds like you still have some catching up to do and look," I said doing a Vanna White to my outfit, "I have on my pajamas already."

"Lord woman, it's only six o'clock, not time for pajamas yet. Oh come on, please! I'm tired of these boys, and I have a good feeling you and I would get along just fine!" she begged.

Weighing out my options of television and an early bedtime against live music accompanying a spectacular Caribbean sunset was a no brainer. Besides, I needed to be around people again, and Hope seemed nice enough. Secretly, I wanted some of that sass to rub off on me.

I smiled big and yelled back, "Sure, sounds good!"

"All right!" she hollered, as she took a swig of one of the beers. "We'll be at the Soggy Bottom round eight and believe me, it's casual," she called back up to me. As she turned to walk inside, I heard her squawk, "She'll be there, Kess!"

Uncomfortable was an understatement. *Why did he want me to be there? He seemed annoyed when we were on the pool deck, and he barely said three words to me. I was under the impression he couldn't get away from me fast enough. Dear God, I am a thirty-five year old woman with a haggard life at the moment, and I don't have the energy to even entertain these kinds of questions. I'm sure I just misunderstood Hope.*

Now, what to wear? I thought, opening the French doors to a closet full of my Midwest clothes.

KESSLER

After twenty years of setting up a stage, putting our seven pieces of gear in the corner of the Soggy Bottom took all of ten minutes. It certainly wasn't a stage, but I've been playing this corner for a few years now, and it's exactly the kind of performing I intend to do for the next several years of my retirement. On my low days out on tour, I'd think about my boat named Sue and this Soggy Bottom corner to keep my spirits up. When I befriended Hutch, the owner of this fine establishment, he gave me total freedom over my set list, and Wade and I had gone over some of our favorite songs, plus a few the crowds always requested.

My nerves were getting the better of me tonight, and I always thank God that the lighting in this place resembles a seventies jail house. I'm usually fine if people recognize me (even though I hope they don't) but tonight was different, because *she* was coming. Hope had invited my new neighbor to come watch us play, and I had already made a complete ass out of myself earlier this afternoon by acting quiet and standoffish. Playing the ladies man role was never a problem for me, but today, *Christ today*, the words would not form on my lips. I just stood there tipping my hat to her, like some bobble-headed jackass. I tried to act mad and put out to Hope for asking Annie to meet her here, but she saw through me like a linen sheet and boasted, "No thanks necessary."

We took our beers to the corner—after a couple shots of whiskey first—and got the set started with "Louisiana Saturday Night." The tables filled with groups of people laughing and carrying on, but there were still a few empty seats left at the bar, including the one next to Hope, but her plus one just walked through the door. I watched Annie and Hope hug hello like childhood friends, standing at the end of the bar commenting on each other's outfits.

Damn! She looks good. I thought, and it brought a smile to my face and sweat on my palms. She wore her dress and her hair the same, long and flowy, with red toenails peeking out of her sandals. They noticed me looking their way, and Annie gave a little wave. That small gesture made my heart race and the temperature in the room rise a few degrees. It's a good thing I can play guitar in my sleep, 'cause I wasn't paying any attention to what Wade was singing, nor could I have cared less. I was ready to get this set over with and have the chance to talk to Annie.

The hour drug by slower than drying paint, but we finally finished the first set and left the crowd wanting more—hopefully in Annie's case much more. Hope and Wade had their usual fifteen minute groping session, which was awkward for a moment, but it gave me an in.

"You don't have any other choice but to get used to it," I said, pointing at the forty-year old teenagers. "They make-out everywhere they go."

"Oh. I've never been one for PDA, but it's nice they're still in love; rare but nice," she said, looking uncomfortable.

"Please sit," I offered, pulling out her barstool and taking hold of her hand so she didn't trip on the peanut shells scattered all over the floor.

"Look, I'm sorry about crashing your party this afternoon, and I guess again tonight. I didn't mean to get in the way; it's just that Hope has a way of making you her friend from the first hello. Don't worry though, I won't keep popping over on you," she promised.

The stereo suddenly cranked up thirty notches, so I leaned in close to her, fixating on her lips, plump with red gloss. "I know exactly what you mean about Hope, everyone says that about her, and you certainly didn't crash anything. In fact, I'm really glad you came tonight, and I would love it if you stuck around for a while," I swooned, finally feeling a little more relaxed.

"Well, you know it just so happens that I don't have any other plans this evening, so of course I'll stay. You guys sound so good up there. Do you play together often?" she asked.

"We live next door to each other, so a sing-along is inevitable when beers are being passed out on the patio and the chiminea is smoking," I answered her cautiously.

"Y'all gettin' along all right over there?" Hope chimed in.

Annie smiled at me and said, "Yeah, we're fine. Then she turned to Wade and asked, "You guys done making out yet? I'm ready to hear some more songs."

"Oooh, this one's got a smart mouth; I like it! Gonna have to watch that, Kess. Before you know it, she'll have your nuts in a vice and be the only one with a key. My balls haven't seen another face in twenty years," Wade bantered back.

"All right then, on that note, let's get goin' on the second set," I said, pulling my hat down over my eyes, completely embarrassed but used to it where Wade is concerned.

We brought the heat to the second set and fire ignited inside of me; it was the most fun I'd had in months. I spent two years letting that same fire slowly burn out of me; ready to give up on love and filling my days with waiting. Waiting on something or someone to inspire you is taxing on your heart, and it can beat you down so slowly you don't notice it's happening, until one day you just stop getting back up. I didn't realize how much I needed a woman until she was here standing in front of me. My younger self would have played the superstar card without hesitation and only admitted a silent regret when my eyes closed at night, where the truth can't hide. I'm not sure if the instant attraction was mutual, but she was still here listening to me play, so I had to make a good second impression, since my first one was a miserable failure. My thoughts about her were already too far into the future for any respectable guy to admit. I'd known her less than a day, but I liked her, and was already smitten.

We ended our little show with "Long Way to the Top" an AC/DC tune from the seventies; always a pleaser, and the crowd showed their appreciation with a healthy round of applause. When they scattered a bit, we packed our gear tightly in the corner; I'd earned myself a beer.

"Kess, glad to have you back, always a pleasure!" Hutch said, as we shook hands across the bar.

Hutch is a pasty colored Irishman with the cliché, curly mop of red hair. He stands freakishly tall and looks as though his body has been assaulted by freckles. Any man with intense alabaster skin has no business living in a land where the sun continuously shines, giving way to a heat stroke on a weekly basis, but I've never heard Hutch complain about his life, not once.

"You know we wouldn't play anywhere else! Thanks for having us. Hey, this is my new neighbor, Annie, and hopefully we can make her a regular while she's here," I said, putting my hand on her back and feeling the unexpected pleasure of her silk dress on my fingertips.

"Hi, Annie Whitman. So nice to meet you; I'm having a wonderful time tonight," she said to Hutch.

"Francis Hutchinson is my full name and everyone but my mum calls me Hutch, so you should too. What are your plans while in paradise, Annie?" Hutch asked her.

"Well, my girlfriends are coming Friday for a few nights, but I'd really like to do some diving after they head back home. Do you happen to know a reputable dive master I could contact to take me out a few times?" she asked.

"Hell yeah, you're looking at one! I run a small operation out of the hut behind the restaurant, and I'd be glad to take you anywhere you want to go. Kess can vouch for me; I've taken him out plenty. Do you want to see turtles or a ship wreck?" he asked.

"I'd really like to dive the pier. I've seen so many wonderful pictures, and would like to experience it for myself. Do you have a business card I can take with me? When my friends leave town I'll be ready for a big adventure," she said.

"Hey, y'all, Wade's teeterin' on the fence, and if he's gonna drink anymore, I'd rather he embarrassed himself at your house, Kess, rather than embarrass me here. We probably oughta get goin.' Besides, we have to be at the airport by noon, and we're famous for missing our flight. A few days away from the kids makes me think that I could learn to like them again." Hope laughed.

"I'm also going to call it a night. It's a long way from Kansas City, and I've been up since four. Nothing sounds better than sleep right now. Hope and Wade, I have truly loved spending the evening with you, and wish you could have met my friends; they would have loved you both. Kess," she said, as she put her hand on my shoulder and then slid it down my arm as she spoke. "I loved listening to you play, and hopefully will hear more music coming from your patio. I'm sure we'll be running into each other again." She gave my bicep a friendly squeeze. The touch from her fingertips made the hairs on my arm rise and a boyish smile spread across my face.

The girls hugged after we walked out to the Jeeps in the parking lot, and promised to keep in touch. *How can women become best friends or mortal enemies in a matter of hours?* Understanding the psyche of a woman is not something I'll ever get my head around. Hell, I think women are on an hour-to-hour basis of understanding themselves, but they baffle me daily. Seeing Hope hug Annie meant she had the stamp of approval and was already accepted into our little family. There was no need to worry about Mama D's thoughts; Hope was going to give Annie a good report when she got home.

Wade was smoking a joint in the back of the Jeep, which pretty much guaranteed he was going to puke on the way home, but I didn't care, because as Annie got into her Jeep, she turned and smiled at me-specifically at me—and we shared a moment. I was sure of it.

ANNIE

Walking into the Soggy Bottom was like crashing a stranger's wedding. White lanterns hung from beams running the length of the restaurant and row after row of Christmas lights crisscrossed through the open air patio. The smell of booze and gardenias assaulted me as I walked through the archway dripping with blooming flowers. Taking one step at a time down a set of brick stairs that led onto the main dining area, I was almost waiting for someone to announce me, like at a wedding reception—which by the way is horribly embarrassing, and I desperately wished brides would stop requiring that kind of entrance for their guests.

Hope sat at the end of the horseshoe shaped bar and had definitely chosen the seat with the best view. The ocean was within reaching distance, and if not for a brick wall, my chair would be sinking into sand as salty water pooled around my feet.

"Hey!" she drawled, standing up and giving me big southern hug. "I'm so glad you made it! I started to worry you might of changed your mind."

"Never! I need a night like this in the worst way and would have cussed myself for missing it," I admitted. "This place is so random, but truly fantastic. How did you find it?"

"Kess has been playing here awhile, and he always talks about it when he's home in Nashville. I think it's been here since the sixties, but had a bunch of different owners."

Kess and Wade were already situated in the corner of the dining area, playing "Louisiana Saturday Night." Song names I remember, because I love music so much, but putting a person's face and correct name together has never been my strong point. After introducing myself for the third time to someone, I usually walk away completely embarrassed.

"Wow, these guys sound amazing! I expected to hear a couple of college boys playing for beer money, but damn, they sound professional. Do they play at a lot of bars in Nashville?" I asked.

Her face got all scrunched up like she was thinking real hard about my question, and it took a while for her to come up with the answer.

"Um, no, they aren't really into the bar scene. We take turns throwing parties at our houses, and Mama D—that's my mama who lives with us—will throw out a big spread of the best southern food to ever hit your mouth; she cooks for the ones at Kess's house, too. Wade still thinks everyone comes 'cause he throws the best parties, but it's Mama D's cookin' that keeps 'em comin' back."

"So, you've known Kess a long time then?" I asked, trying not to sound like I was fishing.

She smiled and said, "Kess is like family, and we go back twenty years. I'll tell you what though, he's way better looking than he used to be! When I first met him, he looked straight out of the trailer. That boy had the trashiest mullet I'd ever seen and the saddest attempt at a mustache; looked like he glued on all twelve of the hairs that were spread across his lip—truly disgusting. I guess we've all come a long way, but mostly Kess." She looked at me and said sternly, "He's a *really* good man, who in the past has broken a lot of hearts and burned the same number of bridges, but karma upped and kicked his ass one day, and he didn't like it too much. He's been a changed man ever since."

Huh, interesting, sounds like there's a story behind all that.

I raised my beer bottle and said, "Here's to a good ass kicking."

"We all need one." She laughed as we clinked our bottles together.

About that time two handsome cowboys rolled up on us and ordered another round of beers. Hope and Wade were like magnets, their bodies smacked into each other without warning for the rest of us to look away. I hadn't seen two people so oblivious to a crowd around them since college, when it was normal to be at a party and see a girl getting fingered while sitting on a kitchen counter. Party goers walking by to get a beer from the fridge, stopping to chat with friends or requesting a song from the kid working the CD player; never paying much attention to the girl with her legs spread open and her tongue down some guy's throat.

Luckily, Hope and Wade were somewhat tasteful in their display, and Hope's dress wasn't up around her waist. Public protocol was to pretend I didn't notice them, but I couldn't look away, and was in a full blown stare. At the moment, I wanted to be Hope or rather, just in her position. Twenty years with the same man who still reaches for my hand, smiles when I walk in a room, and quite frankly, who still makes my panties wet; that's one hell of a trifecta to be centered on. Instead, I'm riding the scales that dip back and forth from husband dies in a car wreck to husband kills himself, each day reading a different and equally shitty out-come.

"You don't have any other choice but to get used to it. They make out everywhere they go," Kess said, startling me.

Shit, you're so pathetic! I've been standing here getting off on his married friends who are just acting married, and now he probably thinks I'm some freak-ish peeping Tom. God, I suck at being normal.

I made some obscure and lame comments and basically wanted to die, but eventually changed the subject back to music; a subject where I wasn't an asshole. We chatted for a few minutes, and his smile was warm and unpretentious; he was easy to talk with, and I felt relaxed with my new acquaintances, hanging out at my new neighborhood bar.

The guys were back up front doing their thing, and I couldn't get over how enamored the crowd was with them. Yes, they sounded fantastic, but the applause they received after each song was borderline standing ova-tion. Hope was right about the women—shameless, although I could cer-tainly see why. Kess looked so natural with a guitar; his fingers slid up and down the wooden neck like liquid, but he still managed to make each note ring out clear. Curls of sandy brown hair fell out from under his cowboy hat, licking the tops of his ears and sides of his cheeks. The veins in his hands popped out and spread up his forearm while he strummed, and the muscles in his arms lay over the body of his guitar, almost like they were holding it in place; apparently, I was on Team Shameless as well.

Oh, my God, what am I doing? I turned my eyes away from him in shock.

I can't be attracted to him; we just met. I'm not ready for that yet. Am I?

By the time Wade needed an escort to the Jeep, we all agreed to call it a night and walked to the parking lot together. When it comes to friend-ship among women, you usually know right away if you've found a good one. Although once in a while, a decoy can slip pass the goalie and blind side you by stealing your clothes or your boyfriend, but hopefully that's rare. I wanted to keep up with Hope; she was one of the good ones. Be-sides, my clothes would swallow her tiny frame and I had no man for the taking.

"Have a wonderful time here, Annie, and I hope you find what you're looking for," she said as we hugged, then whispered in my ear, "Don't be afraid to take a chance, honey. Your next big adventure could be right next door." Then she smacked my ass and said, "Drive safe, baby!" Maybe it's a southern thing, but the three of them were always smacking each other on the ass, and it seemed more common than a hand shake.

Is he watching me? I wondered as I got into my Jeep. It's a wide-known fact, if two people have an attraction to one another but are parting ways, one will be watching—savoring the last images of that person, and one will turn and look back—for the exact same reason. I was the one who looked back and he was smiling, watching me go.

ANNIE

The back of my head heated up and sweat tickled the space in between my breasts, pooling in the elastic of my sports bra. Mumford and Sons delightfully ruptured my ear drums as I came upon the straight away that lead me to the most Eastern point of the United States. St. Croix is a US Virgin Island and entitled to chisel that fact into an enormous rock that sits atop jagged cliffs and beside an information booth in a circle driveway. I had run five and a half miles, past the golf course and along the narrow strip of pavement; watching the ocean waves pull in and out, sometimes getting the notion to spray itself against the rocks.

"This is a once in a lifetime moment." I felt the need to acknowledge it aloud.

I walked around the gravel circle until my body didn't struggle anymore, and then reluctantly drank from the water fountain at the information hut. After five miles, I wasn't too picky and knew I'd never make it back to the house without hydrating.

A specific playlist is integral in the success of finishing a run. I meticulously coordinate the order of the songs with the mileage planned on running. My mind always gives up faster than my body, so inspirational songs are placed around the point when I know the bargaining will begin.

"Let's just walk a few minutes, or how about we turn around now and sprint the rest of the way home," are just a few of the openers my mind will use when my body is in pain and willing to negotiate. So, the music feeds my will-power and drowns out the whiner inside my head. There is no better circle of self-satisfaction than seriously wanting to give up, choosing to run through the pain and finishing what I started. Digging deep within yourself and achieving your set goal can truly change your perception of life; running was only a small part of the goal to get my life back on track, and I was going to take "digging deep" to a whole new level when Hutch took me scuba diving under the pier.

On the way back, I had to turn the music off because I woke this morning with a case of the guilties and wasn't letting myself move past my flirtation with Kess last night.

Only being widowed six months, I have no business ogling with a stranger. Numerous questions need to be answered about Jack's death, the contents of the lockbox, Jamie's behavior and what I hope to accomplish in St. Croix. This is not a vacation.

On the other hand, I am widowed and haven't even thought about another man besides Jack in six months. I'm just enjoying the view. I'm not going to marry the guy, I've only known him one day. I've been through a hell of a lot already, and from where I'm standing, can't even see the other side.

Yet, maybe I am allowed to enjoy a tiny morsel of paradise.

Thump-swish, thump-swish. The rhythm of my shoes hitting the pavement and the sound of my dry-fit shorts rubbing together between my thighs untangled my guilt.

He's a good looking guy; any woman would find him attractive. So what if I pictured him naked, it's not like anything is going to happen.

Okay, now I was getting closer to the truth, because *I think I did want something to happen.* I hated to admit it, but I did. I pictured Kess's hands running the length of my spine and covering my torso with goose bumps. Putting my hands up his shirt and tracing his muscular frame with my fingertips, leaving his nipples hard to the touch excited me. I needed the strength of a man to collect all my little pieces and tell me, "Don't worry, this is normal—you're normal." I was tired of depending on just my body to warm the bed, and wanted another heat source under my sheets. Most of all, I wanted to feel good because of what someone else was doing to me, instead of what I had to do to myself. I also knew I had the power to make it happen.

If I knocked on his door and dropped my towel when he answered, exposing my naked body, I'd have a pretty good chance at getting fucked today. That's all it would be though; a fuck and inevitably, when it was over, I would feel like a fuck.

This was a truly sick conversation to have with myself and one I was completely unprepared for, because finding another man attractive had never crossed my mind. Only being thirty-five years old and not living even half of my life expectancy yet, textbook logic is that I would find another love in my life. Although, all the thoughts and plans I had about future events were just that, future. Apparently, there is an exact moment where the planes of time are allowed to connect; past and future come crashing into the present, and it looked as though that moment was rapidly approaching.

"I just want to feel okay!" I growled, cutting off the smooth gliding of my running rhythm and stomping my feet on the pavement instead, like a band major leading a parade. The back and forth conversation with myself was getting old. There is only one of me, but I was constantly fighting with myself like I had a twin, and apparently, at this point, was mad enough to have a full blown temper-tantrum in the middle of the street.

When am I allowed to feel like myself again without guilt or sadness or any number of emotions that tap you on the shoulder and say, "Not today, Annie, it's still too soon, maybe another day of sadness. Maybe tomorrow is your day."

Only a half mile to go, and its up-hill the rest of the way home.

My legs would punish me severely tomorrow; this was no amateur's run. Upper cut, right hook, one-two punch; my heart and head kept the fight going. When was the bell going to ring? I was emotionally beat up by the time my feet reached the driveway and finally made it to my stopping point. At the top of the hill I walked off some of the pain in my knees and decided, for my mental stability, to keep it amicable with my neighbor, but picturing him naked was a completely fair compromise. I was just too tired to argue with that.

I walked down the rock path from the driveway to the front door, picking fresh flowers along the way because mentally stable people do this, and *holy shit!* Propped up against the front door was a familiar looking box wrapped in brown packaging, addressed to Andrea Whitman.

"Un-fucking-believable!" I proclaimed, scooping it up and guarding it tightly, shielding it from anyone who could be hiding out among the five-foot tall lemon grass planted on either side of the door. *Very cloak-and-dagger.* I rushed inside and began to rip the paper off the box, but there was so much goddamn tape on it, only tiny pieces fell to the floor.

"Fucking UPS," I snarled, as I pawed at the box like a five-year old at Christmas.

Every drawer in the kitchen got opened until I found the one storing the knives. The tape couldn't come off fast enough; finally, I was in! I set the box down on the counter and sucked in my breath, holding it until the lid was off and the main item accounted for. The black Halloween kitty had a smug and taunting look on its face, so I ripped the ass clear off that cat, the threads popping violently. My fingers made contact with the passport in the belly of the beast, and I gave little kitty an enema that would make a grown man cry. I needed to have another look at Andrea Bozeman.

121

Not so smug now. I thought, tossing the cat back into the box and taking the passport into my room, throwing myself onto the bed. One by one, each objective was being accomplished; excitement was an understatement, but I couldn't lose sight of the mission. Salt began clumping and chafing underneath my arms, forming hardened sweat balls sticking together and scraping across my skin the longer I delayed a shower. Locking the passport in the safe with my other documents, I carefully stripped off my clothes and shut the bathroom door.

The open air shower in my bathroom was modern and luxurious, but the steam easily escaped and that was what my muscles craved. I leaned up against the marble wall and let the hot water from the rainfall shower-head run down my legs in hopes of reliving the cramps that were already settling. A walk on the beach was a necessity in keeping my muscles loose or I'd be clomping around like Frankenstein by nightfall.

I threw on a cotton maxi dress, slapped a piece of grilled chicken on a bun and went outside to take a slow walk on the beach and stretch my legs while eating my sandwich. Purposefully, I walked in the opposite direction of Kess's house, but not before shamelessly sneaking a peek at his patio to see if he was outside.

The sand squished between my toes with every step and the tide then quickly washed it away; nature's own exfoliation. The bottom of my dress had collected a number of sentiments from my walk. I waded ankle deep into the ocean to rinse the hem, and that's when I saw him walking towards me.

He had on loose fitting linen pants, a T-shirt that read "TABASCO" across the front, and his beloved cowboy hat pulled down tight on top of his gold-rimmed aviators. It didn't matter he was still too far away for me to clearly see his face, I knew it was him. Instantly, butterflies replaced the bottomless pit of sad inside of me.

"Hi, Annie!" he called out as he walked up, looking gorgeous as he took off his shades. "You don't have a washer and dryer at your house?" he asked me.

"What? Oh, this," I stuttered as my face flushed. "I was trying to get the sand off the bottom of my dress, but I'm assuming it's in vain, because it's everywhere and I'm already finding it all over the house. Are you coming or going?" I asked, while tying a knot in the bottom of my dress so it didn't drag anymore.

"Both, I guess. Hope and Wade left this morning; it was too quiet at the house so I thought a stroll would be relaxing. Would you like to join me?" he asked grinning so wide that the dimple on his right cheek was pronounced.

"Yeah, I know what you mean. The silence can be deafening; it always takes a little while to adjust to the quiet," I noted.

"Why do you say that? Do you live alone?" he asked as we started walking.

"I do. My husband died six months ago, and I recently gave my wiener dogs to my niece and nephew, so it's just me now. You?"

"Jesus, I'm sorry. You seem so young to be a widow. But yes, I do live alone; been divorced for eight years."

"Oh. I'm sorry to hear that, too," I repeated, as we lapsed into an uncomfortable silence.

"Do you want to talk about this?" he asked, as he shoved his hands into his pockets.

"Not at all," I said, both of us relieved. "How about music? I had a great time listening to you play last night, and it so happens you guys played my favorite song: AC/DC's "Long Way to the Top." Great song and hands down, the best concert I've ever seen. They did a show in St. Paul last year, and I actually peed my pants when they did "TNT." I'm not sure why I told you that, it just slipped out, but sadly it's true."

"Wow! That's an interesting tidbit of information, but don't worry, I'm positive you aren't the only adult to recently pee their pants," he laughed. "I'm glad music does that for you. Who else do you like?"

We walked through the remaining daylight hours, up and down the stretch of beach in front of our houses, talking about life and music in Nashville and Kansas City. We stayed on safe subjects, nothing too personal, just scratching the surface type topics. As soon as I told him about my girlfriends coming, the wind picked up and started pelting us with sand, so we had to make a run for it to the closest shelter. Tiny grains stung my bare legs and arms as I cupped my hands around my face, shielding my eyes as I ran. We ducked behind a row of boxwood hedges that flanked the path to Kess's back door, crouching down until the wind died. Our faces close and breath heavy from the run, both of us obviously avoiding eye contact; I didn't know what to do, what to say, or how to act, the Junior High School dance was more comfortable than this. I would speculate that he'd agree.

When the bushes stopped swaying and the sand laid back on the ground, we stood and quietly began the walk back up the path. "Well, you've met my closest friends, so it's only fair that I get a chance to meet yours. Why don't you bring them by the Soggy Bottom if y'all don't already have plans? I play two nights from now and usually go on around eight, but should finish up about ten if y'all get a late start," Kess said, airing nervousness through his words.

"I'd like that," I answered, as we walked back up the grassy path to the gates that separated our backyards.

We stood at the gates and had another awkward high school moment. His hands were plunged deep into his pockets and mine fumbled with the knot on my dress; neither of us wanting our walk to end.

Again he broke the silence. "Thanks for keeping me company. Besides peeing your pants, you seem pretty normal," he teased.

"Well, you caught me on a good day," I replied, as we both laughed.

"Since neither of us have plans, would you like to have dinner with me tonight? We can eat out on my patio and keep it casual," he assured me.

Oh, my God, is he asking me out? Does dinner at his house count as a date? Am I going on a date? Should I change? Does he mean right now?

I could actually hear the plane in a downward tailspin as I'm screaming from the cockpit, *"Pull up, pull up! Mayday, mayday, I'm a fucking idiot!"*

Take a deep breath and get ahold of yourself. He said casual, so don't over-analyze his every word. Set your tourettes aside and just try to be normal.

"Casual, huh? Well, what are we having?" I asked, relieved my voice was relaxed.

"I have no idea, but we can figure that out together," he replied, making his dimple pronounced again.

KESSLER

Her scent of washed cotton fresh from the laundry was intoxicating, and I found it difficult to concentrate on the job of cutting vegetables and boiling pasta. My coolness continued to escape me while fumbling my actions and words, as if I'd never been alone with a woman. She, on the other hand, seemed mellow, gliding around my kitchen oblivious to the fireworks going off in my head. I kept fading into the daydream of our arms around each other, but she's a widow, so out of respect, she would have to make the first move. I was more than willing to wait.

"Beer or wine?" she asked, as she comfortably scrounged through my fridge.

"Always beer. I don't even know why the wine is in there; it's probably expired."

"So you like beer, you're from Louisiana and you live in Nashville, but I haven't asked you what you do or even your last name," she said, as she pulled the bottom of her dress up to her knees and used it as a bottle opener for the beer, which I found incredibly sexy.

Shit, I knew this was coming. I like this girl and don't want to lie to her, but I have to know she's interested in me and not the lifestyle my money can provide for her. If this relationship goes further, she'll just have to understand and forgive me when I tell her the truth.

"My last name is Kroy," I lied, blurting it out without any forethought as to how ridiculous the whole name sounded.

"Wait, your name is Kess Kroy?" she asked with raised eyebrows, immediately picking up on the stupid.

"Kessler. My first name is Kessler, but my friends call me Kess. I worked for River Rock Records on Music Row, but you could say I'm unemployed, or will be shortly. My job isn't as fulfilling as it once was, so come January, I'm ending my employment with the company."

Pretty close to the truth. I thought, trying to justify my lie.

"Your turn," I said.

"My full name is Andrea Whitman, but as you know, people call me Annie, and honestly, I haven't done much since Jack died. Kind of pathetic, huh?" she asked, looking up at me with large chocolate eyes while continuing to stir the pasta.

"Well, I haven't been in that position, so I'm really not one to judge," I reassured her.

We agreed on The Black Crowes for our listening pleasure, and took our food and conversation to the table outside. While balancing our plates and drinks through the sliding glass door, I noticed Annie was limping on her left leg and trying her best to disguise it.

"I actually have a physical therapy degree from LSU; it's been a long time, but I can take a look at that ankle for you. In fact, if you're already limping, you should be alternating ice and heat," I said, sounding official.

"It's nothing that won't go away. I just ran too far today, but I'll let you know if I need something. Besides, I'm hungry. Let's see how we did on this pasta. Cheers!" she said, holding her fork out in front of us.

We dove into likes and dislikes about everything except politics, and I stole glances of her when she was busy scooping pasta onto her fork or taking a swig of beer. Her smile needed to be branded in my head, so when I went to bed tonight, I could see it like a picture. We talked through the sunset, and she laughed at all of my stories about Wade, so I just kept telling them. After another beer, she got up to go to the bathroom and her ankle had doubled in size; it was too painful for her to walk on.

"Listen, I really should go, but thanks so much for inviting me. The cooking and the conversation were really nice. Next time, I'll host," she said, while quickly getting up.

"Wait, you really shouldn't walk on that ankle; at least let me help you to your door."

"No, no. Really, I'm fine." She hobbled down the stairs, holding tightly to the railing.

I followed her down, making sure she didn't fall, but it was obvious she was in pain, and I didn't understand why she wouldn't let me help her. Once she got down the stairs, she would have to make it across the pool deck to the gate without something to hold onto and there was no way that was going to happen; her ankle was too swollen.

"At least hold onto my arm so you can balance yourself."

"Nope, I've it got." She rejected me again as she started to hop across the concrete floor towards the railing that separated our backyards.

"Just let me help you," I said as I followed behind her; my tone becoming sterner as my frustration grew.

"I told you I've got it!" she snapped, her voice becoming louder as she hopped.

"Jesus, what's your problem?" I yelled as I bent down and scooped her up; her arms hung around my neck and her legs dangled to the side as she let out a groan, but I just kept walking to the gate.

"Why won't you let me help you?"

"Because I'm afraid I'll kiss you!" she exploded back at me, quickly covering her eyes with her free hand.

I stopped and set her down on the wide concrete railing, our faces close enough to exchange breath.

We stood in silence staring at one another in our own Mexican stand-off, gaining composure—or in my case—balls. As I prepared myself for her "Why we should just be friends" speech, she completely surprised me—and I think herself—when she suddenly filled her hands full of my hair and pushed our lips together. Our noses and teeth bumped as she slightly opened her mouth. Breathing became heavier when her fingers tightened around my curls as she pulled me close to her, smashing our shirts together. I ran my hands up her neck, squeezing it gently, then down her back; desperately wanting to cup her ass in my hands, but stopping myself. Apart, together, apart, together; the pressure of the kissing became stronger, until I couldn't hold back any longer. I plunged my tongue into the sweetness of her mouth and her legs instantly wrapped around my waist, suffocating the space between our bodies. Through closed eyes, a soft light filled my head and a sensual state of relaxation came over my body; everywhere but my dick, my dick was another story. With every tug of my hair my erection got bigger, until Annie had him at an embarrassing length which I was unable to conceal. We stood at the fence kissing and touching each other's skin while the breeze rattled the palm trees above us. At one point, I tried to remind her that we needed to ice her ankle, but she just softly shushed me, and I was happy to obey.

The wind picked up again, blowing her long hair around our faces, trapping us in our kiss. I ran my hands up and down her bare arms, which were trembling and covered with chills.

"Let me take you inside. You're shaking; you must be cold," I whispered.

"I'm not cold, just happy I think, but it's hard to tell because it's been a long time," she confessed with a shy smile.

In that moment, I was humbled. We've known each other about thirty-six hours and that's the second time she's let her guard down.

"Me too," was all I came up with, but I truly meant it. I gently swept her hair away from her face so I could see her eyes and keep us in this moment.

After I got Annie back home and settled into her bed with her ankle elevated and heavily iced, I surrounded her with books and a laptop, making a kind of nest in case she got bored.

"Your water is on the nightstand with some Ibuprofen, and you should probably take that soon to help with the pain. Is there anything else I can get you before I go? Do I have to go?" I asked her, with a perma-grin plastered on my face.

"You've already gone above and beyond, so thank you, Kessler. And yes, you have to go, but I'm hoping you'll be back," she whispered with the same grin.

I *loved* hearing my name coming from her lips, and now I was the one getting the chills. Kneeling down beside her bed, I smoothed away the hair from her eyes, which was just a lame excuse to touch her skin again, and said, "I don't know about you, but that was the most amazing kiss I've ever had," and leaned in for another small one. "Can I call you or come by to check on you later?" I asked, hoping she would say yes.

"Tomorrow, okay?" she replied, as she meshed our fingers together and gently rubbed her cheek with my hand. "And yes, I'd say that kiss was up there."

Taking the steps two at a time and in a full sprint by the time I made it up the rear steps to my house, ears buzzing and blood pumping, excited for the sun to come up. I needed to see her face again and fuss over her, if she'd let me. My God, I hadn't felt this boyish and young in a long time, probably since I was. Isn't it just like a woman to come out of nowhere and knock you on your ass! I wasn't complaining, just happy I finally found a woman who could.

ANNIE

The swelling in my ankle had subsided over night, but I'd continue icing the rest of the day, and expected to be back on two feet before dark. Only total devastation of the earth could dampen my spirits today, and I was fairly certain that wasn't going to happen, at least not on this day. My girls were coming this afternoon, and last night, I'd kissed a boy.

I replayed every detail a thousand times over; fingering his thick, brown hair, the blue in his eyes that only Crayola could mimic; both of us caught in a state of panic and pleasure when I brought his face towards mine and his swelling erection that grew along the length of my thigh the more we kissed. Our embrace was pushing perfection, and I felt silly and girlish from the moment I woke up this morning; quite a change from the last six months. My only goal of the day was to allow myself to fully enjoy this feeling instead of beating myself up over it.

I kept busy by putting fresh sheets on the guest beds and clean towels in the bathrooms, which took a hell of a lot longer than expected with the use of only one foot. By the time I finished the chores my ankle was a throbbing mess; it had its own heartbeat. I needed something stronger than over-the-counter to ignore the pain, but that didn't seem likely, so I made a Bloody instead.

It's quasi-healthy with the celery and the pickled okra. I'll eat something later with carbs to soak up the alcohol so I'm not hammered by noon.

The knock at the door was so soft, I barely heard it over the buttering of my toast. It was Kessler, holding a bouquet of flowers he must have picked on the way over, and two steaming Starbucks coffees, one of which had recently spilled and was still burning his hand.

"Oh no, let me get you a towel! Come in, come in," I insisted, as I put the coffee down and ran his fingers under the cold water, both of us smiling at each other, but a bit lost for the right words to start a conversation.

"I didn't know how you'd be getting around this morning, and I was going for coffee anyway, so I hope you don't mind me bringing some over. These are for you," he finally said, as he dried off his hands and offered me the flowers. "I won't stay long, I know your friends will be here today, but I wanted to take a look at your ankle, and also tell you how wonderful last night was for me."

"Thank you, Kessler. Coffee and flowers, are you always this sweet?" I asked, hopping onto the kitchen counter, my leg running the length of the bar.

He smiled and said, "You caught me on a good day."

"It's not as swollen, but the pain is worse today," I confessed, as he gently manipulated my foot in his hands.

"I take it that's what the Bloody is for," he teased. "I brought you some things from my medicine cabinet that might help speed your recovery." He pulled an Ace bandage and tiny packets of Icy Hot gel from his back pocket, getting right to work on wrapping my ankle.

Who does this? Nobody is this thoughtful and caring about someone they just met; nobody this handsome anyway. There has to be a catch. He's got to be hiding some crazy underneath that beautiful face.

"I really don't know what else to say except thank you. I'm speechless and that doesn't happen often, so we should both enjoy it."

"It's really no big deal. All right, you're wrapped up, and it should last the day. Just holler if you need any help, but I don't think you should run on it for a few days," he advised as he turned back towards the door.

Grabbing his hand before he got too far, I pulled him close to me, once again making the first move. I don't know what it is with this guy, but confidence is swimming in the oxygen around me and possesses me with authority. I'm like Annie Oakley wrangling up a cowboy and holding on tight—no fear, only guts.

It's Act II and the story line is the same, but the scenery has changed; we're on my turf now. I quickly found myself melting into his freshly showered skin and suffocating his lips with mine.

His cheeks resembled shiny red apples, ripe with excitement as he ran his hands up and down my thighs, only momentarily stopping to squeeze my skin or trace the outline of my knees. We were escalating at mach speed and could easily be naked in a matter of seconds.

Don't sleep with him, Annie! Don't lose your dignity over wet panties and lack of self-control. He won't respect you lying in a pool of cum after knowing you only two days. Don't be that girl! For God sakes, it isn't even noon!

I found myself in another raging battle of willpower, resulting in no definitive victory for my mind or body when considering the end result.

130

On the bright side though, he wanted me as much as I wanted him, and in a woman's mind, there is no better scenario. As I was about to gently end our kiss, he beat me to the punch.

"Whoa," he stammered stepping back from me, rubbing a non-existent beard on his face and carefully planning his next thought. "I can't believe I'm about to say this, and believe me, it's the first time in my *life* I've ever felt this way, but I need to slow down. Please don't think I don't want to be with you, because it's really the exact opposite. Truthfully, I'm so turned on right now that if I had the chance to get you naked, I'd probably shoot you across the room. Jesus, that sounds terrible. Wait… I didn't mean it like that. Obviously, I'm having a hard time explaining this, but…." he stumbled over his words.

Holding his flushing cheeks in my hand, I cut in and let him off the hook. "You don't have to explain. I think we both feel the same way, but our past is dictating our fears of the future. I'm not offended in any way and actually think it's refreshing, so let's go slow," I said in my sweetest voice, giving him a reassuring smile and a kiss on his lips.

"Listen, I'm not good at dating games; the right amount of time to wait until you call someone, playing hard-to-get or acting casual when I really like someone. I'm just too old for that kind of shit. Could that be any more obvious since I showed up on your doorstep this morning? But, I want you to know I like you."

"I like you, too. Are you going to ask me to prom?" I said with my most serious face.

He laughed. "See! All traces of coolness are completely gone! I'm acting like such a douche."

"No, you're fine, I'm just teasing you," I told him. "How about kissing? Is that off limits?"

"I hope not. I'd hate to think I blew my chances over that little speech about self-control," he said as he leaned in close to me, his hands planted firmly on the counter, instead of near my crotch. Our faces came together again, and I was filled with girlish joy. I actually felt my insides coming alive.

When our lips started to chafe, we decided a break to our separate corners was in order. It was clearly impossible to be in the same room with any degree of space between us, but I asked him to come by later to meet my girlfriends and he said he would.

***

I could hear their voices before they even pulled into the driveway, and I limped outside to the bottom of the steps to greet my guests.

"Hey!" everyone squealed at once, hugging and talking over each other.

"I'm so glad you girls are finally here! Come in and get settled. I'll take you on a tour of the place."

After a short, gimped up tour of the house and the fight for the room with the ocean view—which was won by Claire and Leslie—Jenna whipped up some appetizers in an impressive amount of time, and we took a pitcher of margaritas to the patio to talk over each other some more. This is my favorite part of our girls' trip. We all have so much to say, and we'll be cutting it close with only seventy-two hours available to fill with conversation. One year we invited the husbands on our trip. After that week, it was consensus of both the men and the women that you need to have lady parts to withstand the amount of talking expended in such a short amount of time.

The sun was setting and the candles on our table became brighter when I heard Kessler playing his guitar from inside his house.

"Is that the radio?" Tori asked, looking around for outside speakers.

"No, I think it's my neighbor playing. He invited us to one of his shows at this bar down the road tomorrow night," I said, hoping they didn't see through me.

"If he's any good, I'll go," Jenna spoke up, stuffing an oversized beef-steak tomato into her mouth.

"What *does* everyone want to do while we are here?" Leslie asked the table.

And we're back! I thought, as everyone started talking at once, and we held court on the best eateries and boutiques the island had to offer.

As alcohol quickly over-took the dinner hour, cooking clearly wasn't an option anymore, so we ended up eating sandwiches and chips; no one cared if it wasn't gourmet. I had given up hope of Kessler coming out and didn't blame him in the least, but it didn't stop me from checking to make sure the light was still on in his kitchen.

Hey girls, this is my neighbor Kessler Kroy. I've only known him a few days, but we've already made out a couple of times, and I'm hoping for more as soon as

I'm over my dead husband. Who would want to pass up such a colorful introduction?

"Hi, ladies," he said, as we all let out a startled scream.

"Jesus, Kessler, you scared us!" I shrieked, holding my chest.

"I'm sorry; I thought you saw me walking through the gate." He laughed.

"Girls, this is my neighbor Kess and the person you heard playing earlier," I said as I fought off a guilty smile. "Come over and have a drink with us!"

"Here, Kess, you can sit next to me," Tori piped in, way too eagerly.

He got to know my friends a little and I was more relaxed after they had a chance to meet him. The first meeting between boyfriend (for lack of a better word that describes our newness) and friend is a crucial one. It ranks only second to the infamous parental meeting. All future plans can easily become road kill if either of the introductions go awry, but tonight, Kessler was flawlessly funny and perfectly charming; he nailed it. To see him laughing with my friends made me like him even more.

"Thanks for the beer and the conversation, ladies. I hope to see you tomorrow night. Good luck with the rest of the wine tonight," he teased, as he shot me a devastating smile and sexy wink.

I watched him walk all the way back to his veranda, and the outline of his muscular physique was apparent even through the yellow patio lighting.

Once he was safely inside his house, Tori turned to me and asked, "What the hell was that?"

"What do you mean?" I asked, forcing myself out of a sexual coma. "My neighbor?" I was blowing it.

"Something's going on there. I saw you two giving each other googlie eyes across the table. You're fucking him!" she drilled me.

"What? God, no! Why would you say that?" I tried to sound appalled, like the thought had never crossed my mind.

"Annie, you're trying to bullshit me, and I can smell it a mile away. Don't forget, I conveniently walked in on my husband fucking that coffee slut on his desk, and you're a fool to think it was a coincidence. I knew that asshole had been fooling around for months, but was forced to stand outside his office doors listening to their bodies slapping against each other just so I would catch him red-handed and have the evidence to clean him out during the divorce. I know when people are fucking! I'm an expert by now," she slurred, but I don't think it was just from the liquor; some of it was residual pain.

"Okay, its two-thirty, and I'm done. Who's coming with me?" Claire asked. Little mother hen trying to round up the chicks and herd them inside for a respectable bedtime.

Perfect timing, Claire. I could have kissed her.

ANNIE

The quiet house and thick fog of my hang-over made it difficult to remember if my friends had arrived yesterday or if I had drank myself into a dream. The familiar caveman walk to the bathroom to puke up an entire bottle of Pinot Noir—which I'm pretty sure had permanently stained my insides purple—took me back to the mornings in Kansas City after Jack's funeral, when a hang-over was as routine as a morning cup of coffee. I drank too much, too often, and justified my drunkenness with the pain of a tumultuous summer. I needed to get a handle on it. With each body-wrenching convulsion that watered my eyes and left me too short of breath to prepare for the next, I felt like Alice tumbling down the rabbit hole. Crying wasn't helping my situation, but like the wine from last night, the tears kept coming.

The moment when your conscience supersedes any previously successful internal bargaining methods used in talking yourself into a bad idea, you're toast. All bad choices after that ah-ha moment are made with malice, there's just no way around it.

Sitting on the edge of the bed with my eyelids thumping and continuing to water, I stripped off my sweaty and sticky clothes that reeked of my former self and threw them in a pathetic clump in the corner. I was a master at self-criticism—almost enjoyed it—but I was tired, not sleepy tired, just so goddamn tired of who I had let myself become, and needed something substantial to mark the occasion of this reckoning. I drew a cold water bath and forced myself into the tub. The icy water was physically painful but sickly exhilarating on my skin, all the way into my bones, and it awakened me on a spiritual level. There would never be another time in my life when cold water didn't instantly slap my mind and snap myself back to this bathroom, where I witnessed my rebirth. I promised myself this was the start of a purge of toxicity from my life, and the last of the leftover wine, begging to escape my stomach, was the first to go.

Having emptied my insides into a lovely porcelain toilet, I dried off and dressed, then went into the living room to see Leslie sprawled out in a lounge chair on the patio, smoking.

"Oh, my God! Honey, are you okay?" she gasped, wide-eyed at my jaundiced skin and overall frightful appearance.

"Ugh," was all I could muster as I fell into my own chair beside her.

"The girls took a ferry into St. Thomas to shop for the day; they should be back around four," she told me. "They didn't want to go without you, but I gave them the go ahead and hope that's all right."

"Lord, thank you for doing that. Shopping sounds like the threshold of hell right now. Why didn't you go?" I asked in whisper.

"Carl would flip his shit if I spent the day blowing money, and they were excited to go to the Nicole Miller store. Even if I could spend six hundred dollars on a dress, I wouldn't have anywhere to hide it when I got home, so it's less heartbreaking not to know what I'm missing. Besides, the quiet is priceless, and I wanted to make sure you were okay," she said. "So are you okay?"

"It's just a hang-over. I'll be fine by the time they get back," I said, keeping my epiphany to myself, not wanting to mark the occasion with anyone else.

"I wasn't talking about your hang-over. Smoke?" she offered.

"Sure." I accepted, pulling a Camel out of her pack. Smoking was on the purge list, but one thing at a time. "Can we please not talk about me? I'm sick of thinking about myself. Let's talk about you," I begged.

"We can talk about me, but only if you agree to switch the subject back to you when we're done," she pestered.

"Man, you're tough." I sighed, cracking a smile.

"Yes, I am. My clients in group call me the Dragon Lady. It's so frustrating to work with addicts. Shifting through the bullshit to move past the addiction and uncovering the real reason they started using in the first place. It usually takes months before a breakthrough, but sometimes the stories can be inappropriately amusing. I have a new client—a battered woman—who takes revenge on her husband at dinnertime," she said with an inept giggle.

"What do you mean?" I asked, my head beginning to pound again.

"She has put everything—and I mean *everything*—disgusting and harmful to the body into his dinners. Cleaning products, potting soil, shaved metal; you name it and she's sprinkled some in. She once told me, after her husband spent the day beating her severely, she doused his drinks with Ipecac syrup and watched him spend the weekend wriggling and thriving on the bathroom floor, but she still accepted all the blame for instigating the beating. Her genius bought her three full days free of beatings from that asshole, since he was too sick to barely get out of bed," Leslie bragged, airing a quiet sense of pride.

"God, that's awful, and it also sounds like a lot of work. Why doesn't she just leave?" I asked.

"Annie, if I could figure that part out, beating a woman wouldn't be considered a syndrome anymore. Humans are creatures of routine, no matter how unthinkable that routine is. A woman may leave her abuser an average of seven times before she leaves for good. She just continues living the hell over and over, and when you throw in years of degradation at the hands of the one you once loved, but don't have the resources or safe haven to make the break, you eventually just succumb to that routine. Let's take you for example. How devastating was it for you when Jack died and your routine for the last decade ended? Did you have a hard time finding a new routine?" she asked.

"That's different. Jack wasn't beating me. Jack died," I said. *Jack's dead. Was it getting easier to say or was it my hang-over? Not sure; can't analyze that right now.*

"It's no different, Annie, not for these women. Leaving the life and the routine they've been living is equivalent to a death. In some cases, an actual death, whether it's his or hers, is easier than leaving."

We sat in silence, smoking and pondering the logic and ludicrousness of the subject.

After a time, I admitted, "Yes, Jack's death turned me into the cliché of a tragedy. It's not just the sadness of losing the man I had pledged to love for the rest of my life, but everything that defined my life was also about Jack. After ten years of marriage, the lives of husband and wife are completely intertwined; separation seems impossible. When I first came home from the funeral, it was comparable to the feeling a first time mom has when bringing a newborn baby home from the hospital. 'Now, what?' was my only thought. Everything had changed for me mentally, but physically the only thing different was Jack's absence. Everywhere I looked and everything I touched resembled a different time, taking me back to a place where I was married and happy, but now living a completely different life, someone else's life. For some reason, I couldn't remember who I was before he died, and had no idea who I was supposed to be going into the future; but each day kept happening, the sun kept rising despite my disgust for it, and like you said, a routine was born."

"Believe me, we could spend weeks on the complexities of women scorned, but I just wanted to get you talking," she confessed. "Now, are we going to talk about your neighbor or are we still pretending that nothing's going on there?"

"Is this business or pleasure for you? Will I be getting a bill in the mail for your psychoanalysis of my mental stability?" I asked with a crooked smile.

"Nope, no bill; especially since you're dodging the question. As your friend, I say go get 'em; you only live once. Since you said his friends were a lot of fun, there's a good chance he isn't a psychopath. I saw how you looked at him, and quite frankly, it's the only time I've seen life in your eyes since Jack died. You're hiding, Annie, probably a number of things I haven't figured out yet. It's okay if you aren't ready to talk, but no one can hide forever; even dead people can't always keep their secrets. Kess seems to be a gentleman, and God knows the world needs more of those, but I've got to tell you, I feel like I've met him before. He just looks so familiar," she said.

She always nails me, even if she doesn't know it at the time. I want so much to let this volcano of information erupt from inside of me; spewing facts and feelings among the people interested, like ash raining down on a village, but I'm just not ready. I'm secretive, and I'm a liar. When did this happen? Why can't I just let go? If I actually thought Jack died in a freak car wreck, I might have played the grieving widow role perfectly, but there's so much shame attached to being the wife of a man who took his own life, who chose death over me.

As tears brimmed my eyes, I wanted to run to my room and hide, but instead chose to confide in my friend.

"Leslie, I do want your help," I said, wiping the corners of my eyes. "I would love it if you would just lie down with me. My head is throbbing, and my body desperately needs sleep, but I don't want to be alone. It sounds childish, but I just really need someone right now."

"Okay," she mused with a motherly smile. "Let's take a nap."

I drifted off to sleep with drying tears crusting around my eyes and a full heart, along with a promise of reform, which I intended to keep.

The girls returned from shopping and performed a fashion show of all the clothes they'd bought. We took our time getting ready for a nice dinner out and maybe Kessler's show at the Soggy Bottom. Leslie and I shared my bathroom, and while primping, she gave me an umbrella wink; letting me know, as far as she was concerned, I'm covered.

***

138

There was nothing particularly special about La Noche on the outside, but once we entered through the one-hundred pound wooden door, we were hooked. The interior of the restaurant felt like a luxurious Spanish adobe; not a right-angled wall in the entire place. The cryptic décor coupled with chestnut furnishings enveloped us into the darkness—the lighting, the wood, the tile, everything seemed to smolder. This restaurant was a hidden little inland gem to which only the sexy people were privy.

"Who wants wine?" Claire asked.

"Count me out. I'm still shitting purple," I grumbled, forcing a laugh.

"Nice, Annie. Can we just pretend to be fancy for one night?" Jenna begged.

"Sorry, love. Since you're the professional chef, I think you should just order for all of us," I said.

"A step in the right direction," she agreed.

The waiter wheeled out the contents for our Caesar salads on an antique bar cart and made an impressive display of assembling the salads at our table. Claire, being in the antique business and having an eye for fine furniture, used what little Spanish she knew to find out absolutely nothing about the cart or its origin; apparently our waiter knew about the same amount of English.

"Hey, how's death cat? Is he still torturing your clients?" I asked Claire.

"Oh, God, that cat!" we all chimed in.

Claire has this very beautiful black and white Persian cat with a real shitty attitude. On our last girls' trip to Charleston to visit Claire, it attacked each one of us randomly throughout the week and actually drew blood on Tori. The cat lures you in with soft purring and gentle weaving throughout your legs, but once you lower your hand within striking distance, it goes bat-shit crazy on you.

"He's banned from the store. One afternoon, he bit a little girl who thought he was a stuffed cat and reached out to touch him; that was his last bridge to burn. I still love him though, and if you had ratted hairballs stuck to your ass, you might be grumpy, too," she pouted.

"Why don't you take him to a groomer?" Jenna asked.

"Well, he's banned from there, too," Claire said, as we all erupted with laughter.

It was typical of Claire to unconditionally love something that kept hurting her—even making her bleed—and it was reminiscent of my feelings for Jack. How long was my love for him going to make me suffer? When was it enough?

As dinner wound down and we paid our tab, I put out a feeler to see if anyone wanted to make Kessler's show. Leslie was the only one who wanted to go, but I'm smart enough to know she was just keeping me company, and I loved her dearly for her dedication to our friendship. We dropped the girls off at the house and made the short drive to the Soggy Bottom.

His second set was almost over by the time we arrived, but just hearing the roughness of his voice and catching the smile that swept over his face when our eyes met instantly made me feel better. Leslie was smiling too, watching us fall all over each other in our minds, and she genuinely looked happy for me; normality was a possibility in my life again.

I'd promised we'd only stay a half hour or so. When it was time to go, Kessler grabbed my hand, gave it a light squeeze and walked us to the Jeep.

"Thanks for coming by tonight. I really appreciate it." He beamed.

"I'm really impressed with your music. How long did you say you've been playing?" Leslie asked him.

"Well, pretty much all my life, at least as far back as I can remember anyway," he told her.

He leaned his face in close to my ear, parting my hair back with his nose and whispered, "You look beautiful tonight." He lingered long enough for the warmth of his breath to cling to my neck, and trickle all the way down to my toes.

As we pulled out of the parking lot, Leslie asked with more of a statement than a question, "You like him, don't you?"

This time I didn't lie. "Yes, I do."

KESSLER

While in the Islands, sleep was supposed to be a main priority, but waking up every two or three hours at night forced me to take naps in the afternoon, which contributed to the lack of sleep the next night. I was caught in an irregular sleep cycle that seemed unbreakable. As my retirement date closed in on me, so did my claustrophobia. For the last ten years I've been focused on my next project, cursing myself for never living in the moment. Now, when there's no future project to consume me, I can't seem to enjoy the thought of retirement. Two albums worth of songs are sitting in a notebook, but with no official plans to record any of them. I was a little lost.

I found myself thinking more and more about Annie and the divine intervention of our meeting two thousand miles away from home. The thought of her sleeping alone next door made me itch. I wanted to be next to her, skin to skin under her thin cotton sheets, but it was comforting to picture her face in my mind. Her peach colored skin surrounding those large autumn eyes made my stomach warm and my heart settle. As I finally started fading into sleep with the sun on the horizon, my house phone rang.

This can't be good. Only a handful of people know this number and a phone call at six in the morning never starts out with good news.

"Hello?" I answered.

"Hey, buddy, sorry to wake you, but you better get your ass back to Nashville; they're calling a meeting and the cats out of the bag," Wade informed me.

I didn't need clarification because that could only mean one thing; River Rock Records had gotten wind of my intent to retire. First, they were going to schmooze me into staying, and if that didn't work, they would drop a novel of legal papers in front of me to scare me out of leaving.

I sat up in bed, so my brain would start thinking business. "It's all right, I knew this was coming. I haven't e-mailed in any song ideas or corresponded to any artists they want me to work with on an upcoming album. I thought I'd have more time but should have known; they work quickly. How many people are involved so far?" I asked

"Just the suits I think, but they asked me to sit in on behalf of the company to try and talk you out of it," he said. "I told 'em to go scratch cause I ain't their errand boy. You've made them twice the money that they've made you, and they signed you after your name was already out on the scene, so it's been a two-way street for the both of ya. I think I'm uninvited to the meeting at this point, but I'm not sure 'cause I ain't takin' their calls."

"Settle down, Wade. This isn't your fight. I'll have my pilot get the jet ready and try to get a flight out today. If I get back at a decent hour, I'll come by."

"Sounds good. You know Mama D's just *dying* to cook for you, so I'm sure the whole kitchen will be filled with all things that Kessler Carlisle loves; it sickens me. Hey, how's your neighbor?" he asked sarcastically.

"Not the best time, buddy," I said as I hung up the phone.

I didn't move. I was caught off guard and needed some time to put the pieces together. The business aspect of the shit storm ahead didn't faze me; I would have never come out here without knowing exactly what to do when this ball started rolling, but I never expected to meet Annie. I never planned for her to be a part of my puzzle, and even though I'd only recently met her, I knew that she was it; the real reason I was here.

My first call was to Lloyd, my concierge, and I asked him to make arrangements for a flight out today and to take care of the house since I didn't know if I would be back anytime soon. The second call was to my agent, and I loaded him full of all the bullshit I knew he wanted to hear. I'm a quick study and learned early on in this business to deny, deny, deny, and then come clean. He's done a great job for me over the years, but I guarantee there's a twenty something up and coming artist who's punching his fist in the air right now because this morning, he got the phone call he's been dreaming about his whole life.

My phone rang again. "Hello?"

"Yes, Mr. Carlisle. The plane will be ready for boarding at eleven this morning, and the car service will be at your disposal. I will see to the details of your boat and home myself. Everything will be handled with the utmost care," Lloyd assured me.

"Thank you, I appreciate it," I responded and hung up.

Now, what to do about Annie. I had about four hours until I boarded a plane. I had no idea if I was going to see her again and that possibility made me sick. I needed to talk to her, alone. I grabbed a quick shower to wake myself up and then packed a small carry-on bag. Walking through the house turning off lights, I thought about what I could say to her that didn't make me look like a complete asshole.

Should I tell her the truth? At this point, I've only really lied about my job and my last name, but I guess that's kind of a big deal, since it's basically who I am. She might not even think twice about me leaving; maybe she doesn't even care. Goddamn it, why did I lie? I'm such a pussy; although, I blame some of that on my plastic ex-wife. She fucking ruined me.

Stop! I screamed a reminder to myself.

She has nothing to do with this and that was a long time ago. This is a situation I created, and I'll just cross my fingers, promise to never lie to her again and hope for the best.

Jesus, that was exhausting.

I set my bag on the front porch and made the long walk of shame to knock on Annie's door. This wasn't the most appropriate time to have this conversation, but it was the only time I had, and I didn't want to remember her like a figure in a snow globe—shaking her up, watching her twirl in confetti when I needed a fix; the only real part of the image being regret.

Cowboy up, as my mama would say.

The chattering of women's voices was in full force as I approached the door. *Super, I'm gonna do this in front of everyone.* I knew I deserved it.

There was silence after I knocked. A leisurely morning mess of a woman answered with a blond bird's nest of hair sitting atop her head. She wore a light pink one-piece romper I'm assuming she slept in, and had on no make-up; the rims around her eyelashes were the same shade of pink as her pajamas. The crow's feet barely fanning the outside corners of her eyes showed her age and proof of life. She was the woman of my dreams; real, natural and unedited.

It's bullshit how women say they try to mold themselves into what a man wants; Botox, fake tits and lip injections become necessities to please a man, blaming their physical woes on the men who expect too much. Bullshit. The majority of men in America would be ecstatic to find a woman who occasionally cooks their favorite food or orders take-out without first asking a thousand questions, lets them watch football on Sunday, doesn't nag if the toilet lid is left up,

and every once in awhile says thank you for a hard day's work. Real women with
real skin that hasn't been poked and paralyzed is always sexier, so stop trying to
pin that shit on us.

Annie put her hands in front of her face like she was shielding her eyes
from the sun and gasped. "Kessler! What are you doing here this early?"
She shut the door half way, completely blocking herself from my sight.

"Would it be okay if we talked for a few minutes?" I asked, as I
clutched her hand from around the door and gently pulled her out
enough so I could see her face.

"Why don't you come in and let me get dressed first?" she pleaded,
still trying to hide behind the door.

"I can't stay very long, and I was hoping to talk to you in private.
Could you come outside, please?" I begged again, starting to get nervous.

"All right, but at least let me grab my robe," she said, as she pulled it
off the back of the barstool.

I couldn't help but notice her lightly tanned legs standing shoulder
width apart as she wrapped herself in a white silk robe dotted with
blooming colorful flowers.

"I've gotta go back to Nashville today. Remember how I told you I was
going to quit my job soon?" I didn't wait for a reply. "Well, it's happening a lot faster than I anticipated, and I have to go back and deal with it. I
don't know how long this is going to take, so I can't tell you when I'll be
back. This is a shitty way to leave things with us, and absolutely not what
I had planned, but it's my reality right now."

My words were becoming faster as I was forcing my way through the
speech I'd whipped up on the walk over.

"I can't stop thinking about you, Annie. I like myself when you're
around me. I like the way my skin heats up and my face hurts from smiling. You look so good to me, and I want to know you, know as much as I
can about you. I'm clueless about your feeling towards me, but I couldn't
leave without telling you mine," I said with a strangled voice at the end of
my breath.

I completely skipped over the part where I was a liar. I just couldn't do
it. I couldn't take the disappointment on her face after coming clean, and
didn't even want to think about it, so I put it out of my mind.

She stood there smiling at me, folding in the corner of her bottom lip
to make a U shape and then tugging gently at it.

I wanted her so badly. This woman with ratty hair and no make-up, standing on the front porch in her robe, smiling as I spilled my guts to her; she's the one I want, I choose her. I slid my arm around her waist, pulled her close to me and inhaled her signature sent of washed cotton. I kissed her lips softly; her embrace felt like home to me.

She pulled away and put her hands on my shoulders. "I totally understand that you need to go handle your business, and I hope it works out exactly how you want it to. This past week has been strange and exciting and it's made me feel like a teenager again, which was wonderful! I'd be lying if I said I hadn't been thinking about you a lot or that I won't miss you after you leave, but neither one of us expected this romance to happen, so you don't owe me anything. There's nothing to feel bad about here, no strings attached," she said, and then ran her fingers through my hair. "You've made me feel alive again, Kessler, and I'm forever grateful to you for showing me that love is possible."

She said my name again! What if I never hear her say my name again? I made her feel alive! Don't go, you dumbass! Who cares about getting sued? Don't leave her and ruin your life!

I spun her around and pushed her up against the wall; our tongues twisted in their own embrace, slipping in and out from between our lips. With her breath hard on my chin, I couldn't stop myself from tucking her robe back and running my fingers along her perfectly shaped ass.

"Kessler," she whispered, stating my name, not asking me a question, but still managing to melt my shoes into the concrete.

I loved being with her, and I didn't want it to end. I wanted to ask her to come with me, leave the past behind her and start a new life with me, because I couldn't wait, and I didn't want to waste another day of my life without her.

"Oh, lord, you don't know what you do to me," I crooned into her neck, covering it with my lips.

The reality of us making out in her front yard was suddenly a little embarrassing when I noticed her friends peeking out from the blinds in the kitchen window. We both heard them giggling like school girls who had just witnessed their first kiss. It ruined the moment, so I faked a laugh, and got to see her smile again.

"Can I call you?" I asked her.

"Kess, we live in different states. How would that ever work?" Her voice was soft.

"I don't know. I haven't gotten that far yet. I just don't want to let you slip away," I confessed.

"This house is rented until mid-December, so you know where I'll be if you start to miss me too much," she teased, lightly slapping my arm. "Let's not say good-bye, just see you around," she added, as she snuggled into my chest.

"All right, Annie Whitman. I'll see you around." I sighed begrudgingly as I took her hand in mine, and she kissed me one last time.

As I turned to go back to my house, my feet were almost as heavy as my heart. My brain was firing signals to my legs to get moving, but a shuffled step was the best they could do.

When Annie opened the door to go back inside, I heard, "Ooohhh!" from the girls then an eruption of laughter.

I've never had a hard time leaving a woman. God, my divorce was easier than saying good-bye to Annie. Clearly I was bummed, and planned on getting drunk as soon as I got in the air.

ANNIE

As soon as the door closed behind me, I burst into tears. I'm not sure all the girls thought Kessler was the man I currently needed in my life; however, my friends rushed me and covered me with their love. Since I had left them in the dark about my real feelings for him, they also asked tons of questions.

"What's wrong? Why are you crying? You guys were just kissing; did something happen with Kess? What can we do?" Were the questions I heard, but everyone talked at once, and I wasn't sure which person asked what, so the tears just kept coming.

My façade of strength ceased, the acting became too daunting. It was time to fill them in on the confusion of the last six months. I collected myself and began to tell them my story.

"I haven't been completely honest about what's been going on with me and why we are all here in St. Croix," I said to my four best friends, who all had pitiful looks on their faces. "It started a few days after Jack died…"

I spent an hour going over the high points: the possibility of Jack committing suicide, Jamie's outburst at the changing of the Will, the box and its contents I found in my basement, the picture of the flag under the pier and Andrea Bozeman's passport I had in the wall safe.

"I know this seems so crazy, but I have to figure out what all of this means. I have to find some answers. Are you all mad at me for bringing you out here?" I asked.

"Annie, go home. Forget all of this—even Kess—and go back to Kansas City, or you're going to get yourself hurt," Tori surmised.

"I agree," Jenna interjected. "This sounds too dangerous. Fly with me to Denver tomorrow and stay in my guest room. You can take a break from your life, and you'll be safe at my house."

"Claire, would you like to weigh in?" I asked.

"I just want you to be okay, so if that means staying, then stay, but promise us that you'll be careful," she urged.

"I'll be as careful as possible, and love you all for loving me, but I am staying. I'm already here, and girls, I'm on to something big. I have to see it through," I said.

Leslie didn't chime in with her opinion, but that was probably coming in a private conversation later, so I didn't ask her in front of the others.

"Okay," I said, dragging the word out as the stress released from my mouth. "I feel better already. Now, let's take our stuff down to the beach and enjoy the rest of the time we have together. We can make some sandwiches, and there should be some rafts in the shed next to the pool house." They all just stared at me. "Really, I'm going to be fine, so let's just make the most of today, since you're all leaving tomorrow morning."

I'm pretty sure I had ruined our last afternoon together, but I really did feel better telling the truth. It's weird how secrets can begin to change you. They slowly instill paranoia, forcing you to pretend all the time like an actor in a play, and I was feeling more and more like a liar than just someone keeping a secret; it was becoming exhausting. More than anything else, I was grateful to these women who didn't judge me and only wanted the best for me.

"Let's go!" Tori hollered, standing at the patio door with large beach bags hanging off her arms.

"I'll catch up with you. I have to make a call first," I said, pulling out Francis Hutchinson's (or Hutch as his friends call him) business card.

I waited until the familiar chatter that only a group of women can make together became softer and finally non-existent, as they made their way down to the beach.

"Soggy Bottom. This is Hutch speaking," he rumbled over the noisy bar crowd.

"Hi, Hutch. This is Annie Whitman. My friend Kessler introduced us at your bar the other night."

"Um, yeah. Oh, hey, Annie," he said, as though his memory became clearer. "What can I do you for?"

Why do the majority of old guys say, "What can I do you for?" Is it an attempt at a joke or are they just trying to keep up with the slang of a younger generation? The generation behind me uses a word to describe someone like me (single in my mid-thirties) and it's cougar, so I could give a shit about keeping up with that.

148

"I wondered if you had some time to take me diving at the pier in Frederiksted?" I asked.

"Sure thing, be happy to! My weekends are pretty busy, and I have to open the restaurant tomorrow, but I have the next afternoon free. Round twelve o' clock, if that works for you?"

"Yes, that's perfect! Do you want me to come by the bar or just meet you at the pier?" I asked, getting excited.

"Come to the shed behind the Soggy Bottom, that's where all my equipment is stored. I'll need to get you fitted for a BCD vest and flippers. Your car will be fine in the parking lot for the afternoon."

"Okay, sounds great. I'll see you in a couple of days," I replied, hanging up.

Reeling with excitement, I pulled on my swimsuit and slathered my Midwest skin with sunscreen. My gut told me this dive was a step in the right direction, and I was praying that something of interest was underneath the pier.

As I walked out of my bedroom, Leslie sat on the edge of the couch with a concerned look on her face. Obviously, we were about to have our private conversation.

"Hey, I thought you went down with the rest of the girls. Whatcha doing?" I asked, still surprised.

"I think I have something to show you, and I'm not sure how you're going to react," she cautioned.

"Listen, if it's about the phone call that I'm assuming you heard, then I'd be happy to explain it to you," I responded.

"No, no need to explain. I know you aren't leaving with us tomorrow, and I really didn't expect you to even entertain the idea. I know you too well," she said with a smile. "It's about Kess, and I think you need to sit down," she noted, as she pulled out her iPad with a large picture of him on the screen. The caption read: Top Grossing Country Artist of 2011.

KESSLER

Wade waited inside the metal hangar as my Cessna landed at the Nashville airport. High winds and sketchy weather conditions made our arrival an hour late. The pilot handed Wade my bag and told him good luck since I was a hot mess of whiskey. The unseasonably cold air for the beginning of November gave way for a chance of snow, and I forgot to bring a jacket with me in my rushed packing this morning. As the wind whipped through my T-shirt, stinging my chest and hollering in my ears, Wade helped me to his car, laughing the whole way.

"Well, ain't this a fun change for us? I get to be Mr. Responsible for once, and I can't wait for Mama D to get a look at you! How does some shrimp and sausage egg casserole with bacon butter beans sound right about now? Maybe you could wash it down with a big ole glass of whole milk!" he shouted.

I let him have his fun; he'd earned it by picking me up and besides, hell must be freezing over if Wade's the sober one, but I wasn't in a talking mood. The silence made our ride home seem impossibly long, and about ten miles outside of Franklin, Wade finally spoke.

"Ah, Kess, you can't be this worried about the meeting tomorrow; your contract is up. They might use some scare tactics, but there ain't a lot they can do about you leavin.' The only real issue I see is the people you're leavin' behind who have worked for you all these years, but you can't live your life based on other people's dreams; you gotta focus on your own. Everyone and everything's for sale at the right price; just take care of the people who have taken care of you," he assured me.

"Yeah," was all I said.

He dropped me off at my garage door, and I went inside to take a shower. My mind was a washing machine, spinning my regret around in circles; my heart drowning in soapy water.

She seemed so nonchalant when I left. She didn't beg me or even just ask me to stay. I thought we had something between us, a fire of some kind. How could I have misread her so wrong? The way she looked at me on that first night we kissed, running her fingers through my hair and squeezing her thighs around my waist; that wasn't just a regular kiss. The tremble in her hands and rising breath, every time I put my arms around her, told me she wanted me. I just don't understand. Did she change her mind? Did she find out who I am? Oh shit, does she know I lied to her?

I tortured myself with these kinds of questions and obviously, wasn't going to get any answers from Annie, who was two thousand miles away. I needed to get a woman's perspective, so I got dressed and went next door.

"Oh, my baby's home!" Mama D screeched as she met me at the kitchen door with a bear hug.

She stepped back to take a look at me, and her face immediately turned sour. "Uh-oh, what's wrong, sugar?" she asked.

I had planned on playing it off like it was no big deal and maybe casually ask her advice later on after dinner, but instead I blurted out, "I think I really screwed up, Mama!" I was just as shocked as her because I've never talked about women with Mama D. Her eyes glowed with the nurturing warmth of a lioness, ready to pounce on my problem. She ate this stuff up.

Mama D led me to the couch in the living room and told the boys to scram until dinner. Hope walked past, caught a glimpse of me and yelled, "Hey, look who's back!" before she actually saw my face.

So there I was with the full attention of the two women I respected most in this world, about to tell them what an asshole I had become. Hope had already told Mama D about Annie (just like I knew she would) and that she thought there was something special happening between us, so I filled them in on the rest.

"No, you shouldn't have lied to her, Kessler. Your mama brought you up better than that, but, baby, it isn't like you killed someone. You're trying to protect your heart, and I think anyone can understand that, but you do owe her an explanation. Once you explain, she'll soften a bit," Mama D implored, with Hope nodding her head in agreement. "Besides, you don't even know if that's really the issue. Maybe she's just guarding her heart, too."

"What do you mean?" I asked perking up, intrigued by this point of view I hadn't considered.

"Well, darlin,' you two are all hot and heavy, kissing and giggling with each other and then *bam*, you tell her you're leaving, and you don't know if you'll be back. What's she supposed to do with that information? She

151

supposed to beg you to stay and profess her love to you, just to have you leave anyway? Maybe she knew you were leaving either way, and she didn't want to be standin' a fool and watchin' you go," she said sternly, with Hope still nodding in agreement and this conversation increasingly becoming a lecture for me instead of a pity party. It was obvious these women were starting to turn.

Mama D started in again. "Now, I suggest you handle your business here in Nashville, then you ride that fancy airplane of yours back to St. Croix with your tail between your legs, tell her who you are; give her your whole life story if she wants it, tell her you're falling in love with her, and beg her for forgiveness. After that, it's in God's hands, baby, and at least you'll know you gave it your best."

"I *am* falling in love with her, but what if she turns me away? I don't think I can take that kind of rejection," I confessed.

"Yes you can, Kessler. You'll never regret falling in love, but you will regret not giving it a shot. Life is full of all kinds of disappointment, so if you have a chance at happiness, you gotta fight for it. If you don't have love, baby, you ain't got a pot to piss in. Love creates happiness, so go out and get your happy," she gleamed. "But first we gotta eat; can't send you to a big downtown meeting with whiskey on your breath and an empty belly. Uh-huh, bet you thought I didn't notice. Drinking in the afternoon? Shame on you, Kessler Carlisle. You go fallin' in love then acting all kinds a fool," she muttered under her breath as she walked into the kitchen and started pulling plates out for dinner, still lecturing me even though I was in a different room.

I smiled at Hope. She patted my leg and said, "You know, I've got her number. She gave it to me the night before we left St. Croix. You wanna call her?"

"Not yet. I want to talk to her face to face. She deserves that."

About that time, Wade poked his head in the living room. "Can I come in yet?" he asked, only giving me wink, not a hard time.

Dinner with my family was a welcome feeling, and I sat quietly as the boys gave me the highlights of football games and the start of basketball practice. Mama D updated me on the feud she'd been having with the woman up the street over her booth at the Farmers Market; apparently this lady is trying to get out of paying her monthly fee, very scandalous. Wade filled me in on the progress of his next album and showed me the different artwork options considered for the cover. This was as close to my Norman Rockwell, picture perfect life as I could imagine; the only thing missing was Annie.

ANNIE

The pre-dawn breeze of another museum-worthy sunrise blew through my bedroom windows, banging the plantation shutters against the glass, prematurely waking me up. The covers were completely kicked off my body, mangled and twisted into a violent heap at the foot of my bed, as my face laid on a wet pillow case soaked entirely from my own sweat. I had been dreaming of Jack.

Dreaming was a terrible—and wonderful—ordeal for me, and after waking up, it always trapped me in a fake reality where the emotions of my dream are real, but the reality of the dream is false. It fucked with me—a lot.

I can smell my stink.

Reaching for a clean nightgown from my pajama drawer and then changing my mind, I grabbed running clothes instead.

I'm just going to end up tossing and turning in sheets that need to be washed, and I already need a shower, so I might as well go for a short run.

I loved pulling on running shoes; my nylon armor protecting my feet from the vast elements that Mother Nature might try and throw at me. Tying the laces (always in a double knot) meant that it was time to work and this always felt symbolic. I've never been good at enjoying a hobby strictly on a fun basis. Always starting out with the best intentions, but inevitably, turning it into a competition with myself, the hobby eventually becomes a job. Even though this sounds insane, running works for me on so many levels. Imagine a woman sitting motionless on a couch in her living room staring at the wall with the stereo blaring music into her face. Not the happiest image. Now, imagine driving through an average American neighborhood and passing by a woman jogging—super normal. The mental aspect of the two women in these scenarios are the same, so I might as well use running to sort out my head instead of staring at a wall.

The front door creaked closed in the dense darkness of the house, but outside presented the polar opposite as the ocean birds squawked the sun awake. I found a playlist that suited my mood and then was off and running to Kessler Carlisle's latest album. Last night, I downloaded every album that Kessler had released over the last twenty years, and planned on listening to them all. The gruffness in his voice soothed my mind like aloe on the skin and strangely enough, wrapped him around me, but I guess that's probably how stalkers start out feeling, too. Nevertheless, Kessler helped me run my three miles this morning, just for fun.

When Leslie showed me his picture yesterday, I spent a few minutes in shock, but honestly, I got it. I understood why he lied about his profession and gave me a fake last name.

Some woman must have done a real number on him.

When I read the mass of articles about him and scrolled through hundreds of his pictures online, it made me sad for him; he was running from a character that he had become within a circus of a life he was living. Watching him on YouTube acting in a video or playing for the audience was a different person than I knew, and he really didn't even look the same, even though he was still wickedly handsome. Leslie can second this because she's the biggest country music fan I know, and she's seen his show four times, including the one a few months ago in Kansas City; it still took her three days to figure out his little secret. However, the pictures of him and Wade together were genuine; the way they looked at each other was real—like brothers.

I certainly wasn't mad at him for his charade. I mean, Jesus, I'm the queen of secrets; especially concerning Kessler. I have a whole slew of information I had chosen not to tell him, and it wasn't a small time scandal, like being a celebrity. He'd asked for my phone number, which I had denied him, and I doubt he's listed in the phonebook, so I guess if I wanted to see him again, I'd need to buy a ticket to the show. I already missed him and couldn't stop smiling when picturing his face. This wasn't the right approach to take when trying to forget someone, but truthfully, I wasn't ready to forget him just yet. Hearing his voice in my ears and pretending he was singing to me was good enough for now, but no sad songs. I wasn't ready for those either.

My ankle felt healed and didn't give me any trouble on my run today, but I didn't want to push it; I'd be in St. Croix alone, and want to do a lot of running to pass the time. Plus, I had a very important date with some fish tomorrow afternoon, so I turned back early and headed home.

The girls were awake and in the midst of eating breakfast, drinking coffee, and collecting their things strewn about the east wing of the house. With the opening of the front door, the kitchen went from a hen house to a funeral, as four sets of eyes cloaked me in sadness.

"Hey," Jenna said lovingly as she scraped eggs off the bottom of a pan. "You okay?"

"I'm good. A run always helps to brighten things," I said with a smile.

"I wish we didn't have to go today. I don't feel right about leaving you here by yourself," Claire added as she gave me a hug.

"What about Kessler? Do you think you'll see him again?" Tori asked.

"I really don't know, but can't think about that right now. Concentrating on myself and finally closing this chapter in my life; knowing the truth about Jack, about his life and his death means everything to me and it's what I'm going to focus on. I just have to know," I said. "What time should we get you girls to the airport?"

"We have two cabs coming to pick us up in an hour. We didn't want to trouble you, and this way we don't all have to try to squeeze into your Jeep. Plus, I hate good-byes at the airport; seems too final. I'd rather just wave to you in the driveway," Leslie said with an uncomfortable smile.

"Oh, no! I could have taken you! Really, it's no big deal," I promised.

"No worries, but we need to finish packing and get our mounds of stuff to the front door," Jenna barked as they all suddenly scattered to their bedrooms, like they forgot they were on a schedule.

In no time the cabs arrived and just as fast as they came, my girlfriends left, and I was alone. In a matter of only minutes, the life and laughter that filled the Cotton House was sucked out the door with my best friends. My only acquaintance on the island now was Hutch, who was taking me diving soon, so I decided to rummage through the pool house to see if an equipment run was going to be next on my list.

ANNIE

S hifting gears in the Jeep was exhilarating and gave my mind some focus as I matched the anfractuous hills and bends in the road with my foot pushing the accelerator; a therapeutic relaxation between me and the three empty seats. No random braking or rubber-necking a wreck on the side of the road, which is an everyday occurrence while driving the highways of Kansas City; only a narrow open road, free from the urban assault of vehicles and their road-raged drivers. With an empty day ahead of me and no plans except for a run—which had already been accomplished—I decided to drive around and take in the beauty of another gorgeous day on the island. The palm trees seemed to blow in the same direction I drove, cheering me on to keep going, until I found myself coming to a stop in the parking lot of the Soggy Bottom.

Such a creature of habit.

The Christmas lights twinkled and a low murmur from the small lunch crowd hovered over the dining room as I took a seat at the empty bar. Hutch busied himself wiping down liquor bottles and cleaning the cash register when he noticed me through the mirror hanging on the corner wall of the bar.

"Hey! My next diving client, right?" he questioned.

"Yes, Annie Whitman. We met the other night," I said, standing up and shaking his hand across the bar. "I was out for a drive and found myself on your doorstep, so I thought I'd come in and have a bite to eat."

"Glad to have you, Annie! My recommendation is the conch fritter salad with our house dressing; best on the island. Do you mind if I keep you company while you have lunch?" he asked.

"Of course not! That would be fantastic. I could use a little company right now, and it just so happens you're the only person I know on the island at the moment," I stated.

"Well, I guess we should get to know each other a little better then," he replied, slapping the bar top with a menu. "Where do you call home?"

"I'm from Kansas City, but have a house rented here for a few months, so I guess St. Croix is my temporary home," I answered.

"St. Croix was once my temporary home, too, but that was about forty years ago." His laugh was booming. "Are you here on business or pleasure?"

I didn't really know how to answer that question, because oddly, the answer is both. The business of Jack's death was my main reason for being here, but Kessler Carlisle had recently added some pleasure to my life and now there was no definitive answer to such a simple question. Although, the lines became muddier the longer I stayed on the island.

My silence said enough for Hutch, and he winked at me with kind validation. "That's okay; sometimes no answer is the right answer."

"Wow, forty years. I guess you're considered a local now. St. Croix is kind of a random place. How did you end up here?" I prodded.

"Do you want the story I usually tell people or do you want the truth?" he asked me frankly.

"Whichever you want to tell me, I guess," I replied, feeling a little confused.

"I grew up in New Jersey, but after one tour in Vietnam, I knew I could never go back to city living. As our plane landed in San Francisco, the cries of joy from every soldier was indescribable; we were finally home. Unfortunately, like wee lambs, we could not have known this final destination was the lion's den. My first moments back on American soil— the greatest country in the world—a woman with dirty hair and soiled clothes came up to me in a rage, screaming that I was a baby killer, and then she spit on me, right in my face. I'll never forget the look of hatred in her eyes. I just stood there, so shocked I had waited a year to come home to this. I flew back to Jersey and tried it for a week, but every time a car backfired or the news helicopter circled over my apartment, I went into a state of panic, and that's when I decided this wasn't the way living was intended and certainly not for the rest of my life. I bought a map and chose a place I thought would be free of the realities the rest of world had to experience, and I'm still here today," he reveled, with a big white smile.

"What a sad story. I'm so sorry that happened to you. I don't really know what to say. It seems terrifying to just pick a place to start your life and hope it works out, but it does look like you chose wisely," I agreed, also thinking about the events in my own life that led me here.

"After a year in Vietnam, nothing is too scary. Sometimes, when we are faced with adversity in life, the most important decision we can make is to just listen, and God will show us the way."

"I'm not a very religious person, especially these days," I informed him, a bit embarrassed.

The waitress brought the salads out and refilled our water glasses, giving Hutch a pat on the back and turning to me, saying, "If he's giving out advice then you'd better listen, because as annoying as it is, he has a tendency to be right."

"Are you in need of some advice right now?" he asked, with one eyebrow raised.

"I guess everyone could always use good advice."

"Well, what I would tell you is that you don't have to be religious to hear God, you just have to be willing, and there's a big difference between the two. If you have time, I'd like to tell you a story, and you can take whatever you like from it," he declared, as he wiped his mouth and took a huge swig of water from a mason jar.

"I'm all ears," I said, grateful to be having a meaningful conversation with someone, even if we didn't know each other that well.

"One night while patrolling the low foothills of the jungles in Vietnam looking for the enemy who we called Charlie, my company commander decided to split us up for the night. Both groups set up night-loggers, and we enclosed our perimeter with claymores, which are basically small boxes loaded to the gills with explosives. At about two o'clock in the morning, all hell breaks loose, and the trip flares started going off around us, warning us that someone was closing in. The thing about Charlie is that they never wasted any of their men. They only attacked if they thought they had the upper hand on you, so we bore down for a fight. For two or three hours the only light I saw was the explosions of the frags we threw across the ravine at each other—fireworks in the darkness. Besides the frags exploding, the other thing I heard was men digging what we called foxholes; we used them to take cover and jump into when grenades got too close. I went about my business, digging a hole large enough for my lanky body to fit into. After a time the exhaustion took over, and my arms became like little packets of jelly, so I sat still to take a rest and catch my breath, when I felt a frag fall into my foxhole. Obviously, the surge of adrenaline shot me six feet out of that hole. As soon I felt the earth under my feet, I bared down on the ground smashing my

159

ribs into the dirt, waiting for the blast, waiting to be blown into several pieces. But nothing happened; the bomb never went off."

I'd stopped eating and my eyes were the size of quarters as I took in all the details of Hutch's story with a twinge of pain, because I realized how selfish I had become in my obsession with my own life.

"With the break of daylight," he started again, "the explosions stopped, and the only sounds were of men groaning and thriving in pain. I hadn't moved in hours and was afraid if I tried to, it would become apparent I had no arms or legs. Paralyzed with fear, not just for the lack of body parts but also because I'd been there three weeks—only twenty-one days—and I didn't know how I was going to make it three hundred and forty-four more. It seemed hopeless and impossible that I would ever leave Vietnam alive."

He noticed the tears welling in my eyes, patted my hand and said, "I promise, the story gets better and there *is* a point."

I nodded silently, caught up in his story.

"Okay, where was I?" he mumbled to himself.

"The next morning—when the sun came up the next morning," I blurted out, enamored and horrified with his vivid account of events.

"Yes, yes. So the frag never went off, and my curiosity got the better of me; I had to find out why. I crawled over to my foxhole and peeked inside. I couldn't believe my eyes, because it wasn't a bomb at all, it was a can of vegetables and the reason the bombs stopped going off altogether. The Vietcong had run out of explosives, so they started throwing soup and vegetable cans until they could get their men out of the area. Written in black print right on the front of those green beans was, "Provided to you by the United States of America." I just sat there and cried; cried for myself and for the men around me who would never go home, because even though I fought with hundreds of men, I didn't really know any of them. We all came from different parts of the nation, were given guns and told to protect one another. Vietnam was a war of one person, each individual trying to stay alive and by far, one of the worst ways to fight a war. Even if Charlie didn't kill you, there were still times that you wished you were dead.

"But, I managed to survive that day, courtesy of the United States, and the next afternoon, a Protestant Chaplin happened to be flown out to our makeshift basecamp to do a prayer service. They did that every once in a while.

"Believing in God had never really crossed my mind. Growing up, my parents never mentioned religion, so it just wasn't something I thought about, but twenty-one days of people shooting at me and knowing that someone had lost their life because of my actions can make a person believe in almost anything. It was my first prayer service *ever*. The only time I'd been inside a church was for a wedding or a funeral, but somehow, I just knew what to do. I was happy to do it, not because of the Chaplin's instructions, but because I needed help, and I was more than willing to receive it. Planting my knees firmly in the ground, I asked God if I was going to make it out of Vietnam alive, and to my surprise, he answered me.

"Suddenly, it wasn't one hundred and ten degrees outside; coolness just kind of washed over me, sending chills right to my bone. I'm surprised I couldn't see my breath. It wasn't an actual voice that said, 'Yes, Francis Hutchinson you're going to live!' but more of a peace that came over me. I felt the hands of God upon my shoulders that day, and knew I would be okay. It was the most defining moment of my life, and it's beyond fascinating what we can hear if we are just willing to listen."

I sat frozen with shame and *could not* have felt any smaller. This man, basically a stranger, had shared a life changing experience with me, and I had spent the better half of six months lying to my best friends and treating people almost as poorly as I had treated myself. A change in the way I lived my life was in order. I needed to start making a difference; I just didn't know how yet.

"That was the most touching story I've ever heard, and can't express to you how much it means that you would share it with me," I professed, dabbing at my eyes, trying to pretend like I wasn't crying.

"Happy to do it, just don't let it be in vain," Hutch said, as he gave me a fatherly smile and patted my hand again. "Now, you look like you could use some rest. Why don't you go on home and relax so you're raring to go tomorrow when we head out to sea."

"More good advice; you're a wealth of knowledge," I said, as I pulled my purse off the back of the chair and threw down a twenty.

"Well, I'm old, and I've done a lot of living in my years. I'll see you tomorrow afternoon, Annie," he said as he gave me a squeeze, his sasquatch hand engulfing my thin shoulder.

"I can't wait," I replied, giving him a wave as I walked out the door.

ANNIE

The gravel lot was half full when my Jeep pulled into the Soggy Bottom around eleven forty-five. Fat with sliver-green clouds, the sky looked as if it had an upset stomach and would hurl a storm any minute.

"Only a light rain, nothing to worry about," said a voice from inside a tiki hut with a thatched grass roof.

"Hey, Hutch! Good to see you again!" I beamed, walking over and giving him a hug.

"Did Kessler come with you? I forgot to ask about him yesterday," he inquired, looking around.

"No, he was called back to the States on business. I'm not sure if he'll be back to the island," I said uncomfortably, staring down at my feet while drawing a circle in the gravel with my shoe.

Hutch must have sensed my reluctance to discuss Kessler, so the questions about him ended. However, he did offer his opinion on the subject.

"Huh." He looked perplexed. "You know, I've known Kessler for near five years now, and he's never introduced me to a lady friend of his before. In fact, you're the first woman I've ever seen Kessler take an interest in. Now, I know it's none of my business, but both nights you came to the bar, he must have asked me ten times if a woman matching your description had shown up yet. Almost pained me to have to keep telling him no, but I saw his face when you finally walked in; made a point of it, cause by that time, he had me almost as interested in you as he was, and my curiosity got the better of me about this mystery lady," he declared, as he leaned his elbows on a small wooden cabinet. "I certainly see what the fuss is all about." He grinned as a toothy smile stretched across his pasty white face.

I smiled back, not sure how to accept the compliment.

"Any who, let's get down to business. Have you been diving before?" he asked, completely changing the subject.

"Yes, but it's been awhile."

"How much do you remember?"

"Not a lot of the technical stuff, but enough to do a shore dive at the pier."

"Well then, let's get you suited up," he stated, as he pulled out a wet-suit and measured me for a weight belt.

The island of St. Croix is shaped much like a foot, with Cotton Valley situated on the toes. We made the forty-five minute drive along the ball of the foot, over the arch, around the ankle and finally we arrived at our destination, the Achilles' heel.

How appropriate that the pier is in the exact spot the Achilles' heel would be located on a foot? The irony is uncanny.

Greek mythology never interested me, but I've heard the legendary story enough to understand the modern translation is one of weakness even in immeasurable strength. It was beyond the inspiration I needed, and my spirit flooded with a potent dose of moxie as Hutch's little pickup rattled to a stop in the parking lot across the street from the pier. We made small talk during the first fifteen minutes of the trip, and I told him that I hadn't been able to stop thinking about the story he'd told me yesterday.

"Well, it wasn't meant to keep you up at night, but the stories that really speak to us somehow do," he pointed out, never taking his eyes off the road.

Neither one of us had much to say after his poignant comment. Small talk seemed pointless and somehow beneath us, so we let the air from the open windows do the talking for us until we were ready to unload.

"Start getting your gear organized. I'm going in here a second to get a little help," Hutch said, as he pointed to a tiny yellow restaurant behind us.

Once I started taking my duffel bags out of the back of the truck, I re-alized it would take more than one trip across the street before all of my gear was on the beach. Just then, Hutch came out the back door of the restaurant with a big burly man whose chest and arms were covered in tribal tattoos.

"This here's Donnie, and he's going to be our pack mule to the beach. I'll lock up the truck, so leave anything you aren't diving with in the glove box," Hutch instructed me.

With the help of our tribesman Donnie, we had everything in a pile on the sand in only one trip. Hutch gave him a twenty dollar hand shake, and he made his way back to the restaurant, never speaking one word to either of us.

I thought I'd be uncontrollably nervous by this point; I'd been thinking about this dive since Gail and I concocted this plan in her living room almost a month ago, but I was more anxious to just get it over with than anything else. I zipped up my wetsuit, put my mask and snorkel on my head and opened my duffel bag. With his back turned, Hutch hooked up the air to my vest as I pulled out my knife and retractable-shaft shovel, and laid them next to my flippers.

"Oh, you won't need those," he said, pointing to my knife and shovel as he turned around noticing them. "These are protected waters and are considered a National Monument. Whatever you pack in, you have to pack out and nothing more; no souvenirs."

I just stared at him in silence as I hooked my knife belt onto my thigh, sliding the jagged blade into the holster once it felt tight. Picking up my shovel and jamming the pointy edge down into the sand so it stood erect on its own; the silence between us came to a head, causing a meeting of the minds. We stood there for a minute or so awkwardly looking at each other while the sky grew greyer and thicker with moisture.

"We aren't going diving for fun, are we?" he surmised.

"I'm afraid not," I answered.

"Um, I'm not sure what you're after, Annie, but like I said yesterday, my curiosity has a tendency to get the better of me, so I'll go along for the ride. I could use a mission to get my blood pumping, like back in my Vietnam days. Just know, if anyone is patrolling the beach when we surface, we don't know each other. Got it?" he stated emphatically.

"I got it," I calmly replied.

We put on our buoyancy control device, or BCD, which is a vest worn while scuba diving that inflates and deflates depending on whether the diver wants to sink to the bottom or rise to the surface. The ample vest coupled with the weight of the air tank made out-of-water movement difficult, as we gaggled towards the water like moronic penguins, trying to retain an ounce of dignity. I was aware that Hutch kept glancing over at me and shaking his head with choice words he kept to himself.

The water was waist high when he turned to me and said, "It's your show, Annie. You've got a little over an hour of air, depending on how well you regulate your breathing. I've got less since I'm twice your size; just tell me where you want to go."

"Let's kick out on the surface to the end of the pier, and save our air for the dive. We're going to the last column on the right side, and once we get down to the bottom, I'll take it from there," I said in a surprisingly authoritative voice.

"I'm assuming you already know it's like swimming five football fields to even get to the edge of the pier. That's a hell of a long way. Can't we just walk to the end of the pier and jump?" he proposed.

"No, we'll be less noticeable in the water, and the extra oxygen tank is too heavy to carry that far. Don't worry about me, but if you need to stop and float for a while, just tell me and I'll be happy to rest with you," I answered, as it started to rain.

"I didn't realize we are trying to go unnoticed. Is there a chance you're going to tell me why?" he asked.

Again, I answered with silence.

"Well, I didn't think so," he mumbled to himself.

I couldn't have asked for a better weather scenario than rain. People instantly packed up their conversations and fishing rods, and the pier was basically vacant except for one man who seemed more interested in his fresh catch than us; the less people the better.

Hutch fit the shovel in between the back of my wetsuit and vest, so I didn't have to drag it through the water. Biting down on the mouthpiece of the snorkel, I echoed, "Let's swim!"

Totally underestimating how exhausting the swim out to the pier was, we had to stop three different times to rest. As we bobbed up and down with only a hundred yards to go and taking our final rest, I was reminded of the day that Jack died. I felt this exact same sensation of floating when I passed out in my entry way. At the time, I had considered myself weak, much like the Achilles' heel, but today, out here in the ocean, I knew I was more like the arrow that brought the Greek God to his knees. I couldn't help smiling as the rain pelted my face, slipping off my cheeks, and becoming part of the ocean. I liked this new Annie, and she would be sticking around.

"You mind telling me what's going on right now in that pretty little head of yours, 'cause I'm already wiped out, and you seem almost giddy. Do I at least get to know what you plan on doing once we get down there?" he sputtered, as water ran off his beard in a continuous stream.

"Time will tell." I smiled. "Last push, we're almost there."

165

When finally reaching our target, we worked together to strap the extra air tank around the column in case one of us needed more air, and to also use as a descending line. Hutch went under first, and I took the extra few seconds to clear my mind and steady my breath.

Breathing underwater is entirely unnatural. It takes a moment to wrap your head around the process of sucking in air when your brain is fully aware; oxygen isn't available below the surface. It takes even longer to begin to relax. Humans are the minority below the waterline, and even if it never crossed your mind before the dive, once you are submerged, it's extremely evident; even a small mistake can cost you your life. I had a habit of fidgeting with all of my gadgets the first few minutes of a dive, much like how a batter fits and refits his glove before each pitch. It was my check system, and it always helped to calm my nerves.

I deflated my vest a tiny bit at a time, watched the bubbles rush to the surface breaking free of the ocean, and in return, started to sink. With one hand on the descending rope which was attached to the column, and the other hand pinching my nose, equalizing my eardrums with a popping sound every few feet, the bottom became more visible. Hutch kept requesting an OK sign made by my fingers, to let him know that I was, in fact, OK.

The colors under the ocean are insanely bright and each dive is like seeing them for the first time. Up there, the pier is just gray concrete, but down here, it's an underwater aquarium, kept secret from those who aren't willing to take the risk and sneak a peek. I allowed myself to enjoy the scenery of a watery city bustling with fish and other odd-shaped swimmers. Once my feet touched the bottom and the stirring of sand quieted, Hutch pulled on his tank knocker to get my attention.

"Tink, tink, tink," the knocker sounded.

He pulled out his underwater wipe-erase board and wrote, "Now what?" Shrugging his shoulders in an exaggerated motion, he moved in close enough for me to read his note.

I wrote back, "Let me look a sec," and he gave me his favorite OK sign.

Please be here. I came all the way to St. Croix; please let me be right.

I circled the ten foot radius of the column covered in barnacles and tall seaweed; nature's graffiti splashed upon the concrete like neon's in a bar. Random plants and overgrowth surrounded the base, and tiny fish darted out of their suburban homes as I ran my fingers through the gulfweed.

166

Then I saw it, a small patch of bare sand on the ocean floor where nothing grew, except a miniature, shredded, yellow fringed, American flag. My breath grew shallow with excitement as I struggled to plunge my fingers into the salty grains, but continued to float up and away from the floor. All the air in my vest was already drained and I still couldn't keep my feet in the sand. Hutch noticed, and expertly slipped ten extra pounds in my weight belt, immediately sinking me back down to the bottom.

Annie, you smart, smart girl! I screamed at myself from inside my mask.

Anything underwater is hard to accomplish; we are slow moving blobs with relativity no strength. Hutch helped me pull out the shovel that was still wedged on my back and even that small task took two of us. I hovered over the bare spot, stuffing the flag down the front of my wetsuit; law or not, I was damn sure leaving with this souvenir. I began wiping away the sand, but of course, most of it just fell back into its original spot. Next, I tried digging an actual hole which seemed to work somewhat better, but after each new attempt, I had to wait for the sand around my mask to clear before digging again. The job seemed endless.

The knocker again. "We are digging?" he wrote.

I shooed him away and had finally started making some progress when the current suddenly kicked up. The coral blew backwards, almost completely lying on its side, and the sand whirled in circles as a wave pushed past us. Hutch grabbed the shovel out of my hand and clipped us both to the descending line with a D-ring as I filled my free hand full of seaweed and held on tight until the series of waves passed; both of us like plastic bags kicked up by the wind, twirling and dancing under the water.

Hutch was immediately in my face, vigorously giving me the OK and expecting it back. Once it was over, I thoroughly enjoyed the rush of adrenaline, and was actually having fun.

The knocker. "Let me," he wrote, and then held up the shovel in one hand and his oxygen gauge in the other.

I held up one finger to signify that I had one thousand pounds of air left, about thirty minutes and again the OK; he went to digging, doing a better job than me.

It seemed like an eternity of bobbing up and down clipped to the line as time drug slower than a prison sentence, when I finally heard, THUNK, THUNK, THUNK. The density of the sound was thick and slowly traveled through the water, like someone throwing dirt onto a casket. I unclipped and threw myself onto the hole that Hutch had made.

167

He stepped back, resembling an astronaut walking on the moon with sand floating up around his flippers.

I reached into the hole and fingered around until I found a handle. *Holy shit! Jack, you son of a bitch, what have you got for me?* A surge of power raced through my nervous system. *Screw that dismal woman-child, shriveling on her couch like a Boston fern wearing the same heinous sweatpants day after day. I'm intelligent and strong, and I will never wallow in self-pity again. Stay calm, Annie, keep focused!* I reminded myself.

Jiggling the handle back and forth, just like with the box in my basement, I traced my fingers around the hard rectangle shape. Wiggle-trace, wiggle-trace; I moved in a measured pattern until I looked down at my air gauge and noticed it was at five hundred pounds. My air was low because in all the excitement, I'd forgotten to steady my breathing, and we still had to ascend slowly to the surface to avoid a sickness called "the bends." But I'd rather die from the bends than leave this box behind. Keeping to my sequence, with a small tug later, I freed the box from its watery grave in the Caribbean.

As I ecstatically pulled some sort of hard case out of the ocean floor, I turned around to see the expanding whites of Hutch's bulbous eyes, like two scratch balls from a pool table had been shoved into his scuba mask. I pointed up and started to ascend, but he grabbed my wrist tightly and shook his head no. We had to follow the rules of ascension, and he wore a watch which beeped if we moved to the surface too quickly, so I let him lead the way.

As we got closer to the waterline, I heard the rain coming down, splattering into millions of droplets across the water above. It reminded me of the sound a record player makes when the needle gets to the end of an album, like soft static; it was beautiful.

When we popped up on the surface, I looked around to make sure we were alone and then let out a squeal.

"I take it you found what you were looking for?" Hutch asked while spitting water, unable to control his excitement for me.

"We'll see." I giggled.

The swim back to the beach was long, but we were already half way there by the time we actually surfaced. I held onto the case so tightly, my hand almost fell asleep. When we finally reached the beach, we both crumbled into sandy piles of exhaustion. I was physically spent, but also filled with hope. I have found, even if you have nothing but hope, you somehow find the strength to keep going. However, instead of pondering the possibilities of the contents of this box, I could only picture Kessler's face. This was the most exciting day I'd had, maybe ever, and strangely enough, it was him I wanted to share the excitement with instead of Jack, and the feeling caught me off guard.

"Well, aren't you going to open it?" Hutch asked excitedly.

"Can't. Don't have the key," I said smiling. *Not yet anyway.*

"I'll be the first to admit that I don't have a fucking clue about today, but it sure was fun!" he raved, slapping his thighs and gathering our gear.

The drive was pretty quiet until the truck came to a complete stop back at the Soggy Bottom parking lot, and Hutch turned to me and said, "Annie, we've only started to get acquainted, but I learned a lot about getting a feel for people when I was in the military; in fact it was my job, and you seem to be good people. I've got to tell you though, I don't think you have any idea what's in that box, but you went to an awful lot of trouble to get it. It's none of my business; nothing much is, but if you ever need help with anything, please consider me your ally, and know I'll do what I can for you."

"I appreciate that, Hutch, and I'll take it to heart. Thank you for taking me out today. I don't think you'll ever know how much you've already helped me," I said, handing him his payment for the dive, plus a two hundred dollar tip.

KESSLER

River Rock Records is the tallest building on Music Row, with green glass covering the outside of the partial brick building, giving off a pompous stench that's frequently discussed amongst musicians, especially those who were passed up on a record deal. There is some truth to the gossip though; it just doesn't fit into the history that saturates Music Row. On the other hand, it's a shining example of the kind of future expected for the Nashville Sound.

Music Row is a ten block radius of interconnecting alleyways that house hundreds of businesses related to country music, and centered upon two main streets, Sixteenth and Seventeenth Avenue-Music Square East and Music Square West. It's the heart that beats inside the chest of anyone who cranks up the volume to their favorite country song; they just don't know it. Record labels, recording studios, licensing firms, publishing houses and radio stations all come together in this small radius, to entice you to love a song enough to buy it. Music Row is to country music what Cooperstown is to baseball. All that said, I have created a wonderful family through ten years of memories in these ten blocks, and I was sure as hell gonna miss them.

I caught my reflection walking up to the glass double doors, and saw a haggard man staring back at me. The bags under my eyes, a pastel color to my face, and an overall slouch in my demeanor was not the way a twenty-five hundred dollar Tom Ford suit is meant to make you feel. I dressed in it this morning because I usually felt like a rock star in this baby, but maybe firing your music family is more Big Smith overalls, rather than a Tom Ford suit kind of day.

Six years ago, I signed a Three Sixty deal with River Rock, and to say that I had fulfilled my contract is an understatement; I blew it out of the water. I signed an album deal guaranteeing to record four records with the option to make more if we both wanted to keep going, otherwise I would be a free agent. In the old days, being famous was very compartmentalized, but now record companies are offering Three Sixty deals which are an all-encompassing package, where no job is outsourced; everything from the album, tour press and online media is handled in-house. With this kind of deal everyone is on the take, and we all make more money by cutting out the middle man. I was ready to get off this merry-go-round, and I knew a lot of other people's jobs would end with mine. I just needed to rip the Band-Aid and get the hell out of there, so I asked Wade to meet me at our favorite Mexican dive, SATCO, in an hour. I didn't plan on staying any longer than that.

I'll be goddamned if it wasn't just business as usual, and then our partnership was over. It's not like I expected them to beg me to stay (well, I kind of did) or throw me a going away party, but I couldn't help feeling like I'd just been fucked then kicked out of bed.

That's it? I've been working myself into knots over, "Our lawyers will send over the paperwork." Jesus, maybe Mama D was right, and I think too highly of myself, 'cause that was a kick in the balls.

I changed into jeans and my favorite LSU hoodie and headed down Twenty-First Avenue to meet Wade. He was already into his first stack of tacos when I walked onto the deck and saw him through the window.

San Antonio Taco Company, or SATCO as the locals have dubbed it, is a little Tex-Mex joint located right next door to Vanderbilt University and Music Row. You order your tacos like you would sushi, and every time I'm downtown, I never miss an opportunity to eat here.

"Well, how'd it go? You a free man?" Wade asked, with a mouth full of taco.

"Yeah, I guess so, but I thought you told me they were gonna beg me to stay," I stated.

"They were, but if your answer is no, then they gotta move on. Shit, man, what do you care anyway? Isn't this what you wanted? From what I heard in the living room yesterday, sounds like you've got yourself a little lady problem you should be turning your attention towards instead," he said, with a know-it-all smirk across his face.

"Annie," I crooned, as my face lit up and a smile spread to my cheeks that I couldn't have stopped, even if I'd wanted to.

"Oh, shit," Wade scoffed, shaking his head. "Please *do not* tell me you think you love this girl."

"I know I do, Wade."

"As a guy, I'm gonna tell you that you're acting like a pussy; getting all sloppy over some chick you barely know, and it's disgracing our entire gender. As your friend and someone who talks a big game but's been faithfully married to the same woman for twenty years, when you know—

you know. What I don't understand is, why you're sitting at a Mexican dive at eleven o'clock in the morning eating tacos with me, when you should be high-tailing it back to St. Croix to fuck your brains out for the next two weeks," he said with a smile.

"I gotta go, buddy." I quickly stuffed my uneaten tacos into a bag to take with me, then stretched my arm across the table and smacked Wade in the mouth. He was right, and I loved him for his honesty, but mostly, I just wanted to piss him off.

"Now, dammit, I told you to stop slappin' me!" he hollered, as he threw his taco down on the table. "If there's a picture of that in the newspaper, I'm gonna be all kinds of pissed!" he yelled, but I was already through the doors and sprinting to my car. I had to run home first, but I could be landing in St. Croix by three o'clock, and I was overwhelmed with excitement to make it happen.

ANNIE

I sat stewing in disbelief on my kitchen counter, staring across the room at the black box that was virtually empty except for a Ziploc bag. The weight of the case fooled me into thinking treasures would be spilling out of it when I finally got it open, but there were only two things locked inside—a picture and of course, another key. I guess I thought the contents would be a little more exciting. The picture was of three men and one woman sitting at a table in a café. It was faded and looked like it was taken at least a decade ago, probably in the nineties, and the only reason it held my attention was because a young, handsome, and tanned-faced Jack Whitman was in it. My breath was literally taken away to see him again. After Jack died, I tried to get my hands on any picture he was in, especially if I had never seen it before, and they were hard to come by. Jack was never the kind of husband who whipped out the camera and said, "Let's take a picture!" I usually had to beg him, and that always annoyed me, but once again, Jack isn't smiling at the camera; no one in the picture was smiling. In fact, it looks like none of these people even knew their picture was being taken. On the back were two separate lines written in pen, both containing random numbers.

Enough with the numbers! I was a Parks and Recreation major in college, not a fucking mathematician.

I researched a Pelican Case on Google and found it is made to be submerged underwater while protecting the contents; the information didn't disappoint because the inside of this box was as dry as crappy merlot. I was one hundred percent sure the key I found in the lockbox from my basement was going to be the same key that unlocked this case; I was right. Once again, I didn't fully understand the contents, but I did know if this picture needed to be buried in the ocean, I'd better keep it safe.

Every part of my body screamed, *"Stop what you're doing! This is not a normal day in someone's life. Let go and move on!"* But my mind would just continue to spin scenarios until I eventually drove myself crazy or until someone came looking for this case. I pulled on my shoes and turned up the music; I needed to run.

Approaching the last hill, which I had dubbed "The Beast," I was mentally exhausted with still no real formulation of a plan for myself. I had another key, but no clues to guide me in the right direction.

What do I do next? I asked myself over and over as I ran along East End Road.

Once the hill crested, I caught a glimpse of a car in my driveway. My initial reaction was to turn and run, but honestly, I just didn't have the energy. I crouched behind a palm tree to get a better look; it was a red Jeep.

Oh, my God! It can't be!

My heartbeat felt like stones skipping across a pond, and my face instantly stretched into a panicked smile, totally forgetting about my little dilemma.

He came back. Holy shit, he came back for me!

I stood at the top of The Beast, pinching my hand to make sure this was really happening when I saw him; arms folded over his chest and feet kicked out, leaned against his Jeep, making sexy look effortless. Finding him standing in my driveway felt like seeing my best friend in a crowd of strangers, and it was confirmed at that moment—I was falling for him. He noticed me and started walking towards the edge of the driveway. I'm not sure what came over me, and I've only seen this done in movies, but I took off into a sprint and jumped into his arms, wrapping my legs tightly around his waist. He picked my five-five, hundred and twenty pound frame up into the air with such ease; my heart and body were literally soaring.

We smothered each other with our lips, while broken sentences tried to escape. I guess we had both thought about each other a lot over the last few days.

"Baby! I'm so sorry! God, I missed you! I haven't stopped thinking about you!"

I'm not sure who said what, but I knew I didn't want to let go of him.

"Stay with me, Kessler. Take me inside," I whispered, as he was already carrying me to my front door, his entire face filled by his smile.

We stumbled through the doorway, hands and lips heavy on the other, when he stopped and pulled away.

"Wait, stop. Annie, I have to tell you something; I lied to you. My name is Kessler Carlisle, and I'm a country music singer, and if you'll just let me explain...."

"Shhh," I breathed, putting my finger to his lips. "I know."

"You know?" he said, sounding ashamed. "How?"

"Leslie clued me in on your little secret; it's okay. I'm not mad, but I don't really want to talk about that right now. In fact, I don't want to talk at all," I emphasized. "Now how's that country song go? Something about things getting hotter after the sun sets. Is that right?"

"Yeah, that's about right." Kessler chuckled, smiling so big that his dimples were the size of nickels.

"Well, it's the middle of the afternoon here, and we're about to make a liar out of that song." I slid my fingertips inside the waist of his shorts, making an involuntary gasp escape his lips, as I turned and led him into the bedroom.

The concepts of space and measured time seemed to blur over the remaining daylight hours. I couldn't tell where my body started and his body stopped; a mass of sticky, wet flesh, pulling each other as close as physically possible, but still trying to get closer. His erection was painfully hard; I thought it might burst just by looking at it. I straddled his thighs, taking in every inch of him, filling my insides with this beautiful man. I slowly leaned back, stretching his manhood out and bringing him to a sitting position, whispering, "Yesss, Annie, yesss baby," as he lightly rolled my nipples between his fingers, stopping only to kiss them. We slowed the pace from NASCAR to a Sunday drive, wanting to make this last as long as possible; neither one of us wanting to climax yet.

He fancied watching us in the mirror on the wall as I sat on his lap, with my back against his chest. As ecstasy shut down my brain, I had to remind myself to breathe. Until now, I hadn't realized how much I'd missed being close to a man; his intoxicating smell, rough hands on my skin, and the feeling in my heart when our eyes connected.

"I can't wait any longer, Annie. I need to be inside of you," he whispered into my ear as he kissed my neck and stroked my ass with his free hand.

I liked seeing him feel out of control; more so, I liked that I was the one driving him there.

175

Turning around to face him, my fingers jammed into his thick hair, we kissed furiously as he slid inside me, and filled his hands with my breasts. When my eyes rolled backwards and orgasmic electricity suffocated my insides, I lost the ability to focus on anything other than extreme pleasure.

"Don't stop!" I blurted out as my fingernails dug into his chest, and Kessler wasn't far behind me. The sounds we made at climax aren't describable, but yes, it was that good.

The unmistakable smell of sex clung to the bed as the sheets lay tousled across the footboard. I laid my head on his throbbing chest, enjoying the moment and catching my breath, our legs completely entangled like a human braid.

"Holy shit, that was amazing!" he gushed, turning to look at my face.

As I started to agree, uncontrollable laughter came out instead. I sat up in an attempt to make it stop, but it just doubled me over, and I laughed even harder.

"Damn, that's never a good reaction," he uttered, sounding concerned.

"I'm so sorry! I don't know why I'm laughing. It's just that I don't remembering feeling this good and this light and God, yes, it was perfect!" I assured him, cupping his face in my hands and softly kissing his lips. "Let's do it again."

We lay in bed, exploring each other under the sheets, softly and unguarded; free falling into one another.

The sun had long set when we finally rolled out of bed, both of us delightfully disgusting. While taking a hot shower, it dawned on me that I had spent the last few hours naked in the bright light of the sun shining through my windows, and never once had I worried about my physical appearance concerning Kessler. I wasn't an unfortunate looking person, but I wasn't twenty-two anymore either. Nothing about my body was perfect, and tiny wrinkles had already started their march across my face. Only now, alone in the shower, did it cross my mind.

He's one of the good ones. I let all my superficial worries go, but as soon as I did, a new set popped up.

The reality of my situation—that in fact, I was also a liar—came rushing over me faster than the water from the showerhead. I needed to fully let him into my life, show all my cards and let him decide if he wanted to stay. I hoped he would forgive as easily as I did, because after today, it would break my heart if he decided to go.

"Kess?" I called out, wrapping up in my robe.

I found him sitting at the kitchen table, looking at the Pelican Case, and I knew there was no turning back now.

"Hey, baby," he said, as he wrapped his arms around me, pulling me onto his lap.

He smelled of Old Spice, which I loved—a manly man's deodorant, and his hair was still damp from his shower. This was such a perfect moment I was about to ruin; my new lover who made me feel like a teenage girl when he called me baby, sitting in his lap with his arms around me, both of us fresh from our first sex-capade.

"I'm sorry about snooping, but it was lying on the table. Why would you have a case like this?" he asked as he turned it around in his hands, inspecting the craftsmanship of the box. "Isn't this the kind of gear used by the military?" he asked curiously but unassuming.

"Kessler, I've got some confessions of my own and I want to be totally honest with you; no secrets. Okay?"

He nodded, looking paranoid, like he was ready to jump ship.

I took him through the days after Jack died, telling him about the key that Robert Graville had given me, about unlocking the box I had dug out of my basement, the pictures of the flag—which was the reason I was in St. Croix—and the case and its contents I had pulled out of the ocean—which was the reason I was staying.

"Are you okay so far?" I asked, praying to God that he didn't bolt for the door.

"I'm speechless, and I don't really know what to say. Is there more?" he asked, I'm sure hoping I would say no.

"I'm afraid so, but just a little bit," I told him.

"Okay, then I'm gonna need a beer. Want one?" he offered.

"Yes, please," I said, walking over and kissing his shirtless back as he pulled two bottles out of the fridge.

At this point, I was worried it was all too much for him to absorb, which must have showed in my demeanor, because he put his arms around me, stroked my hair, and said, "I'm still here, Annie, and I'm not going anywhere. Don't look so worried. I'm just taking it all in." He finished his beer in three remarkable gulps and said, "Okay, I'm ready. Go."

"Really, the only other part I haven't mentioned is that I think my brother-in-law has it out for me; to harm me. Oh, and I got a little over two million dollars after Jack died, so don't worry about me wanting to spend your money. I've got that covered," I quickly said, trying to make a little joke.

"*What?* You're brother-in-law? Are you serious? Why?" he asked, almost choking on his words.

"I'm not sure." I sighed. "The only reason I can come up with is the insurance money. Jack changed the Will leaving me the only beneficiary, then suddenly and suspiciously dies three months later. I think it really pissed Jamie off, getting blindsided and totally cut out, but I can't be sure. That's why I had to find out if there was another box, another piece of the puzzle. So I came to St. Croix and the first day here, I met this cowboy and after a very short time, began falling in love with him."

He took my hands and wrapped them around his waist. "First of all, I don't care about the money, Annie. I wanted to find someone who loved me for who I am, not what I have, and I did; that's why I came back. When I first saw you sitting on your balcony, all I could do was tip my hat. I felt like such an idiot that I didn't have the balls to even say hello, and you can bet your ass that Wade rubbed it in all night! This doesn't happen to me—the way I feel when I'm with you—and everything you've told me so far, it doesn't scare me away from you. It's totally messed up and certainly troubling, but it's not gonna make me leave this island without you," he said, as he smoothed the hair away from my face and looked hard into my eyes. "Now get your shit, only the important stuff, 'cause we're staying at my house from now on. You can come back over to grab more clothes, but not alone. From here on out, it's me and you."

"Kessler, you don't have to do this; take on my life and completely disrupt yours. I mean, please don't feel obligated to move me into your house."

"This is who I am, baby, and even though I'm gonna sound like a complete pussy, I've been waiting for you for so long. Waiting for a woman that I would fly two thousand miles on a moment's notice for.

Yes, you have completely disrupted my life because I've finally found you. I'm in love with you, Annie, and I just can't see why I shouldn't go to the ends of the earth to keep you safe. Me and you, baby," he whispered, as he wiped the tears off my cheek and held my hand over his heart.

ANNIE

Kessler cleaned out a few of the drawers in his bedroom and bathroom so I'd have a place to put my clothes and personal belongings.

"I want you to feel at home here, so whatever you need just let me know, but first let me show you something in the basement," he said, as he led me down a flight of stairs carrying my Pelican Case for me. The marble was cold on my bare feet and chills ran up my legs.

We walked down a narrow hallway and through a heavy door that made a suction sound when opened. He turned on the light, and I was surrounded by racks and racks of mahogany shelves filled with wine.

"This is beautiful, but I thought you didn't like wine," I remembered.

"I don't, but I had it built when I bought the house and thought that celebrities are supposed to have wine cellars. I've come a long way." He smiled, shaking his head. "This isn't even what I wanted to show you." He pushed on one of the walls, and it popped open. "This is."

He punched in a code and the door of the safe unlocked. "You can use this for whatever you need and the code is 1492. Columbus sailed the ocean blue in fourteen hundred and ninety-two. Can you remember that?" he asked.

"Yeah, I think I learned that around the fourth grade," I teased him.

"Well, me too, and that's why I use this code for everything. We'll lock up your case tonight and work on it tomorrow. Now, can we please go to bed? You wore me out today, and this morning I woke up in Nashville. I'm exhausted, but really looking forward to falling asleep with you next to me," he said as he kissed me, and we headed back upstairs.

I slipped into one of the hundreds of LSU T-shirts he owns. "Oh, my, gawd, that's sexy!" he cheered, smiling ear to ear. Pulling the covers back for me, he patted the empty side of the bed, "Get on in here, baby."

I snuggled down into the feather bed mattress and found my nook in his arm as my ear rested on his bare chest. I listened to his heart beating and was warm inside and out, until I realized I had one secret left.

Don't do it! Don't sabotage another perfect moment with bullshit from the past.

But I promised him total honesty, and I was all about keeping my word.

"Kessler," I whispered, my voice barely squeaking out his name.

"Yeah, baby," he answered, kissing my forehead and letting out a comfortable sigh.

"I have one more confession."

"Uh-oh. How is that even possible?" he asked.

"Well, I don't know if I should even mention it. I mean, we just got together, and I don't want you to think I'm insinuating or expecting anything, and it's just something that hasn't come up, but..." I rambled, sounding like an imbecile.

"Annie," he cut me off.

"I feel like I should tell you I've had two miscarriages." He sat up, propping himself on an elbow. "And I don't think I can have kids. I'm sorry if this is presumptuous, but we said no secrets, and if you still want kids, then I'm probably not the girl for you because I can't give you any," I said looking down at the sheets, too scared to look in his eyes. I might have just changed everything.

He lifted my chin up until I had nowhere else to look but into his eyes and said, "I'm so sorry that happened to you. It must have been awful, but I want *you*, Annie, and if down the road we want to talk about kids, then let's talk. Right now, I couldn't be happier. Me and you, baby," he affirmed, gently kissing me on the lips.

I laid there in the dark not wanting this wonderful day to end, but feeling grateful for the way the events of the day had unfolded. For the first time in a long time, I thanked God.

***

The sweet smell of breakfast wafted into the bedroom where I was still sleeping at ten in the morning. Kessler whistled a tune I didn't recognize, but I figured country music was about to be a huge part of my life, so I started paying attention.

"Kess, this looks like the breakfast buffet at the Ritz Carlton. You've totally out-done yourself here. Thank you, honey!"

181

"Hey, darlin'! How'd you sleep?" he asked, kissing my forehead, not waiting for an answer. "I know, I got a little nuts, but when I woke up this morning, I felt so good and you weren't up yet." He put his arms around my waist and lifted me off the ground, sitting me on the island, spatula still in his hand. "I didn't want to disturb you but needed to focus my energy on something, so I started making breakfast—which by the way, is a lot more fun to do when you aren't just cooking for yourself. But now that you're up—and sitting on the kitchen counter with my LSU shirt on—all I want to do is take it off you." His voice faded into a whisper.

Leaning into me, goose bumps spreading all over his shirtless skin, I ran my fingers up and down his finely crafted chest. He slid my panties down around my ankles and slowly pulled off my shirt, looking into my eyes, both of us smiling. I'm naked, sitting on his kitchen countertop and for some reason, this did not feel strange; it felt good and natural and meant to be. He lowered me down, the cold of the granite giving my skin a shock, and spread my legs; gently and slowly, building the anticipation of the first touch of his lips on mine. I let out a moan I'd never heard before, from some hidden place inside of me that apparently only Kessler unlocks. My ears rang and temporary blindness set in, along with my first orgasm of the day.

"Jesus, that was amazing! I can't feel my legs," I whispered, trying to gather myself, waiting for the pulsing in my ears to stop.

"I aim to please." He chuckled.

"I think we burned breakfast." I laughed as he helped me off the counter. "I obviously need another shower and I'd love it if you joined me, so I can return the favor."

I'm falling in love and leaping into a relationship with this sweet, amazing man; a scary and wonderful feeling, and I don't want this to end. I loved that he pleasured me without asking for anything in return. Most men would be shoving their cock in your face or continually pushing your head down, because it seems like that's the universal sign for "suck my dick," but he was only focused on me which only makes me want him more.

"I'd love to." He smirked, and I followed him into the bathroom, his full erection leading the way.

Even though we couldn't keep our hands off each other, we were now able to focus on something other than mauling one another and tried to act like normal people instead of sex crazed fools, at least for the afternoon.

182

We went for a walk down the private stretch of beach running behind our houses, his arm hanging around my shoulder and my hand holding onto his waist, walking and talking.

"I've been thinking about all the stuff you've shown me, especially the Pelican Case, and I can't make heads or tails of it, but I know who could. I think you should let Hutch take a look at all of this and tell him your story," Kessler urged. "He's a trustworthy man and has a military background which could be of value to us at this point."

Us? Don't let me wake up from this. I was back to begging God.

"You don't have to sell me on Hutch. I've been thinking the same thing, but I'd feel better if you were with me. Are you up for all this?" I asked, crossing my fingers behind my back.

"Me and you, baby."

KESSLER

As we drove down East End Road towards the Soggy Bottom, Annie was uncomfortably silent and kept wringing her hands together; a side of her I hadn't seen before. I wanted to take away the anxiety plaguing her, and tell her that none of this mattered in our life together because I was going to take care of her, but I knew it mattered to her and I didn't want to overstep my boundaries. Boyfriend was a new role to me, and I didn't want to blow it with her, so I decided to keep my mouth shut today.

Hutch came out from behind the bar to greet us. "Kessler!" he said, smiling and slapping my back. "I thought I might see you back here sooner rather than later! And I see the secret agent is back on the job," he added, as he gave Annie a hug and took her hand. "I'm so glad you called me, Annie. I haven't been able to stop thinking about our little adventure and to tell you the truth, I'm dying to know what's inside that case."

"Do you have somewhere private we can go?" Annie asked.

"Of course, let's head upstairs to my office; it's quiet and we'll have plenty of space to spread out," Hutch offered.

He unlocked the door and led us into a decent sized office with a large rectangular table situated in the middle of the room; the Grateful Dead played on Pandora in the background.

I took a seat in the corner chair of the office but Annie waved me over, patting the chair next to her.

She needs me, and she wants me by her side. Ya done good buddy.

Annie unlocked the Pelican Case and laid out the contents: the key, the picture, the black notebook with the account number, the two lines of random numbers from the back of the picture, the passport with a fake name and the fringed flags. Then, she retold the same story to Hutch that she had already told me.

"Hmm." Hutch sighed as he stroked his bushy and graying beard; looking through and then over his bifocals as he scanned the items. "Lay everything out, exactly in the order you found them," he instructed Annie.

She rearranged the items and replied, "This is the way they came to me."

The room was quiet except for the thinking sounds Hutch made, and Ripple playing from the computer.

"Okay, I'll start with this," he said, holding up the key. "This is a safe deposit box key to St. Croix Banking downtown. The only reason I know this is because of the SCB stamped on the head of the key, and I also happen to have the same type of key. I'm assuming the numbers on the back of the picture are the security code and box number; too short to be more account numbers, but it's just a logical guess since they were found together. The passport is professional and looks completely real; the documents that were used to have this made must have been very authentic. But this, *this* is what I'm most interested in," he proclaimed, as he held up the picture from the café. "What year was this taken?" he asked Annie.

"I didn't find a date on it, but my guess is sometime in the nineties," she answered.

"Do you know any of these people?" he asked again.

"Him. This is my late husband, Jack Whitman," she said, pointing him out in the picture.

"You're sure you don't know anyone else?" he echoed.

"I'm sure."

"Well, I don't know the rest of these people, but I sure as fuck know this guy!" he wailed, pointing to the man sitting in the middle. "This is John Savage, the goddamn head of the CIA, who just so happens to also be the fucking Vice President Elect."

Hutch was now up and out of his chair, pacing the floor and slapping the picture in the palm of his hand. "Do you understand what this could mean? This is *not* good; a picture like this can *never* be good," he mumbled, more to himself than either of us.

We sat in silence, and I stuck to my mouth-shut pledge I'd made earlier, but even *my* heart was racing, so I couldn't imagine what was going through Annie's mind.

"Where did you say Jack worked before he died?" Hutch asked, as he wore a ring in the hardwood floor around the table.

"Whitman Capital Funds in Kansas City," she replied, the words barely escaping her mouth, like a kid who just got called on in class to answer aloud.

Hutch leaned over the table, showing us the picture. "Look at this picture. Look in the background at the other people in the café. Now you tell me, what the hell is a capital funds manager doing with a guy who was just sworn in as Vice President of the United States; surrounded by people in a café who all have turbans wrapped around their heads?"

Annie's hands started wringing together again, and the color drained from her face. I steadied her hands in mine; they were cold, but sweating, and I thought she might vomit. I rubbed her back to try to calm her down.

God, I'm a fucking asshole. Why did I have to lie to her about who I am? Apparently, I'm just the next guy on the list who's lied about their identity to Annie. I've got to show her I'll never make that mistake again.

"Are you okay?" I whispered in her ear.

"I don't know what I am, but I'm definitely not okay," she cried, as she rested her face in her hands.

"Honey, this picture could turn out to be insignificant, but when you dig a case out of the ocean, I wouldn't think it'd turn out that way. I don't want to scare you anymore than I already have, but have you noticed anyone following you? Anyone hanging around your house or driving by too often?" he asked.

"No. I mean, I don't know! I haven't been paying attention to something like that, so I have no idea. Really, the only places I've been are here at the Soggy Bottom and at the Cotton House. The only time I've ventured out is one night for dinner with my friends and scuba diving under the pier with you. I just didn't think to be paying attention!" she vented, as her words turned into tear-soaked mumbling.

I scooted my chair closer to her and pulled her shaking body against my chest. Desperate to take her pain away, but knowing that was impossible, I was damn sure going to keep her safe.

"What about your brother-in-law?" he asked her. "Do you think he knows about the Pelican Case or this treasure hunt you're on? Could he be on the island?"

"Jamie? I don't know. He hasn't contacted me or anything like that; I haven't seen him. How am I supposed to know if he's here?"

Annie was really freaking out now and I just tried to help her keep it together.

"Let me give you two a minute," Hutch said, heading for the door.

"No, you don't need to leave. I'm no stranger to crying, it happens a lot. I'm sorry, honey, but it does. I'm a crier, and you should know that about me," she said, turning her wet brown eyes at me and cracking the tiniest smile.

"Okay, baby, you cry. I got it," I said, feeling hopeful since she was able to make a little joke about herself.

"Listen, maybe you all have had enough excitement for one afternoon, so let's just leave things where they are for now. Kessler, you keep her close, just in case. Annie, call Liz and do some fishing about Jamie, but keep it casual; ask about the kids or something. When you're ready, find out what's waiting for you at the bank," Hutch coached.

Annie hugged Hutch hard, like you would your brother and said, "Thank you so much. I really don't have the right words to express my gratitude for everything you have done for me, but I hope to someday repay you."

"Well, don't go thanking me yet. Just be more cautious and keep an eye out for each other. Let me know if anything else unfolds," he said.

We packed up the case and slid it into a backpack that Hutch loaned us and headed back home.

As I was about to pull into my driveway, Annie said, "Take me over to my house. I want to get something. I'll just be a second."

When she jumped back into the Jeep, she held up a carton of cigarettes. "I'm always smoking or quitting, and right now, I'm smoking. You should also know that about me."

ANNIE

I sat on Kessler's deck and watched the multi-colored sun burn out into the ocean, listening to him play his guitar from somewhere downstairs. His kindness and quiet attention to my well-being showed his nurturing side, which I found to be a rare but attractive quality in a man. I told him I needed to be alone for a while, and he understood; at least I think he did.

How did this happen? Was I really so oblivious to my own life, my own husband, that I never really knew him? All those work trips he took, was he really in the town he said or was everything out of his mouth a lie? Did he ever truly love me, or was I just sufficient to keep him company while at home? Was Kansas City even where he called home? He could have a whole other family out there, kids out there, wondering, "Where the fuck is my dad?" This is such bullshit. Yes, he left me money; a lot of money, but fuck the money. I don't care about the money. I care about the truth. I gave Jack ten years of unshattering devotion and I don't deserve this; not one damn bit of it.

The scenarios ran wild, and I needed to rein in my mind, or I would never get to sleep tonight. I tried to nail down any truthful facts I had starting from the moment I met Jack; at this point, they all seem to be tangible items. I couldn't trust any memory or conversation I ever had with him because I was second guessing all of them. At this moment, the only absolute to be sure of was downstairs playing his guitar. My solitude had given me some clarity and I made the decision to end this crazy goose chase. I'd go to the bank to see if there was anything in the safe deposit box, then truly let go of the past and bury my memories with Jack to make room for the new ones I was hoping to make with Kessler. No more boxes, no more keys.

I finished sulking, followed the music downstairs and watched Kessler play from a hidden corner. He sat in an oversized rocking chair, surrounded by guitars and singing softly, but stopping to jot things down in a notebook. After listening for awhile, just letting his voice take me away, he finally noticed me.

"Hey, baby," he said with his sexy, signature grin. "Get on over here." He motioned to me as he put his guitar in its stand and patted his lap.

"You sound so good, honey. Whatcha working on?" I asked, as I put my arms around him and pulled my legs in tight, snuggling up close.

"I don't know yet, but you'll be the first to hear it when it's ready. How are you feeling?" he asked, as he softly leaned his head against mine.

"Surprisingly, I'm all right. I believe I have a plan, but can I fill you in tomorrow? I'm tired of thinking tonight. Right now, I want you to play me a love song and get me all hot over you." I giggled.

"Love songs, huh? Okay, let me see. I've got one..."

He played the first few riffs of AC/DC's song "TNT," singing, "Oi, Oi, Oi;" just to mess with me.

"That's so mean! I should have never told you I peed my pants at that concert!" I laughed, slapping his arm. "Come on, give me something good; woo me!"

He sang something sweet yet unfamiliar, but it didn't matter because through the words of the song, I heard truth and unquestionable love. My eyes became wild and my body more alive by the time he started on the second chorus, and before he could finish, I was back in his lap, my lips sealed against his, ready for him to take me upstairs.

We made love in the dark, feeling our way around each other, stirring under the sheets and enjoying the newness of being together. I was awake long after Kessler had fallen asleep, grateful for the sound of his breath and the way his hand managed to keep finding my skin. He looked so good to me, and again, I stopped to thank God. At that moment, it hit me; I'd spent the first months after Jack died cursing at God for giving my life such a terrible turn, yelling at him for his lack of compassion towards me, and waiting and waiting for him to reveal himself. Looking back, as it turns out, God was waiting for me.

ANNIE

"Hello?" Gail answered.

"Hey, friend!"

"Annie! Hey! I was wondering when I was going to hear from you again. What's happening in St. Croix? Have you gone on the dive yet? Seen any striking gentlemen you can give my number to?" she teased, rambling on.

I couldn't help but laugh.

"You sound almost chipper! There must be a story behind that, and if it involves a man, don't leave out any details! I'm drying up here in the Midwest and could use a hot romance story to get me through the winter." She laughed.

"Well, which answer do you want first; the one where I get the box or the one where I get the man? They're both pretty long stories."

I had to hold the phone away from my ear because of all her screaming. "Both! I've got nothing but time!"

I filled her in on all the details of the dive and finding the Pelican Case, and then I filled her in on Kessler; the best part of this trip.

"Oh, Annie. I'm just so happy for you, and you should know that you really, really deserve this kind of man. I'm so glad you found each other!"

"I should be thanking you because you helped me realize this trip, and I promise I'll find a way to pay you back," I vowed.

"The best payment I could ever get is a good looking cowboy like the one you found for yourself. So you just head on back to the available men store and pick me up a few!" she said in her sassiest voice.

"Listen, I've got to talk shop with you for a minute. Have you noticed if Jamie has been back to his office?" I asked.

"Not during business hours. The place is cleaned out, and has been empty for a few weeks now. Why? Do you think he could be in St. Croix?" she asked, sounding, concerned.

"I don't know, but I'm starting to consider the possibility. Did you find out anything about that farm and feed store?"

"Nothing. I drove up to Platte City last week and it's just a rundown building sitting on of a patch of concrete, weeds pushing up through the cracks in the parking lot. It looks like it's been ten years since the last customer bought anything there," she said.

"Okay, well, thanks for checking it out for me. I guess I'll have to put that one on the back burner. Thanks for everything, Gail. I really appreciate it," I told her.

"You can thank me later; just take care of yourself and tell me what you find at the bank when you get a chance," she insisted.

"I will. Let's talk soon."

My next call was to my sister-in-law, Liz. I didn't practice what I was going to say, for fear of it sounding rehearsed. I needed this conversation to be totally organic and completely believable, which shouldn't be too hard since I really did miss my niece and nephew.

I dialed and waited, getting her voicemail. "Hey, Liz, its Annie! I was just calling to check on you guys and make sure everyone is doing okay. I should be home pretty soon; hopefully we can get together and catch up. Tell Max and Mia hello for me; talk with you soon!"

That will have to do. Now the bank.

ANNIE

Although I had moved most of my things over to his house, the danger of my constant shuffling back and forth to the Cotton House exchanging clothes didn't sit well with Kessler. Regardless of how many times I went back, I always seemed to need something else, so yesterday he helped me move the rest of my things. I certainly considered him my lover, but when two people move in together, they take a big leap of faith on each other, and it took some convincing on his part for me to actually make the permanent move to his house. Once I got settled in the change seemed minute, and I really loved being a partner in a relationship again. Yes, Jack has only been gone for six months, and it seems too soon to be this deep into another man, but I now believe in fate. Kessler was wrapped up in a big beautiful bow and handed to me on a silver platter. He's silly and fun, and we laugh a lot despite my circumstances. Catching his stares from across the room or the way he holds his hand out and gently swipes my back as he walks by, wraps me in normality and gives me hope in establishing new roots.

I didn't pack a nice suit with me—because why the hell would I need a suit in St. Croix—but here I am feeling like I should be wearing one, heading into the bank. The nicest outfit I'd brought to the Islands; a classic red, Michael Kors, boat-neck crepe dress with gold heels for a little flare was my choice. I certainly had Kessler's attention sliding this show stopper down my body—the material hugging my torso and holding tightly to my hips, but sex wasn't on the forefront of my mind today. Applying the last coat of matching red lipstick, I caught Kessler's eyes light up in the mirror, intensely watching my application.

"Can I help you?" I asked, smiling.

"I'm beyond help, but maybe you can put some more of that on when we get home," he bargained, giving me a wink.

I leaned in close to his ear and whispered, "I aim to please." Smacking his ass, I walked out of the bathroom, my heels clicking on the marble.

We parked his Jeep in the St. Croix Banking parking lot, and Kessler turned off the engine.

"Everything's going to be all right, Annie. If you're truly ready to move on, then this should be the last time you'll have to feel a pit in your stomach. I love you, and I want to take care of you—if you'll let me—and I promise you, I'll never make you feel this way. You ready, baby?" he asked, as he rubbed my hands between his.

"You always seem to say the right thing, and yes, baby, I love you, too," I said, leaning over and kissing his lips. "Okay, here I go." I sighed, letting a gallon of air escape from my lungs.

"You look amazing, and I'll be right here waiting for you," he reminded me, giving me a little wave.

I brought my Louis Vuitton Palermo PM Tote with me because I had no idea what would be in the safe deposit box, and because it was an expensive bag that made me feel inclusive to the club of people who would even need a safe deposit box.

The bank was a beautiful, colonial structure with sweeping views of the ocean from every window in the lobby. The teller offered me a seat as I waited for the manager, in a stiff leather armchair that was so low to the ground, my knees were shoved into my chest; style over function was a poor design decision when furnishing the lobby. Louie gave no assistance to my situation, and I felt like a Shriner in one of those tiny cars, sitting in this chair that was quite possibly made for a child.

"Mrs. Bozeman, the manager can see you now," the teller said from behind her counter.

Okay, Mrs. Bozeman, let's get this done.

Henry Miller, bank manager, lead me into his office to verify my identification, signature, security number and most importantly, my key. I couldn't help noticing a picture of his family on the desk; a wife and two kids smiled back at me, and I wondered if I would ever have the chance to be in a picture like that. Mr. Miller came back into the office and snapped me out of my daydream.

"Everything looks good," he said, handing my passport back to me. "I have to say, we will certainly miss doing business with you here, but please keep us in mind for any of your future financial needs, Mrs. Bozeman."

"Thank you, that's very kind of you to say, and I certainly will," I responded, having no idea what the hell I was talking about.

193

"Now, if you'll please follow me, I can take you downstairs where the safe deposit boxes are located."

We walked down a long and narrow corridor with concrete walls and psychedelic carpeting, stopping at a large metal door which Mr. Miller unlocked by swiping a card. Behind that door were aisles and aisles of shiny silver columns housing hundreds of small compartments. The further into the room we walked, the bigger the compartments became, and we finally stopped on the sixth row at box 1049; that's when my dress completely pitted out.

"Your key please, Mrs. Bozeman."

I didn't like being called, *Mrs. Bozeman*. It made me nervous and sick. I had to wonder if Jack was supposed to be Mr. Bozeman, or if I was always a widow in this scenario. So many answers I'll never have, and hopefully, someday will no longer question.

We inserted our keys at the same time; his on the left of the box, mine on the right and the door of box 1049 swung open.

"I'll carry your box to the viewing room for you where you'll have privacy and a table to lay your items on. This way please," he instructed, as he pulled out the interior box of the safe.

We entered a small room with the same hallucinogenic carpeting as he advised, "Please take your time, I'll just be outside. Feel free to come out when you're ready."

"Thank you," I replied.

This is it; the last box I'm opening which concerns Jack Whitman. Please be key-free; I don't want to find another damn key in here.

Thankfully, there were no keys, but three purple Crown Royal bags— the ones you get when you buy the bottle of liquor—sat together, lined in a row. A light dust had settled on the outside of the velvet pouches, and I untied the gold rope on the first bag. As soon as the sack began to open, illumination shot through the top like a flashlight had been left on inside.

Oh, God! I thought as I peeked in, sucking up my breath hard. *Oh, my, God! What is this? What the hell is this?*

The light from inside the bag shone insanely bright, and left a sparkling trail all the way to the ceiling, hundreds of tiny prisms dancing on the walls. Diamonds filled the velvet pouch; slipping and sliding over each other the further I opened the bag. I dipped my hand in and let the cold, hard gems cover my palm and slide off my fingers; making clinking sounds like coins dropping into a full piggy bank. I quickly but carefully opened the other two bags and my experience was the same; each time my phone booth sized room became more phosphorescent until seemingly, I was standing in the middle of a disco ball. The twinkle of the prisms and the glare from the bags became nauseating in this microscopic space, and I physically began to see stars. I held on to the metal counter top and slowly lowered myself to the floor, the walls eerily closing in. My skin became extremely hot and the air too thick to inhale; there wasn't enough oxygen to supplement my state of panic.

Breathe, just breathe. I though, concentrating on getting myself right again. *I've got to get out of here without making a scene. Stand up dammit! Get your ass up and get out of this room!*

I picked up the bags and triple knotted each one of them ensuring nothing spilled out, carefully placed them in my tote, wiped the sweat from my face with a tissue, smoothed my hair back, and applied a new coat of lipstick. I tried to masque my sickness and look as fresh as possible walking out of there; lipstick was the best I came up with.

Don't fuck this up. I told myself as I opened the door and sucked in some fresh oxygen from the next room.

"Mr. Miller, thank you so much. I'm finished here."

"Are you feeling okay, Mrs. Bozeman?" he asked, looking a little startled at my ashen appearance.

"Oh, yes, I'm fine. I've been under the weather a bit lately and probably need to go home and rest. Thank you for asking."

I followed him back to the vault and handed over my key as he slid the empty container back into the metal shell of box number 1049.

One foot in front of the other, stand tall, chin up, and don't trip.

I couldn't actually hear his words over my thoughts, so I just smiled, nodding my head in agreement, like a tourist in a foreign country.

"I'll just need you to sign one more document stating your safe deposit box is officially closed, so if you'd please follow me back into my office, we can finish up," he instructed, offering me another seat.

While sliding the paper requiring my signature in front of me, calmness washed over my face, steadying my hands and settling my stomach. With that said, I couldn't get out of there fast enough. I fumbled for my cheap, imitation Jackie O sunglasses, but broke them in my purse as I opened the front doors to the outside. The ocean breeze blew my dress around my knees and across my face; the salty air getting lost in my hair. *Keep moving, keep moving* was my mantra as I turned the corner and followed the concrete walkway to the parking lot. As soon as Kessler saw my face, he jumped out of the Jeep and ran towards me.

"Baby, what's wrong? Are you okay? What's happening, Annie? What was in there?" He seemed panicked, yelling a barrage of questions at me.

I'm sure I looked a fright, and kneeling next to the Jeep leaving two large piles of puke beside the tire did not set his mind at ease.

"I'm okay," I choked, wiping the vomit from my mouth and spitting tiny pieces of breakfast off my tongue. "Let's just get out of here. I need to go home."

Kessler pulled out of the parking lot, not pressing the issue. When we finally pulled onto the highway, the wheels made a roaring sound as they spun around, the wind of the road rushing in. Finally, I cooled down.

He suddenly turned sharp onto a side road which led up into the jungle, putting the Jeep in park but leaving the engine running.

"What happened in there, Annie? Why did you get sick?" he demanded. "Talk to me, baby!"

I pulled Mr. Vuitton onto my lap and removed one of the Crown Royal bags, opening it a smidge and watching his eyes first turn to slits, wincing at the brightness, and then growing wide, like two garlic bulbs had replaced his eyeballs.

"There are three of them," I said, patting the bottom of the bag in my palm, feeling the weight of the diamonds clinking together.

"Holy shit!" he exclaimed, dumbfounded.

"This is it; the explanation," I said. "This is what Jamie wants. He must know about these but had no way to get them because Andrea Bozeman is the only name on the account. He needed me to get them out of lockdown, and I think he knows exactly how this scenario is playing out. Jamie has been two steps ahead of me since the day Jack died. Let's get the hell out of here and get the bags into the safe at home. I have a feeling he's not done with me yet." I speculated, more in charge of my emotions than ever.

We stood inside the wine room in Kessler's basement, each fondling our own bag of diamonds, letting the reality of this insane situation sink in.

"What are you going to do with them?" he asked as he locked the safe.

"These aren't mine, Kessler. I don't know where they came from or to whom they belong. There has to be millions of dollars in these diamonds, and eventually, someone is going to come looking for them—if they aren't here already. There are no more clues—I've collected them all, and this has to be what Jack wanted me to find, but I don't want them. My bank account is already filled with plenty of money, and with the right kind of investing can last me a lifetime. My family was ripped apart over these diamonds and I spent months wallowing in the foulest shit of daily life because of these goddamn things. Finding you was the best gift I could have hoped for, and for me you're enough. I've been praying to God for the longest time, and he answered me with a gift, a *real* treasure—a normal life with a man I love and hope to grow old with, not these diamonds. I'm happy in this new life, right now with you, and I don't want to mess it up, not over money."

He grabbed me and kissed me hard, both of us getting emotional and professing our love for one another in a room filled with mahogany and diamonds.

"Okay, then, what do you want to do with them?" he whispered.

"These diamonds could change a lot of people's lives, so I'm going to do just that; change some lives and make things right," I said smiling, knowing exactly what I was going to do.

ANNIE

T he faint crash of the rolling tide seeped in with the sun through the patio doors. Kessler's lips softly kissed my naked skin and his fingernails gently scratched my back as he whispered, "Annie. Baby, wake up."

I let out a morning moan and popped an Altoid in my mouth; it was obvious what he had on his mind.

I didn't even bother opening my eyes because as soon as I turned over, he slipped underneath the sheets and began kissing me, starting with my breasts and working his way down my body. His erection slid the length of my leg, and it felt like he'd been waiting for me awhile; he just couldn't wait any longer. Kissing my lips and applying pressure with his tongue sent my knees in opposite directions, spread impossibly far apart, my fingers entwined in his thick head of hair, gently guiding the way. He only had to put forth about three minutes worth of effort, when my orgasm snuck up on me and struck without warning.

Morning sex is the absolute best! I haven't figured out why, but then again, I don't really care; I'm just happy to be having it.

He popped his head out of the covers and stretched his legs, with a smirk hanging lazily on his face; obviously awaiting his turn. I grabbed my clutch off the nightstand, and pulled out the same red lipstick from the afternoon before, silently applying the kryptonite as Kessler's face lit up like a school boy watching his first dirty movie. Kissing his ears and licking his lobes, I worked my way down his stomach, leaving a cardinal trail, with only momentary pauses to escalate his excitement. Easing my way back up, my nipples ran the length of his torso, barely touching his skin, and I braced myself against his chest as I slowly rocked back into him.

"Gawd, baby, you're so sexy!" he moaned as I straddled his manhood, his hands holding onto my ribcage.

I pulled the ponytail holder off my wrist and tied my hair up into a large bun on the top of my head as I slowly rocked him inside me. Apparently, naughty librarian is his fantasy girl.

"Oh, that's gonna do it," he stated, pulling his knees up and pushing himself as far into me as possible, letting out a massive groan. "How's that for a wakeup call?" he asked as he rolled over out of breath and with a goofy smile on his face.

We leaned our faces together with our foreheads touching, saying, "I love you, baby," over and over to each other until our overlapping lips quieted our words, but I meant it; I loved him and felt lighter every time I said it.

"I'm gonna jump in the shower and then let's get breakfast!" he gushed with enthusiasm. "Wahoo! That's the way to wake up!" he yelled, clapping his hands together, his naked and perfect ass disappearing into the bathroom.

JAMIE

The waitress refilled my coffee cup, leaning over a little too far and exposing a healthy amount of cleavage directly in my line of vision, giving me a wink when she caught me looking. I was a lot of things, but never a cheat; at least not since I'd been married to Liz, and that was one of my good points. It was also probably one of my only good points, but who's counting.

I set up camp in a sweet vantage point, the ocean in front of me and Annie's two favorite breakfast joints on either side of me. Kessler and Annie had been eating breakfast at both of these restaurants for a few weeks now; they were already so predictable, especially for someone in my line of work. Although I was used to being the man behind the scenes, today was going to be fun, switching it up and watching this play out from afar.

The chorus of birds became louder as the sun began to make its debut and people slowly trickled in for coffee and pastries; no one but the waitress giving me a second glance. I checked my watch.

Any time now.

In a few short weeks, the nightmare of the last six months was finally wrapping up, and my family would be cleared to move away from Kansas City. We could totally start over; new home, new location and new identities. This wasn't the first time I'd left my life behind me, but Liz and the kids would need some time to adjust, barring she doesn't divorce me. It might take them longer than I expect, but patience has become one of my mastered virtues.

Ah-ha! I watched a boat pull in close to the harbor, but mooring on a buoy far enough out that a quick escape was inevitable. The massive, forty-five foot Beneteau Oceanis sailboat was a seamen's dream, and the sun gleamed off the stark white hull sending fragments of light into the water around it. The name on the back read, "The Odyssey."

"Right on time, Achilles," I whispered into my newspaper.

He positioned his boat so a clear shot from the port side window was easily accomplished, then opened the hatch in the cabin and inconspicuously peeked out the top. How I wished I was a cup on the counter of that galley; watching him meticulously lay out his potential weapons and narrowing down his choices after surveying the six hundred foot distance from the boat to the restaurant. My estimation on the murder weapon would be a .308 Caliber Winchester, with a Swarovski scope for accuracy, but it's just an educated guess.

His marksmanship is renowned in certain circles—a steely eyed assassin, and his precision is unwavering. If you happen to be the poor bastard in his sights, he'll ruin you either physically or financially, and surprisingly, most of the targets make the choice of a physical death over suffering a social or political one; it's much less painful. The adage, "Hind sight is 20/20," is not so true for everyone. There are some that commit to a graveyard destiny from the first assignment, and these are the scariest monsters among us—depending on which country you work for.

Through my binoculars I watched him ready himself, scurrying around the boat, popping in and out of the cabin door, and staying under deck a minute or two each time. All the while, I had not lost sight of the patios I sat between, with no sign of the lovebirds yet. However, they must be getting close, because the shades on the boat just dropped, and Achilles is always one step ahead of his target.

I saw them approach the diner doors but lost sight of them until they emerged onto the patio, taking the seat closest to the sand. It was strange to see Annie holding hands with another man, watching him lean in close to kiss her or wrap her in his arms. I surprised myself with the sympathy I felt for Jack. As a husband, I would have killed that fucking guy the moment I saw Annie wrap her skinny legs around him on her patio that night. At this point, I'm detaching myself from this mess, and normally I'd tell Jack that it was his problem, but Jack Whitman is dead, and after today, I'm officially retired.

The show was finally starting as Kessler yelled at the waiter; my adrenalin sent me pacing back and forth in front of my table.

Any second now!

The lovebirds were up and out of their seats in a standoff with the waiter.

Kessler isn't the biggest guy, but farm boys are some of the toughest men out there, and I certainly wouldn't want to take a punch from him. I'm sure he can hold his own, unless he's up against a trained killer, and then, it's probably not going to turn out too well for him.

My head nodded back and forth from the boat to the restaurant, like I was watching a tennis match, but in this game, someone was going to die.

The silencer prevented me from hearing the gun go off, but two delayed seconds later, he dropped to his knees with his arm reached out trying to grab ahold of Annie; her screams pierced the boardwalk. The motor started and within minutes, his rifle was broken down and put away, the boat trolling safely towards open water. I grabbed my newspaper and wiped away my fingerprints from the outside of my coffee cup; better safe than sorry.

Now that he's out of the way, I've got to get back to Kansas City and convince my wife that I'm not a monster.

KESSLER

For breakfast, I picked my favorite beachfront diner on the East end of the island with panoramic views of the harbor from the deck. A plethora of boats littered the docks of the marina and sailboats revved their engines as they pulled in and out of the slips. The seagulls squawked furiously at each other while dive bombing abandoned plates, and fighting each other over the scraps in the sand. I couldn't stop staring at Annie and thinking about how much I loved being with her; especially between the sheets.

I don't know how this happened to me, but I am a lovesick fool for this woman; head over heels and shamelessly in love with her. I can't seem to stop touching her; I've tried and I just can't stop. Mama D was right again; damn that woman's always right. Coming back to St. Croix, back to Annie, was worth my pride.

"Annie, I've been doing a lot of thinking the last few days about a problem I've got, and I've finally come up with a solution."

"What's wrong, babe, what problem?" she asked sounding concerned, worry stamped across her face.

"Well, your lease at the Cotton House is up soon; I'm usually heading back to Nashville about this time to start a new album and spend Christmas with the Rutledge Family. Even though I'm not with a record company now, I still want to record some songs at my home studio. I can't stay here forever; Nashville is my home, and I want to keep it that way. You live in Kansas City, and for me, that's a problem," I said.

Her face immediately started falling, looking disappointed.

"Here's my solution; I love you Annie, more than I ever knew I could love another person. I've always seen taking care of someone as a chore, not a privilege. That is until meeting you, and I would be a broken man to taste this kind of life with you only to have it taken away from me. I can't do it, and won't do it. Come with me to Nashville; start a new life in Tennessee with me. I know I'm not asking you to marry me, but I'll make those same vows of honor and cherish, in good times and bad, right here to you, if you'll just say yes."

Of all moments, the waiter picks the exact worst time to take our order. He caught me off guard, with his two blackened eyes and fat lip, the cut in the middle still fresh and barely starting to scab over. *Damn, that guy got his ass kicked.* He went on about the breakfast buffet and drink specials, with an accent so thick I could barely understand him. I just wanted him to go the fuck away, but of course, Annie was too nice to shoo him off.

"Hey, man, I don't mean to be rude, but we're in the middle of something. Can you please give us a minute?" I asked as politely as possible.

He looked confused about my request; stumbling over his words and looking around the patio, not sure what to do but still standing there.

"Dude! Please! A second!" I yelled.

He darted back inside, but his eyes stayed focused on us.

"I'm sorry about raising my voice," I said calmly, taking her hands, "but this moment has been planned out in my head for days now, and it's not going as smoothly as I thought it would. Annie?" I said, shaking her hand and trying to get her attention, but she kept looking at the door the waiter ran through. "Annie!"

She finally turned and looked at me, her face as perplexed as our waiter.

"Baby, did you hear what I said? What do you think?"

"Yeah, did our waiter seem funny to you?" she asked.

"What? I don't know, annoying not funny."

"No, I mean funny like out of place," she said, starting to wring her hands together, still looking around the patio.

"I didn't notice. What's wrong?" I asked, giving up hope of getting back to our previous conversation.

She turned to me, her eyes growing wide as she lowered her voice. "Hutch said to keep our eyes open, question things that don't seem right and trust our gut. My gut says this isn't right. Look around the patio. There's hardly anyone here, and no one but the seagulls are clearing the dirty dishes from the tables. Our waiter is Middle Eastern. Have you seen any other Middle Eastern men on this island? He barely spoke English. Why would you wait tables if you don't speak the language? He doesn't have a uniform or pad of paper to take down our order, and he hasn't even set our table. This is wrong, and I want to go, something doesn't feel right," she said, as she immediately stood up and grabbed my hand, yanking me out of my chair.

"Jesus!" I yelled, not expecting the strength of her jerk and almost toppling over. "Okay, we'll go," I said looking around, beginning to feel paranoid.

As soon as we stood up, the waiter came out of the double doors, quickly moving towards us. I took Annie's hand, pulling her close to me, standing on the opposite side of the table from him.

"We're leaving," I said to him.

He just stood there staring at us, blocking our way out.

If he wasn't moving, then I was going through him. As I lunged towards him he made the strangest face, like someone had punched him in the ribs, and a stain appeared on the chest of his white, v-neck T-shirt. I stopped, confused about what I saw.

What's on his shirt, and why is it spreading? What the fuck is with this guy?

About the time I realized blood was soaking into his shirt, Annie screamed violently, and the man dropped to his knees. He held one arm stretched out towards her and the other hand in his pocket; a buck knife fell out as soon as his face hit the deck. The backside of his shirt sported an identical bloody pattern to the one on the front, with a gaping bullet hole through the middle.

ANNIE

I never heard the gun go off, and was only standing ten inches away from him. We could have been killed. I could have lost Kessler.

Was someone shooting at me? Were they shooting at Kessler? What the hell is going on? I came to eat breakfast, not witness a murder!

Panic and chaos filled my insides. Trying to think and react, tunnel vision set in and everything fuzzed out of focus. I was so far out of my element, out of the goddamn atmosphere of Holly homemaker from Kansas City, and now can't really remember how I even got to this point, but here I was—bullets and breakfast.

Kessler held tight to my hand and screamed, "Run!" But as soon as we reached the patio doors, Hutch fiercely swung them open on us, almost taking me out.

"I knew you'd be here!" he yelled in my face, taking off his sunglasses to reveal a black eye and puffy cheek.

"Someone's shooting on the patio! We've got to get out of here!" I yelled back at him like a raging lunatic. "Don't just stand there! We've got to go, Hutch!" I screamed and pulled at his shirt until he started to follow us.

We ran through the diner and out to the parking lot. Kessler started the engine before Hutch and I were even in our seats. The Jeep made an evil screech, tearing out of the parking space and leaving thick black marks in our wake.

"What happened in there?" Hutch yelled over the noise of the Jeep racing down the highway.

"It was all wrong! I just did what you told us to do and everything on that patio was wrong this morning!" I yelled back. "You're hurt! What happened to your face?"

"Some fucknut came around asking questions about you two last night, trying to intimidate me, so I beat the shit out of his face! He managed to land a few!" he hollered, clearly smiling over his victory.

"Middle Eastern? Was he Middle Eastern?" I shouted.

"How did you know?" Hutch screamed back.

Our waiter, it was our waiter that went to see Hutch. Maybe those are his diamonds.

"Llyod! This is Kessler Carlisle! I need you to immediately get my plane ready for departure! This is an emergency!" Kessler yelled into his phone.

We came to a violent stop in the driveway; all of us being thrown forward when Kessler slammed on the brakes.

"You two get what you can carry, and I'll drop you off at the airport. Hurry!" Hutch said.

I ran around Kessler's house throwing my clothes in a bag; stuffing in as many toiletries that would fit.

The diamonds! What am I going to do with them? We can't leave them here and I can't show up at the airport with a purse full of them. How am I going to get them on the plane? Think! Think!

"Hurry, Annie!" Kessler yelled from another room.

I ran downstairs and punched in the code 1492, and the safe door popped open. I carefully took out the bags of diamonds, the picture and my fake passport and headed back up to the kitchen where Hutch and Kessler were waiting for me.

"What's the check-in process when you fly private?" I asked Kessler, still shouting, with adrenaline pumping through me.

"We walk through a private security scanner, and then out to the runway and get on the plane. It only takes a few minutes. Why?" he asked.

"When do they scan our carry-on luggage?" I repeated, beginning to calm down.

He smiled, staring at the purple velvet bags and finally catching onto my line of questioning.

"When you fly private, freedom in traveling is a huge perk, especially when you're a celebrity. We don't have to follow the same rules as the rest of the world. Pack 'em!" he yelled.

I reached into the cabinet and pulled out my carton of smokes, discarding the packs out onto the counter.

"Get me a sharp knife and some tape. I have a plan," I said.

I turned over each box of cigarettes and cut a slit across the bottom, gently pulling the box out of the cellophane, so it looked as though the pack had never been opened. Dumping out all of the smokes on the counter, I replaced the empty box with a handful of diamonds and slid the pack back into the cellophane, taping the bottom back together and putting it back into the carton packaging.

"Nine more to go," I said watching the color drain from Hutch's face, remembering I hadn't told him about my trip to the bank yet.

"Holy, Mary, Mother of God! *This?* This is what was in the safe deposit box?" he asked in a whisper as he peeked inside one of the bags.

"I know; I felt the same way," I said, trying to stay focused. "You're taking it way better than me though. I almost passed out, and then I threw up."

"This is incredible! I've just never seen anything like this!" he stuttered, finding it hard to push the words out of his mouth.

Kessler jumped in to help me, and we made quick work of assembling a multi-million dollar carton of Camels. I didn't want to fill the packs too full for fear of the cardboard busting open, so we ended up with a handful of diamonds leftover. I taped and re-taped the carton closed, making sure it was secure before I set it in Louis; my faithful traveling companion.

"Hutch, thank you for your service—not only to our country during Vietnam, but also to me. You're a good hearted man with values and life experience going way beyond what most people in the world will ever give you credit for," I said as I handed him a Crown Royal bag, a handful of diamonds still resting in the bottom. "Keep these and do what you please with them. We have more than enough, and since you have been such a big part of my journey, they are just as much yours as they are mine."

"No, please, I can't take them. It's too much!" he said, trying to hand them back to me.

"I told you, buddy! I said from the first day I met her that she was a keeper!" Kessler said putting an arm around him, then slapping his back.

"Let's just call it cab fare and get the hell out of here," I told him as I ended our kum-ba-ya moment; manually closing his mouth with my hand.

***

When we arrived at the airport, I could have never predicted the amount of people who recognized Kessler. The entire time we've been together on the island not one person has even looked at him twice, but now, every ten feet we were stopped by another adoring fan wanting an autograph or a picture, and he signed every one of them, despite the events of the morning. I had yet to experience this part of his life and I'm sure there will be times when I'll want him all to myself, but right now, I was in awe of his stature and friendly disposition in the middle of this growing crowd. Security stepped in when our jet was ready for boarding, a perfect excuse to end the meet and greet with the fans.

Security check was the last roadblock, and I shoved my hands into the deep pockets of my long cotton skirt to prevent the incessant wringing of my fingers. Kessler and I easily slipped through the metal harbor, and as he reattached his green-bezel Rolex, the security officer grabbed my arm, saying, "You, wait," as she held my purse in her hands.

Shit! Shit, shit, shit!

Panicking inside but trying to camouflage the fear, I walked to the small section blocked off by tables, behind the metal detectors. A stout woman in an overly-tight uniform motioned for me to come closer, her biceps squeezing her shirt with each movement. As I obeyed, she pulled out my carton of Camels, and that's when I just about lost my shit. She pointed to an ugly metal chair and I immediately sat. As she bent over me, cupping my chin in her hands, a crowd of women began to fill in the empty space around us, trying to get a picture of Kessler.

Bracing myself for the next moment, when cuffs went around my wrists or her fist through my face, she said in the sweetest voice, "You're too beautiful for these. This will suck the white from your teeth and the joy from your life, leaving your man exposed to these leeches." She pointed to the gathering of overly anxious women. "You should think about quitting. Okay?"

Floored but elated, I agreed, "Yes, ma'am, I will."

"Okay, then. You have a nice day," she added, as she replaced the carton into my tote.

I couldn't see Kessler's eyes behind the dark lenses of his Ray Bans, but the sweat from his palms that mushed against mine as he grabbed my hand was indication enough. That was the epitome of a close one.

Once we were safely in the air, finally starting to relax, I realized that we hadn't talked about where the plane was going. In all the chaos, it had never crossed my mind to make that decision. I heard every word that Kessler said to me at the restaurant, and was disappointed his profession of love was ruined, because it took a lot of balls to say what he did, and I decided to make it up to him.

The pilot turned around and said, "Looks like nice weather all the way to Nashville. We should be arriving in approximately three and a half hours."

Kessler turned and looked at me with pleading puppy eyes.

I stroked his face, pulled off his ball cap, running my fingers through his hair, and said, "Yes, baby. Let's go home."

ANNIE

The first week in Nashville was a whirlwind, and I was overwhelmed by the amount of introductions that came along with being Kessler Carlisle's girlfriend. Having no personal items of my own, Hope took me shopping downtown one afternoon and we had a really great time together. Having a girlfriend close by seems essential at this point in my life.

I loved the role that Mama D played in Kessler's life, and understood why everyone always ate over there; the food is unbelievable! Even though I was nervous to meet her (I had a lot to live up to) from the first hello she welcomed me with open arms, like I'd been living next door to her my whole life. Wade was busy getting ready for his next tour, but still spent plenty of time on shenanigans, and therefore, plenty of time in trouble with the women in his life.

Kessler has tried so hard to make me feel like his town is now my town, his home is now ours, and the effort put forth was beyond anything I ever expected. Always hugging and rubbing on me, and every time he looked at me, I saw the love in his eyes; it's enough to make any woman melt. A family was slowly being built around me again, and I knew I'd made the right choice about the man and the location.

Christmas was only a week away, and the house felt naked without decorations dripping from every corner.

"If you want, we can hire someone to decorate the house for you," Kessler offered.

"That's sweet, honey, but that's not how I roll. The point of decorating is making memories together, and if you'll help out and be my co-pilot, then I promise not to get too crazy; at least not this year."

He pulled me in close and whispered, "Let me show you to my cockpit," followed by an outburst of laughter, feeling extremely proud of his terrible joke. I'm pretty sure at that moment he was picturing me naked.

"I've gotta run to the store and get some new strings for my guitar, but I should be back soon. I already drug the lights out and they're sitting in the garage; I knew you'd come for them sooner or later," he said as he kissed me good-bye.

I've learned to appreciate the small gestures made by men, because in their eyes, they are larger than life.

I started with the miniature Evergreen trees which line the side of our house closest to the Rutledge home. They would be able to see the lights from their kitchen, and Mama D would love that I was already putting Kessler to work.

While busy stringing lights, I heard the car door shut and the sound of footsteps coming around the corner, the frozen grass crunching under his shoes.

Kessler must be back already. He'll get on board the decorating train when he sees how nice the lights look.

"Hey, baby! Don't you love..." I started to say, until I looked up and saw Jamie standing on my lawn.

I tried to scream, but my voice caught inside my throat and only a hollow screech managed to escape. As frozen in my boots as the grass to the ground and holding on tight to a strand of Christmas lights, my mouth hung open in a silent scream; visible breath my only sign of life.

He spoke first. "Hi, Annie. It's been a long time."

"W-What do y-you want?" I almost had to manually rip the words out of my neck. "P-P-Please leave me alone. Please!"

He took a step towards me, as I took a step back.

"Jack really made a mess of things in our little family, didn't he?" he asked me with an arrogant smile, shaking his head. "He never should have married you. I told him not to marry you, but as you can see, Jack always does what Jack wants with little regard for anyone else."

He took another step forward, and I matched him with another step back.

I have nothing but Christmas lights to defend myself. Oh fuck, this isn't good! I really started panicking, realizing that I would have to make it to the house and lock all the doors for a chance at survival, but knowing how slim that chance actually was.

"There's so much you don't know about the Whitman boys, Annie. Although, you've done very well for yourself over the last six months; fattening up your bank account with those diamonds and running around St. Croix with a celebrity. Kessler Carlisle? Really? I never pictured you as a country music fan."

"You were in St. Croix. You killed that man, our waiter," I stated.

"Yes, I admit I was there, and yes, that man needed to die, but I wasn't the one who pulled the trigger," he said.

This time I heard the gun cock.

"Don't move you limp dick shitweasel or I'll fill the back of your head with bullets and splatter your ugly face all over these pretty decorations; even Santa Claus won't recognize you!" Wade yelled as he stood up from the waist high, cat-tailed grass just a few feet from us; his face hidden behind a shotgun, ready to fire.

Jamie held his arms in the air "Now, let's not lose our heads! Everyone calm down! Everything's okay, and no one's getting hurt today!" he negotiated, obviously backtracking.

"Yeah, she's gonna be just fine, but I gotta say mister, it ain't looking good for you," Wade boasted as he stepped over the tall grass, shotgun still in position. "Get inside the house, Annie, and lock the doors; you don't wanna see another man die, not like this."

"Whoa, whoa! Nobody has to die today! I'm not armed! Everyone please stay calm!" Jamie pleaded.

All of a sudden, a red blur shot past me running at full speed and tackled Jamie, laying him out with his face in the ground. In four maybe five seconds, Kessler had Jamie hogtied, his feet and hands jacked up behind his back; he looked like a yoga pose gone horribly wrong.

"Yee-haw! And time! Unbelievable, Kess, you still got it, farm boy! That had to be some kind of record!" Wade yelled, whooping and hollering, stomping his feet.

Jamie sucked hard at the air, coughing and sputtering as he tried to regain his breath.

Kessler hurried over to me, first pulling me in tight and then holding me away from him, checking me over. "You okay?"

"Yeah, I'm okay, I'm okay," I said, finally wrapping my head around the last five minutes.

Kessler walked back over to Jamie and kicked him hard in the ribs, then yanked his hair back, revealing his face as he clocked him; blood sprayed the ground in front of him.

213

"Stop! Please stop!" I yelled, running to Kessler, pulling him off Jamie. "Please don't, I can't stand to see you do that to someone. That's not who you are, so just stop," I begged him.

Kessler turned and spit on him; walking away with the final word.

"Let me shoot 'em, Kess!" Wade bawled in the background, probably enjoying this confrontation a little too much.

"Please! Let me explain!" Jamie begged from the ground.

"Explain what?" I asked, crouching down beside his head, smearing his blood further into the grass.

"Just untie me first! Please, I can't breathe!" he complained.

"You better start talking, because if you haven't noticed, Wade over there is trigger happy, and I can't hold him off much longer," I touted, enjoying the power I finally had over him.

"I'm not Jack's brother!" he yelled reluctantly.

"Liar!" I screamed at him, pointing my finger in his face.

"I swear to God, Annie! Jack and I met at West Point about nine years before he met you. We were partners, *not* brothers. You and I aren't related," he revealed.

"What do you mean partners?" I asked, still not believing him.

"We worked for the government! Please untie me and let me explain. I came here to explain things to you, *not* kill you! I never wanted to kill you. Believe it or not, I was protecting you from the shit storm that Jack put you in giving you access to those diamonds."

I sat back on my heels, my body suddenly three hundred pounds and impossible to hold up; this was all just too much.

My past actually keeps getting shittier. Is it possible to continually feel worse and worse over a dead man? Time heals all wounds is the biggest fucking joke anyone could ever tell me, because the more time that goes by, the bigger this wound gets.

"Untie him," I said, feeling somewhat defeated by my past.

"What? No! What if tries something?" Kessler yelled at me.

"Untie him, Kessler! Wade, if he makes a move, you can shoot him; I don't care anymore," I said, walking over to the patio and sitting down with my head between my knees.

Kessler did as I asked, but Wade kept one eye through the sight and the double barrel on the back of his head.

Once I collected myself, I motioned him over to have a seat and spill his guts, hoping he had proof to back up any of his accusations.

"I'm going to ask you some questions, and I swear to God, if you hesitate even one second or make me think in any way you're lying, then you're dead, and I won't shed one damn tear for you. Got it?" I demanded.

"Do we have to do this in front of them?" he asked, motioning to Kessler and Wade. "I'm divulging very sensitive information; can we go somewhere private?" he asked, somewhat hopeful.

"You have blood running down the front of your head and a shotgun pointed at the back; consider your cover blown," I fumed, irate that he would ask for any kind of special treatment.

He nodded his head in agreement.

"Is Liz really your wife and Max and Mia, are they your kids?"

"Yes, but Liz knew as little as you did until last night when I came clean with her. I don't know if she's going to stay with me; divorce was mentioned," he mumbled.

"Yeah, I bet it was!" I snapped. "Who do you work for?"

"We were brokers, of some sort, for the CIA. Jobs were assigned to us, and Jack was the go man; I filed and filtered the money that we took from our target. We didn't really have a job title because as far as the United States is concerned, we don't actually exist; we were created by a Homeland Security board, and basically, the last ten years we spent outside of our homes were somewhat fabricated. Well, all fabrication," he alleged.

"The CIA? You expect me to believe that?" I sneered.

"Just think back over the years, Annie. Have you met Jack's parents? No, conveniently they're dead. Where are his friends from high school or college? Do you really think anyone is so much of a loner that not only do you never meet an old buddy, but they don't call either? What about your house and the things inside? Nice, but not too nice? Do you pay by cash or credit card? Have you ever known Jack to stick out in a crowd? Parties, pictures, even his wardrobe; has he ever called attention to himself in the eleven years you've known him?"

I didn't answer because he was right, and didn't even need time to consider the questions.

215

"How did you find me?" I asked.

"Did you not just hear what I said? If you live on this planet, I can find you; especially if you don't know you need to be found. Plane ticket to St. Croix-easy, cell phone calls—even better, and then you downloaded about a hundred dollars worth of music from the same artist—a Mr. Kessler Carlisle, who happens to own the house next door to the one you rented. You're a good looking woman, Annie, and the fact you two ended up together didn't take a genius IQ," he boasted with a snarky tone.

"Not the time to get cocky, ass-wipe!" Wade yelled, poking him with the barrel of his shotgun.

"Why were you in St. Croix? You said you were protecting me; from what?"

"The people who own those diamonds, the same people Jack stole from. I only recently found out about those; Jack had secrets from me too, and when I cleaned out the office at the Plaza, I finally put all the clues together. Wherever he got the diamonds was kept from me, and with the publicity surrounding his death, the rightful owner would come looking for them. It's just too much money to let go. And obviously, I was right," he answered.

"The waiter?" I asked.

"Yes, the waiter," he echoed.

"Why did you freak out at Robert Graville's office?"

"Because Jack was dead, and for all I knew, I would be next. I've wanted out of this job for years, and only recently found out because of Jack's death they are releasing me. I'm sorry Jack's gone, but when you have more enemies than friends, bad things are bound to happen. I've made all the exit arrangements to put that part of my life behind me, and just turned over all of my identities and any paper trail created over the last ten years. A person needs an iron stomach, nerves of steel and no conscience for this type of life; I've been extremely stressed the past six months," he whined.

A surge of anger came over me. "You've been stressed? Are you fucking kidding me? Do you realize that you haven't even said the words, 'I'm sorry?' You and Jack have lied to me for over ten years, which by the way, led me to almost getting killed, and I think you should at least say I'm sorry, you self-centered prick!" I screamed in a shrill voice.

"Annie, I *am* sorry, and that's why I'm here, to tell you the truth about your past so you won't question any kind of future you might have with someone else. You deserve a better life, a better man than Jack—you always have. I told Jack not to marry you. Liz and I were different because I was only a glorified accountant, but Jack put you in danger. That never sat well with me. I just didn't have the balls to say so," he added.

"Do you think he committed suicide or is murder now on the table?" I asked.

"I don't know if either of us will ever know the answer to that question," he replied.

"Did he love me?" I asked, not turning to look at Kessler's face, but feeling his stare and knowing that question probably hurt him. But I had to know the answer.

"Yes, Annie, of course he did; you were his wife. That's why he left you the money, so you would always be taken care of financially and never need to worry about finances again."

"Well, Jamie, maybe in the next chapter of your life, you should try to remember you can't buy a family. A real family is something that you earn, with honesty and compassion, not with money," I said, standing up and putting my arms around Kessler's neck. "I'm done here. I don't want to hear any more about my past; I'm so fucking tired of my past. Me and you, baby, the future," I said, lightly pushing my forehead against Kessler's.

"I hope it works out for you, Annie. I really do," he said. "Are we done?"

"Tell your children I love them, and will for the rest of my life. Just because I'm done with you doesn't mean I don't want to see them, because I do. You tell them that!" I yelled, as I poked him in the chest. "But don't you ever contact me again; I don't ever want to see you," I said.

"Understood," he replied, as the three of us watched him turn away and walk back up the hill to his car.

I was exhausted—bloated with toxic information that might take years to completely expel from my mind. All I wanted to do was sleep.

"Just in the nick of time, Wade," I said as I hugged him. "Thank you."

"Happy to do it, but I really thought I was gonna get to shoot 'em," he whined, disappointed in the outcome.

"Sorry, buddy, maybe next time." I patted his arm, and the three of us walked inside—locking the doors and turning on the alarm.

ANNIE

With my decision to make a permanent move to Nashville, there were some ends in need of tying in Kansas City. My house was on the market and the realtor held an estate sale for me. I wanted to retrieve any items of sentimental value and bring them home before the random population rummaged through the belongings I had spent a decade collecting. Walking into my old house was easier than I expected; there was no love lost, only good riddance. Kessler begged to come with me, but I gave him an adamant no. I didn't want him to have any affiliation with that part of my life—complete separation—like a severed head detached from its body. He did, however, let me use his jet, and I could see how wealthy people become totally unattached from the rest of the world; it was glorious! My journey of gratitude was beginning.

The first stop was Gail's house; she had another cup of her homemade marvel waiting for me when I arrived.

"This coffee is beyond addictive! You should have gotten your ex hooked on this and maybe he would have given up the coke," I joked.

"Ha! I don't think he would consider anything to be better than cocaine. Besides, that would just mean he'd want me to make him coffee every morning, which would also mean I'd have to see his face every day, so no thank you! But, maybe one day I'll give up the glamorous life of insurance and start my own coffee house; a girl can dream," she said smiling up to the ceiling, casting a farfetched wish.

"You never know," I insinuated, unable to conceal my smile.

We sat and chatted, drinking coffee. Gail let me go on and on about my insane life and insatiable lust for Kessler. I hated to cut our visit short, but I saw the time and needed to get going. I had two more stops to make.

She walked me out to my car and sighed. "Damn girl, you did good. I'm really going to miss talking with you."

"I'm just a phone call or plane ride away. Why would we stop talking?" I asked, somewhat confused.

"Out of sight, out of mind, I guess. Sometimes friendships just have a way of dying out," she answered.

"We have an open door policy, and you're welcome anytime; plenty of cowboys are just waiting for your arrival in Nashville! Oh, I almost forgot!" I said, pulling a pack of Camels from my purse. "These are for you; a gift from the Islands."

"Um, thanks. But, Annie, I don't smoke," she said, looking confused about how I could have missed that.

"Go inside and open them; you just might start!" I yelled through my open car window as I waved good-bye and pulled out of the driveway.

Leslie's house was my next stop. Her girls were at school, and this was her day to work late so Carl would be the only one there, working out of his home office. He was actually the one I wanted to see.

Carl peered through the window in the door and surprised me with a giant bear hug greeting.

"Annie! What are you doing here? I thought you were in St. Croix," he said, clearly out of the loop.

"I'm only back for the day, and I wanted to come by," I said as we walked into the kitchen.

"Well, Leslie is working late. Can you hang around until she gets back?" he asked.

"No, I really need to get going, but I wanted to give you something." I pulled out a piece of sticky paper that read: Nicole Miller/ size 2/ $500 minimum, and oh, yeah, a box of Camels from my purse.

"What's this?" he asked, as I stuck the paper to the refrigerator door.

"This is the website you're going to visit after you open this pack of cigarettes. Call the jeweler on the business card, and he will tell you what to do. He's expecting your call. I'll be checking your work, Carl, so don't disappoint me!" I said as I gave him a hug and yelled, "Tell her to call me!" as I walked out the door.

I had already sent a generous donation to the Kansas City Renovation Company hoping it would be enough to save some of my favorite downtown buildings with the authentic, painted, historical signs. I passed by a number of them on my way to the cemetery, and tried to decide which one I liked the best, but I couldn't; I loved them all.

This is it, the last stop. I'll say what I came to say and then never look back.

The wind blew the last of the snow around my feet, revealing a sheet of slippery ice underneath. I had a feeling I wouldn't make it out of here

220

without falling on my ass first. I soon found the massive oak tree spitting skeletal roots above the ground, and sitting under it, the cold grey head-stone of Jack Whitman, which was taking a beating from the sharp and leafless branches stretched out almost to the ground. The air was frigid and seemed to blow right through me as the branches from the tree scratched across Jack's name.

"Well, I found them, in case you were wondering. I don't want them, but I found them. I hope this is what you wanted; I hope this is the end result you pictured in your mind. Can you even imagine how this feels? The last time I stood here I buried you, and my world was crumbling right before my eyes. But not today, Jack. I've learned enough over the last eight months to know that instead of freaking out, I'm going to thank you.

"Thank you for giving me a chance to experience the adventure and excitement I never knew existed. Thank you for being the driving force which completely broke me into a thousand pieces, but also gave me courage, allowing my fortitude to eventually break through. Thank you for these journeys that led me to Kessler, because through him, I've learned the heart's uncanny ability to mend. And most of all, thank you for giving me the means to truly change people's lives. I have to admit, that part's been pretty fun," I said with a smile as the snow started falling, sticking to my eyelashes.

"I guess that's about it. Thanks for the memories, Jack; I'm choosing to pretend they were real," I said. As I turned to head back to the car, he stepped out from behind the thick trunk of the oak tree holding a familiar miniature American flag.

"Hello, Andrea," Jack said.

ANNIE

"Oh, God!" I screamed, losing my footing on some ice and stumbling backwards, crashing into his headstone.

Jack's dead. Jack's dead. Jack's dead.

"It's okay, Andrea; I know this is a lot to take in right now," he said as he knelt next to the tree, coming down to my level.

"What's happening? You died! You're dead!" I tried to yell, but my chest was so tight, words and breathing were difficult.

The snow was really coming down now and it covered the ground with a new layer of white. The cemetery was skin and bones, but the blanket of snow gave it an unexpected freshness, like a clean slate.

"I knew this would be hard on you, and I'm so sorry it had to be this way, but I didn't know how else to reveal myself," he said with an uncomfortable chuckle.

His breath came in constant trails of smoke, and the snow had already covered the shoulders of his pea coat and the brim of his fedora, making him look like an actual living ghost.

"Your speech, it was wonderful. Well, everything except Kessler Carlisle. That part hurt, but it's okay, I deserve some hurt from you," he admitted. "I can explain as much or as little as you like, Andrea; I want you to know the truth. Can I help you up?" he asked as he stood and took a few steps towards me, ripping off his gloves and extending his bare hand.

I tried to keep from blinking. I was afraid that the next blink or the next would somehow bring this hallucination to an end, but the snow fall was making that impossible and yet, he wasn't going away. He was real.

I took his hand and lifted myself up, never taking my eyes off him.

"Ann," he said as he smiled. "It's so good to see you again. I've missed you so much!"

"I can't believe you're here! I can't believe you're real!" I whispered, as I took off my gloves and our skin touched for the first time in over eight months.

I saw the longing in his eyes and predicted his advancing embrace as he slid his hands around my waist, picking me up in his arms and kissing me hard. I didn't succumb to his touch at first, but when I finally allowed myself to feel his face against mine, the momentum was unstoppable. The familiar softness of his beard and the smell of his Cartier cologne penetrated my memory, reminding me of the sensation of coming home from a long trip; my will-power was futile.

"How are you here? How did this happen?" I asked, breaking away from our embrace.

"There's so much to tell you, Andrea. Can we go somewhere to talk? My car is just over the hill," he said, pointing towards the parking lot.

"I don't think so; I'm fine here. Say what you have to say right here," I told him, because there was no way in hell I was getting trapped in a car with a supposedly dead man; husband or not.

His eyes turned sad as the realization of our reunion was not what he had pictured in his mind. "You're scared of me," he said, slumping his shoulders and shaking his head.

"Who are you?" I asked under my breath.

"I know I owe you a full explanation, but please try to remember, I love you and nothing I say here today will ever change my love for you," he professed.

"Okay," was all I said.

"My given name is Jack Stallings, but when I was hired twenty years ago by Homeland Security, Jack Whitman was created and Jack Stallings was erased," he revealed, bracing for impact.

"What do you do for the government?" I asked, still shivering from the turn of events, not the cold.

"In a nut shell, I find bad guys and annex their money in an attempt to take down a terrorist platform. The lack of funds either forces their group to scramble, taking years to rebuild, or it dissipates all together. You could say I'm kind of a broker," he added.

"How does that make you a broker?" I asked.

"Well, who do you think gets most of the money I confiscate?" he answered rhetorically.

"So the money you left me is stolen?"

"Depending on how you look at it, but I'll say no, it's not stolen; it came from my employer, like any paycheck would."

"Did you leave all those lockboxes hoping I would find them or was that a coincidence?" I asked.

"Yes, I left them for you, but I underestimated how fast you'd find them. I've got to tell you how impressed I am that you put it all together so quickly! I always knew you were smart," he praised me, leaning in to kiss me again.

When his cheeks got close enough and he expected to feel my lips upon his, he instead felt my hand across his face, accompanied by a loud *smack*. He pulled back in shock; I wanted to hurt him even more, matching the pain he had caused me, so I swung again, this time my fist connected with his nose. He didn't even flinch. I'm assuming he knew it was coming, and he just let me do it.

"How could you do this to me?" I yelled, as I pushed him back with all my strength. "You lied about so many things; our whole marriage was a fucking sham! Do you know how that makes me feel?" I shrieked, pulling a cigarette out of my purse.

"I do, I'm sorry, but I was hoping you would understand on a patriotic level. I was serving my country, Andrea, eliminating the scum of the earth whose only mission in life is to kill Americans. I saved lives, and I'm not a monster! Please try to understand!" he begged.

I saw the disappointment on his face as I lit up my smoke.

"You're smoking again? I thought you quit."

"Oh, fuck off!" I screamed, as I blew a huge cloud of toxins in his face. "You weren't around to ride my ass about smoking. Oh yeah, that's right, you were dead, so I don't really think it's your business to comment on my health," I hissed, ready to claw his eyes out for even mentioning smoking. "What about the diamonds? Who did you steal those from?" I demanded, still smoking and still intentionally trying to blow the smoke right up his nose. Immature, yes, but I didn't really have a lot of leverage going for me, so I resulted to high school tactics.

"The picture you found in the Pelican Case, do you still have that?"

"Of course," I said.

"That picture was taken before September 11th, before we met and about two days before I took the diamonds. I was on a job with my crew to take down some very bad people who were close to executing a massacre in America. My mentor, John Savage—who was then on his way to becoming the head of the CIA and now the newly elected Vice President of the United States—put this mission together. Are you following so far?" he asked.

I nodded my head yes.

"I followed him loyally into every mission, never questioning his motives or morality and never missing my target. I'm the best in the business—that's how I got the code name Achilles—but the day I stole those diamonds, was the day I completely lost my faith in the human race."

I know exactly how you feel about losing faith in people. You of all people will not get my sympathy! I thought, but just nodded my head again.

"Our mission was to bomb the headquarters of a terrorist group, destroying most of their weapons and all of their Intel, but the catch was that it was located in an elementary school. That's how crazy these fuckers are; everyone is disposable for the cause, even the ones who aren't old enough to understand the cause. We were told to stand down. We had received false information, and this school was the headquarters of a lesser cell. My team was thorough though; that's why we're the best. We broke into the school and trashed their offices, taking anything which would be of value to the United States with us, including a large bag of diamonds."

I braced myself for the conclusion of this story, knowing it might not turn out well.

"Some people think because you are a solider or associated with the military that you're this bomb crazy, war happy person, but in most cases, it just isn't so. I remember the relief that came over me when we were told to stand down. This mission didn't feel right. It was rushed and uncoordinated compared to others, but I ignored my gut, thinking at the time I didn't have a choice. I know now I've always had a choice, and this time, my conscience happened to be saved from orders above me, or so I thought."

My legs started to wobble and my knees began to shake from the mixture of adrenaline pumping through me and the wind blowing around me. The only place to sit down besides the ground was Jack's headstone, so despite my discomfort I kept standing, shifting my weight back and forth between my feet.

"Savage knew the diamonds were there," he started again, and I could tell he was sharing this story—verbally confirming the guilt and innocence of the parties involved—just as much for himself as he was for me. "He sent the others to clear the last room in the school and once we were alone, he handed me the diamonds, making them forever our secret. And I've kept it, all these years."

"Jesus, Jack! You're a thief, and you're a liar. How do you live with yourself?" I asked as I began walking to my car with him trailing behind me, begging me to understand.

"Well, up until the last eight months, I had a good woman waiting for me at home, who made my life seem unbelievably normal, and now, that's gone too. All by my choice, but gone just the same," he answered.

I turned to face him with my hands swinging wildly. "Then why did you? Why did you leave me? Why did you run out on our marriage—run out on us?" I didn't wait for an answer because fury consumed my every thought, my every movement. "If you're waiting for me to tell you all is forgiven and everything is okay, then you'll be standing here awhile, because it isn't and it's not," I scorned, really twisting the knife, trying my best to punish him.

"I had to leave! My handler discovered I'm on their radar, and if they are willing to kill innocent people—their people—then killing you wouldn't put a dent in their conscience. Believe me, Andrea, I understand that more than you'll ever know. You see, when I was at the airport waiting for my flight home, the breaking news came over the television with the footage of dead children's body parts littered around that school; he blew it up anyway. Savage bombed that school to cover our theft of the diamonds and then sold his story to the President under the premise that the terrorists struck first. Not to mention, those kids would eventually grow up, embrace their hatred, and kill Americans."

"Oh!" I gasped. "Oh, God, no! I'm sorry, Jack, so sorry for what you went through. I can't imagine how it felt seeing all those dead bodies, and I can't believe you've kept this inside all this time, but that has nothing to do with me. I just don't really know what to say."

"Say you'll come with me! We can start over, go anywhere in the world you want to go; it will be another adventure for you, for us, together!" he coaxed and by the sound in his voice, he actually thought I'd say yes.

I won't lie—for a second I might have said yes, but Kessler's face was all I could see, all I wanted to see.

"I have started over, Jack. I'm already on that next big adventure you're talking about. Of anywhere in the world I'd want to be, I choose Nashville; it's not the city for everyone, but it's the right one for me," I told him. "There's no going back for me; I'd never be able to trust you. Although, I meant every word I said at your grave site. Thank you for the money. Thank you for the ability to change lives, because that's exactly what I plan on doing."

"I knew you would, and that's why I left them to you; something good must come out of this horrible situation. Please think carefully about whom you give them to, and spread them around the country if you can. I love you, Andrea; I always have. To say I'm sorry doesn't begin to explain how I feel, but I am so very sorry. Are you sure you won't change your mind?" he asked one last time.

"I love him, Jack, and it's your fault that I do."

"I know, and I'll never forgive myself. Please don't say no, just tell me you'll think about me, about us," he asked, as he put his hand on my hip.

"Maybe, but I'm not promising you anything, Jack."

The corners of his lips wrinkled with a smile, and his eyes brightened with my response.

"Thank you. Maybe is good enough for me," he said.

"How do I get in touch with you?" I asked as we approached my car.

"You don't. I'll find you, but first, I'm going to start making some of my wrongs right," he said.

I kissed him, knowing I shouldn't but doing it anyway.

"Where are you going now?" I asked as I opened my door.

He stood silent for a moment, looking up and down the long and narrow road which circled around the cemetery as if he was waiting for someone or something. A black Lincoln Town Car slowly made its way around the corner and up the hill, stopping next to Jack. As he opened the door I saw the driver, her unmistakable red wasps' nest hair, and Jack said, "I'm going after the Vice President, and I'm going to destroy him. He needs to suffer a public death first before an actual one, and admit his numerous murders over the last twenty years."

My mouth hung open, but my brain slammed shut at a lack for the right words to say. All the while, the silence between the three of us spoke volumes.

"Are we good here?" Gail asked Jack as he climbed into the car with her.

"Yeah, we're good," he replied, and Gail mouthed an, "I'm sorry" as Jack closed the door, putting his fingers to his lips and then holding them against the window.

I was left standing in the exhaust as the car crested the hill and eventually, drove out of sight.

Acknowledgments

This has been such an amazing journey! So many people have been an integral part of this process and deserve my thanks.

First, an enormous thank you to my editor, Samantha March. Thank you for finding me! You were an absolute pleasure to work with, and I wish every first time novelist could find an editor like you. Thank you so much for your professionalism, kindness, and advice. Here's to a hundred more!

To my mom, Sandra Hiller, my first editor, beta reader, and constant cheerleader who read and reread this book a dozen times, never failing to ask, "What's happening with the book?" Thank you for your love and continual support!

Also, to my dad, John Hiller, who spoke candidly about his tour in Vietnam and graciously allowed me to use one of his many, near-death experiences in my novel. Thank you for fighting for the freedoms that most of us take for granted every day.

To my in-laws, Larry and Cherryl Morrow who took the kids several weekends over the last two years so I could write or sleep. Without those weekends, I'd still be on chapter twelve.

For all my beta readers: Alli Ritchey—the first one to make it a "real" book, Stase Ochoa—my Louisiana transplant and SEC Experience, Christi Nies, Amy Spence, Christi O'Riley, Samantha Halsey, Abbe Montgomery, Fred Seaman, Johanna Morrow, Hannah Dodson, Shana Burblinger, Lisa Rau, Sarah Conroy, Aimee Jeter, and Connie Kilgore.

Thanks, also goes out to Dave Haley for his wealth of knowledge about the music industry in Nashville. He took the time to enlighten me, even on his vacation. Any mistakes made in this book solely belong to me; don't hate on Dave.

For my girls (in no particular order): Lisa Rau, Aimee Jeter, Nancy Vosters, and Jessica Britten. Thank you for giving me fifteen years of detailed backstory! What an amazing history we have together. My life is so much better because you girls are in it. I love you all and can't wait until our next girl's trip!

Huge thanks to Christi Nies, my mentor in writing and life in general. She took every text and phone call over the last two years, even though she had her own life to live. From the moment I walked into her class-room, she has helped me to become a better person, and I would never have finished this project without her honest advice. To only say thank you is such an understatement, but there are just not enough words in the English language to describe my heartfelt gratitude. Thank you for be-lieving in me since the ninth grade.

Max and Mia, thank you for being a constant stream of hilarity in all you say and do. I'm so glad I was chosen to be your mama. My love for you both runs deeper than any writer could ever articulate.

Finally, my biggest thanks goes out to my husband, Lance Morrow. Thank you for taking me to the Cotton House in St. Croix on our hon-eymoon, and again three years later as a family. St. Croix holds so many fantastic memories for us, and it was fun to relive them while writing this novel. Thank you for holding court at the kitchen island—brainstorming storylines, character development, and talking incessantly about this book when you would have rather been playing golf. Thank you for the time, energy, and sacrifice you gave to see this dream of mine come true. So much love to you Sug!

About The Author

Karyn Rae is a member of the Romance Writers of America, and the Columbia Chapter of the Missouri Writers Guild. She resides in Missouri with her husband, son, daughter, and chocolate lab—Augusta Mae.

Find Karyn Rae on her website: www.karynrae.me

Made in the USA
San Bernardino, CA
22 July 2014